Silent Night

By Danielle Steel

SILENT NIGHT • TURNING POINT • BEAUCHAMP HALL
IN HIS FATHER'S FOOTSTEPS • THE GOOD FIGHT • THE CAST
ACCIDENTAL HEROES • FALL FROM GRACE • PAST PERFECT • FAIRYTALE
THE RIGHT TIME • THE DUCHESS • AGAINST ALL ODDS
DANGEROUS GAMES • THE MISTRESS • THE AWARD
RUSHING WATERS • MAGIC • THE APARTMENT
PROPERTY OF A NOBLEWOMAN • BLUE • PRECIOUS GIFTS
UNDERCOVER • COUNTRY • PRODIGAL SON • PEGASUS
A PERFECT LIFE • POWER PLAY • WINNERS • FIRST SIGHT
UNTIL THE END OF TIME • THE SINS OF THE MOTHER
FRIENDS FOREVER • BETRAYAL • HOTEL VENDÔME • HAPPY BIRTHDAY
44 CHARLES STREET • LEGACY • FAMILY TIES • BIG GIRL
SOUTHERN LIGHTS • MATTERS OF THE HEART • ONE DAY AT A TIME
A GOOD WOMAN • ROGUE • HONOR THYSELF •AMAZING GRACE
BUNGALOW 2 • SISTERS • H.R.H. • COMING OUT •THE HOUSE
TOXIC BACHELORS • MIRACLE • IMPOSSIBLE • ECHOES • SECOND CHANCE
RANSOM • SAFE HARBOUR • JOHNNY ANGEL • DATING GAME
ANSWERED PRAYERS • SUNSET IN ST. TROPEZ • THE COTTAGE • THE KISS
LEAP OF FAITH • LONE EAGLE • JOURNEY • THE HOUSE ON HOPE STREET
THE WEDDING • IRRESISTIBLE FORCES • GRANNY DAN • BITTERSWEET
MIRROR IMAGE • THE KLONE AND I • THE LONG ROAD HOME • THE GHOST
SPECIAL DELIVERY • THE RANCH • SILENT HONOR • MALICE
FIVE DAYS IN PARIS • LIGHTNING • WINGS • THE GIFT • ACCIDENT
VANISHED • MIXED BLESSINGS • JEWELS • NO GREATER LOVE
HEARTBEAT • MESSAGE FROM NAM • DADDY • STAR • ZOYA
KALEIDOSCOPE • FINE THINGS • WANDERLUST • SECRETS
FAMILY ALBUM • FULL CIRCLE • CHANGES • THURSTON HOUSE
CROSSINGS • ONCE IN A LIFETIME • A PERFECT STRANGER
REMEMBRANCE • PALOMINO • LOVE: *POEMS* • THE RING • LOVING
TO LOVE AGAIN • SUMMER'S END • SEASON OF PASSION • THE PROMISE
NOW AND FOREVER • PASSION'S PROMISE • GOING HOME

Nonfiction

PURE JOY: *The Dogs We Love*
A GIFT OF HOPE: *Helping the Homeless*
HIS BRIGHT LIGHT: *The Story of Nick Traina*

For Children

PRETTY MINNIE IN PARIS
PRETTY MINNIE IN HOLLYWOOD

DANIELLE STEEL

Silent Night

A Novel

Delacorte Press | New York

Published in the United States by Delacorte Press, an imprint of Random House, a division of Penguin Random House LLC, New York.

DELACORTE PRESS and the HOUSE colophon are registered trademarks of Penguin Random House LLC.

LIBRARY OF CONGRESS CATALOGING-IN-PUBLICATION DATA
Names: Steel, Danielle, author.
Title: Silent night: a novel / Danielle Steel.
Description: First edition. | New York: Delacorte Press, an imprint of Random House, a division of Penguin Random House LLC, [2019]
Identifiers: LCCN 2018050826| ISBN 9780399179389 (hardback: acid-free paper) | ISBN 9780399179396 (Ebook)
Subjects: LCSH: Domestic fiction. | BISAC: FICTION / Contemporary Women. | FICTION / Family Life. | FICTION / Romance / Contemporary.
Classification: LCC PS3569.T33828 S573 2019 | DDC 813/.54—dc23
LC record available at https://lccn.loc.gov/2018050826

Printed in the United States of America on acid-free paper

randomhousebooks.com

2 4 6 8 9 7 5 3 1

First Edition

Book design by Virginia Norey

To my beloved children,
Beatie, Trevor, Todd, Nick,
Sam, Victoria, Vanessa,
Maxx, and Zara,

Thank you for the gift of motherhood,
the lessons you've taught me,
the immeasurable joy we've shared,
the love that makes life worthwhile.
I'm so grateful for all of it,
and for each one of you.

I love you with *all* my heart
and soul,

Mom/ds

"The best and most beautiful things in the world cannot be seen or even touched—they must be felt with the heart."
—HELEN KELLER, quoting Annie Sullivan

"If you're going through hell, keep going!"
—ANONYMOUS, frequently attributed to
WINSTON CHURCHILL

"All things are possible."
—MATTHEW 19:26

Silent Night

Chapter 1

"Your mother is dead, Bethanie. You have to face it. You can't run away from it forever." As a tall, handsome man with a craggy face delivers the crushing message, we see a little girl's face crumple with deep emotion, as though she were dissolving from within. Suddenly her eyes shoot fire, as rage mixes with grief, and she backs away and begins to run. He makes no attempt to chase her. She turns once and looks back at him with fury and determination.

"I hate you!" she screams and we can see that she means it. The girl is barefoot, wearing a blue cotton dress, her blond hair disheveled, her exquisite cameo-like features perfect, her eyes blazing and swimming in tears. She is tiny, delicate, elfin, with an inner strength that nothing he has said can diminish. She runs as far and as fast as she can, trying to outrun what he has said to her. She disappears into a thicket of trees as he watches her with fury in his own eyes, and then he relaxes. All the tension goes out of him, and the little wood sprite reappears, grinning, and skips back toward him, barefoot as she crosses the field. There is applause from a handful of observers.

An unkempt-looking woman in torn jeans and a T-shirt shouts, "Perfect," and the beautiful blond child takes a mock bow, delighted. A moment later, she is surrounded by her fellow actors. She is Emma Watts, the youngest member of the cast of a hit TV series called *The Clan,* a weekly saga of a powerful family living in the Pacific Northwest. Emma recently turned nine and has been on the show for two years. Her mother approaches, looking pleased, as Emma and the man who portrays her father walk back to their trailers, with sound men, costumers, makeup artists, and hairdressers trailing behind them. The director confers with an assistant.

"Good job, Em." Emma's mother, Paige Watts, praises her. "Aren't you glad we worked on that scene again last night?"

Emma shrugs, looking unimpressed. "Yeah, maybe. I swallowed my gum when I was running." Her mother rolls her eyes.

"You're not supposed to chew gum on the set. You know that. You could choke on it."

"But I didn't." Emma is a bright girl, and has become one of the most celebrated child actors on TV, since she joined the show when she was seven. She's a natural, a born actress. She had to give up going to school when she got the part, and is tutored on the set by a teacher licensed by the state of California, Belinda Marshall, a beautiful African American woman, who does voice-overs, commercials, and occasional bit parts on other shows. She wants to be an actress and has both the talent and the looks for it. Her ancestors were Ethiopian and there is a regal look to her, along with her quick mind and warm heart. Emma likes Belinda, as long as she doesn't give her too much homework, which she can't do on nights that Emma has a lot of lines to learn for the next day. It's why regular school doesn't really work for her with the demands of the show.

Emma's mother, Paige, keeps a close watch on all aspects of her career. She coordinates Emma's voice coach, drama coach, speech coach, and dance classes. She takes hip-hop, tap, and ballet, and has a remarkable singing voice. Paige's own acting career never took off, but anyone can see that Emma will be a big star one day. She has given her mother's life purpose, meaning, and direction. Paige had Emma start modeling as a baby, after listing her with an agency nearly at birth. At six, she had Emma start acting, and within a year, she had landed the part as the youngest child on *The Clan*. There are two other children on the show, Adam Weiss, who plays Emma's twelve-year-old brother, and Virginia Parker, who is now sixteen and just got her GED high school diploma, and plays Emma's fourteen-year-old sister. All three of them take classes on the set with Belinda. There's no time for school in the life of a child actor, no play dates, no friends other than fellow actors. Life on the set is intense, with work first and foremost, and their childhoods second. Paige knows what it takes, and also that Emma will thank her for it one day, when she wins her first Oscar for a movie or an Emmy for the show she's on.

They have a decision to make at the moment, a big one. Emma has been offered a part in a Broadway musical, a starring role. She has the voice and the talent for it, and the big question is what will further her career the most: staying with the series or taking a shot at Broadway. She could win a Tony for the part in New York, or an Emmy or a Golden Globe if she stays with *The Clan*. Her mother will make the decision for her, as she always does. Emma wants to stay in

L.A. Paige hasn't made up her mind yet. Emma's career is all consuming. Paige looks a great deal like her daughter, with the same delicate blond beauty, but she never had her daughter's talent. She had given up on her own acting career years before, and concentrated on Emma's as soon as she was old enough to have one.

They are the descendants of Hollywood royalty. Paige's mother, Elizabeth Winston, was the biggest film star of her day. Paige grew up watching her mother on the set of her movies, when she was allowed to. She and her older sister, Whitney, were brought up by nannies. Their mother was always making a movie somewhere. Liz Winston had been a legend, an icon, one of Hollywood's great beauties and most talented actresses. She had won two Oscars, before she died tragically early at fifty-four. Her death had shattered Paige's fragile balance. She was twenty-four and had been trying to start her own career then but got lost in the shuffle in L.A. Her father, Bill Watts, had told her bluntly that she didn't have what it took and needed to find another outlet for her talents. He knew without a doubt that she'd never be an actress of her mother's stature. Her mother had been remarkable on screen and Emma was too. Paige didn't have their gift, and finally admitted it to herself. But she found her purpose in life when Emma was born.

Bill Watts had been the most important film agent of his day. He had discovered Liz, masterminded and controlled every aspect of her career brilliantly, and knew he had found an actress with incomparable beauty and rare talent the moment he saw her. He had never made a mistake with her, and Liz hung on his every word. They married when Liz was twenty-five and Bill was sixty, and she had rapidly become his most important client. She made no decisions without him. He orchestrated every move she made.

Liz had Whitney, their first baby, when she was twenty-eight, and took six months off between pictures. Paige was born two years later, and Liz was an even bigger star by then, and had no time to spend with her. All Paige had ever wanted growing up was her parents' attention, which was hard to come by. And she longed to be as big a star as her mother one day.

Her sister, Whitney, could have cared less, had always hated everything about Hollywood. She wanted nothing to do with a life like their parents'. It was Paige's dream, and Emma had finally fulfilled her dream for her. Paige was convinced now that she didn't have her mother's talent, but that she did have her father's gift for recognizing star material when he saw it. She controlled every aspect of Emma's career, just as her father had run her mother's. Liz hadn't decided what to have for breakfast, let alone what parts to take, without him. He made all her decisions for her. Just as Paige made Emma's. The only difference was that Emma was a child. Liz wasn't, when Bill was making her decisions for her, and running her career and her life.

"Nice work today, Squirt," Charlie Daly, the actor who played her father, said as he walked past and ruffled the almost white blond hair. "At least I didn't have to chase you up a tree this time," he said, and they both laughed. "You're off for the rest of the day, aren't you?" Everyone in the cast loved her, and she had become their mascot. Emma was outspoken and observant, smart as a whip, read voraciously, and was precocious, since her whole life was lived among adults.

"Yeah, but I have school," she said glumly as they reached their trailers.

"Don't tell me your sad stories, you've got Belinda wrapped around your little finger. All you have to do is tell her you have too many lines to learn for tomorrow and she lets you off the hook with no homework. I've seen you do it." He was on to her, and Emma guffawed, with an anxious glance at her mother.

"Don't blow my cover," she whispered to him. But her mother was on to her too. Paige's main interest was in Emma's acting homework anyway. Paige thought Emma could always catch up on school later, though she'd actually never fallen behind. She was up to speed with her fourth-grade work, and doing fifth-grade reading. Despite her own acting ambitions, Belinda was conscientious about her teaching, and everyone on the set respected her. She had the occasional battle with Paige, who didn't want Emma to miss her work with her drama coach, or voice lessons, but Emma always managed to do it all. What she didn't get to do was hang out with kids her own age, or play, except with adults. Charlie had taught her to play chess, and she actually managed to beat him once in a while. He thought it was incredible how smart she was, and how diligent. He shared Paige's view that Emma would go far. Acting was the only life she knew, and it was in her blood. The family talent had skipped a generation but had come out in spades in Emma, and Paige was going to do everything she could to nurture it. It was no secret on the set that Paige was the stage mother of all time. Some of the other actors felt sorry for Emma, she never got to be a child and Paige pushed her hard, but Emma didn't seem to mind. She loved some of her lessons, like hip-hop and ballet. Sometimes she complained that her voice lessons were boring, and she said her drama coach was mean when he made her go over a scene again and again, but he did his job well. Emma almost never missed her lines, and was more accurate than most of the adults she worked with. She often knew their lines as well as her own.

Emma groaned when she saw Belinda waiting for her in her trailer with math homework to correct. Paige ordered her lunch so they could get started. Emma had ballet that afternoon, and a voice lesson that night, which was important if Paige decided Emma should take the role on Broadway. It was all part of the master plan. There were no random decisions about Emma's work. Paige went to return some calls, while Emma did the math with Belinda. There were two messages from the Broadway producer, and Paige closed her eyes for a minute while she thought about it. She hadn't made her mind up yet. There was no room for a mistake. Giving up a hit TV series was a big decision, and so was starring in a Broadway show with major actors, at nine. Paige wondered what her father would have done about it. That was the question she always asked herself, every step of the way. Her father had been infallible in her eyes, and her mother's incomparable career had proved it. She wanted Emma to be as big a star as her grandmother one day. Paige knew that would be her achievement in life, just as her mother's success was her father's.

Emma's career had been a bone of contention between Paige and her older sister, Whitney, ever since Paige had started Emma modeling when she was six months old. Whitney considered it exploitation, and the older Emma got, the more Whitney objected to it. She accused Paige of living vicariously through her child to the point of being abusive. She told Paige she was robbing Emma of her childhood and depriving her of a normal life.

"Don't be ridiculous," Paige argued with her. "Look at her, she's a star at nine, the whole world loves her, and she loves being on the show. Do you think Dad abused Mom by running her career?" They fought about it often, and had diametrically opposite points of view. Whitney had hated their childhood as the children of a major star. Paige had loved every minute of it, or said so now. And she idolized their father. Whitney saw all his flaws.

"Does it ever occur to you that maybe Mom got early onset Alzheimer's at fifty-two, and died at fifty-four, because of the pressure she was under, which he orchestrated for thirty years? She had no life, all she did was work on one film after another, and win two Oscars. She had no time for friends except the people she worked with, and she almost never saw us. She was always working somewhere. Mom did everything he told her to, just like you're doing with Emma now. Doesn't that ever scare you? Aren't you afraid she'll accuse you of stealing her childhood one day?"

"She'll thank me for it when she's as big a star as our mother was, or bigger. With social media today, stardom is an even bigger deal than it was then. It's global now, and everything moves faster."

"It was global then too," Whitney reminded her. Their mother had been an icon like Elizabeth Taylor and Rita Hayworth in their day. But Whitney had never had the impression that their mother was happy. She seemed frightened a lot of the time, except when her husband was making her decisions for her, and she had died so young. She had died two weeks after Whitney graduated from medical school, which had been Whitney's way of escaping her family's Hollywood destiny. She had chosen a career as radically different from her parents' as she could, and she was now a psychiatrist with a solid practice at thirty-nine.

Paige was thirty-seven, and her greatest and only achievement was being the ultimate stage mother and running Emma's life. The two sisters couldn't have been more different, and Whitney always felt sorry for Emma and wished she had a better life with more time to be a child, not just a small adult. But Paige never saw it that way. All she could see was how huge a success Emma would be one day, and she never missed a chance to remind reporters and publicists that Emma was Liz Winston's granddaughter, and even pointed out how much they looked alike. Just reading it in the press made Whitney sad.

Neither she nor Paige had ever married, and Whitney had never wanted to. After watching her father control every instant of her mother's life, marriage looked like a bad deal to her, and she had an aversion to it. She readily admitted she was phobic about marriage. She had no desire to have anyone control any aspect of her life. She'd never wanted children, and didn't consider her childhood a happy one, although her sister disagreed. In Whitney's opinion, she and Paige had had a lonely childhood, brought up by nannies, while their mother was on location somewhere and their father was her constant shadow, so he was gone as well, and too busy to spend time with them when they came back to L.A. He was always setting up his wife's next movie with producers and studio heads.

Whitney loved her career as a psychiatrist, and didn't want to ruin someone else's life, or burden herself with a child. She enjoyed her life among adults, the freedom to do what she wanted, and lead a selfish life if she chose. She liked living alone.

Her determination not to have children had complicated her life for a while. It made her shy away from men who wanted marriage and children, which led her into a series of affairs with irresponsible men who were players and took advantage of the fact that she didn't want to get married. Or she wound up with emotional cripples, incapable of attaching to anyone. As time went on, and the men she met were divorced, she found herself on dates with men and their children on weekends, while they told her their tales of woe about their greedy, vicious ex-wives, and she spent time with their angry children damaged by the divorce. She did everything she could to avoid getting involved with their dramas. She just wanted to enjoy a peaceful, adult relationship with no complications. Her last divorced boyfriend had been the father of thirteen-year-old IVF triplets. It had been a nightmare, with middle-of-the-night threats from his neurotic ex-wife, who he went back to anyway, and Whitney fled as fast as she could when his ex-wife started threatening her. She hadn't dated a divorced man with children since.

For the past five years, she'd been dating someone she considered the perfect man for her. Chad Phillips was a brilliantly successful high-tech venture capitalist in Silicon Valley. He was twenty years older than she, had four grown children she had met but spent no time with, and he didn't expect her to. And he had no interest in re-marrying or having more children. He had a yacht that he kept in the Mediterranean in summer and the Caribbean in winter. They loved taking trips together, and managed to meet once a month for a quiet weekend, or a fun adventure somewhere, which was all either of them wanted. They cared about each other, but Whitney had strong boundaries, and she never let men get too close to her. She didn't need or want a man running her life, and Chad didn't want to have a woman dependent on him again. His ex-wife was still bitter about their divorce fifteen years later, and Whitney wanted no part of jealous stepchildren or angry ex-wives. She and Chad thoroughly enjoyed each other and their adult relationship, and he was fascinated by her work, her beauty, and her history. Whitney was a striking-looking woman, tall like her father, graceful and slim with an exquisite face, porcelain white skin, and long dark hair. The only trait she shared with her sister was their mother's huge blue eyes.

Whitney's relationship with Chad suited them both perfectly, and he was always slightly intrigued by who her parents had been, and how removed Whitney kept herself from the whole Hollywood scene. He thought it was admirable of her. She never traded on it. In fact she never mentioned it, and he had only discovered it a year after they'd started dating, when he read an article about her. Whitney hadn't said a word about it to him before.

He had never met Whitney's sister, whom Whitney described as a flake for most of her life, and the consummate stage mother living vicariously through her child, which sounded unhealthy to him. He loved how balanced and sane Whitney was, despite what must have been an unusual upbringing. Enough so to make her gun-shy about marriage and children of her own, which worked for him. Women had been trying to lure and ensnare him into marriage for all the years he'd been divorced, and it was a breath of fresh air that Whitney never did.

Chad was fifty-nine years old, vital, active, healthy, brilliantly successful, and he and Whitney got along perfectly. They were about to leave on their annual summer trip together, on his boat in Italy. They hadn't seen each other in a month, since a lovely Fourth of July weekend in Lake Tahoe. They shared the fun in their lives, not the headaches. He was already on his boat in Monte Carlo, waiting for her, and she was flying over to meet him in a few days. They spent three weeks on his boat every summer, and she spent another week at home afterward, getting organized to go back to work. There was purpose and planning to everything Whitney did. Spontaneity was not her style. To her, spontaneity always felt like chaos.

Paige's love life had been even more checkered than her sister's while she floundered through the early years of her unsuccessful acting career. She'd had a series of notoriously badly behaved Hollywood boyfriends, the usual bad boys to her lost ingénue. She'd had public breakups, embarrassing cheaters, actors who wanted to get to her father by sleeping with her, hoping Bill Watts would take them on as clients and further their careers, since he was still working in his eighties. Paige had been a mess in the early days, and Whitney considered her embarrassing and irresponsible. Paige was almost as beautiful as their legendary mother, but she had never had her act together where men were concerned.

Their mother's death had rocked Paige's world. She was twenty-four when it happened. And losing her mother had led to a year or two of drugs, and a celebrity rehab, while Whitney was doing her residency.

The worst blow had come when their father died two years after their mother. He was ninety-one years old by then. He had gone downhill rapidly after Liz died. He retired very shortly after her death, and his health began to deteriorate. Whitney felt that losing her had disheartened him so severely, he didn't want to survive. They had had a totally codependent relationship. Paige was twenty-six when their father died, and Whitney twenty-eight. It had been a crushing loss for both of them, but Whitney had weathered it as she did all things, with resilience, strength, and quiet fortitude. Paige had been a lost soul for almost two years, squandering her share of the inheritance, in a free fall of confusion and despair without her parents, and had finally stopped it by deciding that what she needed to ground her and give stability and purpose to her life was a baby. With no meaningful man of the hour to accomplish that with, she'd used an old friend from high school as a sperm donor. He was gay and had been touched by the request. He'd made it clear that he didn't want an active role in the child's life, which appealed to Paige. She embraced the idea of being a single mother, and he did it as a favor for an old friend. Paige was already pregnant when she informed Whitney of what she'd done. Whitney was horrified, and shortly after Emma was born, the baby's biological father got sick and died of AIDS, and Whitney attended her niece's birth with a feeling of overwhelming dismay and sorrow for the child, with a mother who would be incapable of caring for her responsibly, and no father at all. Whitney was glad her parents weren't there to see it, but things had turned out better than she'd feared. Much to Whitney's surprise, Paige was fiercely devoted to the baby, and made her the center of her universe. Whitney didn't agree with her theories about child rearing, but at least Paige was no longer on drugs or endangering Emma in any overt way, even if she was obsessed with making her a star one day. But it could have been a lot worse. Paige cleaned up her act and settled down to mother the baby, and Whitney was pleasantly surprised.

She visited them from time to time, since they both lived in L.A., and Emma was undeniably cute and bright and adorable. She provided a "child fix" for Whitney when she thought she needed one, which was rare. But Emma was her niece, and despite her cynicism on the subject, Whitney had to concede that Paige took motherhood seriously, and her daughter's modeling and acting career even more so. Paige groomed Emma for stardom and often made a fool of herself on TV and movie sets. And admittedly, she had created a successful career for Emma, which Paige thought was desirable and Whitney thought was a grievous mistake.

Whitney still considered Paige a flake about a number of things, but not about Emma's career. Paige was totally focused on it, to the exclusion of all else. She still had the occasional affair with some second-rate actor or other, whom she usually met on the set of the show Emma was on, but her romances never lasted long. She was so intense and obsessed with Emma's career that she drove most healthy, normal men away. For Emma's sake, Whitney tried not to be overly critical of Paige. She loved being with her niece, when they all had time, which wasn't often. Whitney was busy with her patients and her work, and Paige was always chauffeuring Emma from one lesson to the next. "I'm going to be a *big star* one day, you know, Aunt Whit," Emma loved to tease when she was with her aunt and her mother wasn't around. She would do a little pirouette then and laugh.

"You already are a star," Whitney reminded her. "You're on a TV show. What more do you want?"

"I'd like to be on a girls' soccer team, if you really want to know," Emma would say dreamily. That sounded fantastic to her.

"I don't think your mom will let you do that," her aunt said.

"I know, she says I'd get hurt, or knock out a tooth or something. But it sounds like fun to me."

"You can decide all that for yourself when you're older," Whitney reminded her. "You can pick any career you want one day."

"Not likely," Emma said wistfully, "as long as Mom breathes air. She'd kill me if I give up acting, after everything she's done for me." Paige knew how to run her daughter's life with just the right amount of pressure and guilt. "She says she gave up her own acting career to make me a star like my grandmother. Mom thinks I'll win an Oscar someday."

"Maybe you will," Whitney said, "if that's what you want to do." For now, Paige wasn't giving her a choice, and Whitney felt sorry for her. Emma was a slave to her mother's ambitions, but Whitney didn't dare say too much to her niece about it. Maybe one day when she was older, she would. At nine, it was too soon.

"Mom says you're a shrink because you think everyone in Hollywood is crazy," Emma said whimsically, and her aunt laughed.

"I never thought of it that way, but maybe she's right. There are certainly plenty of crazy people in the business," and in some ways, she thought her sister was one of them, at Emma's expense. The life of a child star was not easy or fun. Whitney had several patients who had been actors when they were young, and had paid a high price for it. She didn't want that happening to Emma, but she knew it already was, and there was nothing she could do about it. She just tried to spend a little relaxed time with Emma whenever she could, they had a good time together, when Paige let that happen. Fun wasn't on Emma's schedule, or playtime or other kids.

Whitney hadn't seen Paige or Emma for the past few weeks. She'd been busy and so had they, and she wanted to touch base with them before she left at the end of the week to meet Chad in Europe on his boat. She was looking forward to it. They were planning to sail to Portofino as soon as she arrived. It was one of their favorite spots, a romantic little port town on their way to Corsica and Sardinia and other idyllic locations. Whitney could hardly wait, and had been packing for several days. She knew she wouldn't have time to see Paige and Emma now, but she wanted to call them before she left, to say goodbye.

Paige stopped and picked up dinner on the way home from Emma's ballet lesson. They only had half an hour before her voice coach arrived. She'd bought two big salads, and set them out on the kitchen table while Emma complained.

"I'm tired of salad. Why can't we have pizza?"

"Because you're the star of a TV show, remember?"

"So I can never eat pizza?"

"Of course you can, we had pizza two days ago, you just can't have it every night."

"Why? Because you're afraid I'll get fat?" There was an evil glint in Emma's eye, and Paige did not look amused. What if Emma suddenly started overeating as a way of expressing some kind of rebellion in a few years? It was a horrifying thought.

"You'll never be fat, it's not in our DNA." Both she and Whitney had always been slim, as had their mother, but Emma liked torturing her sometimes, and knew how to do it. Paige was dreading her teenage years. "Besides, if we take the Broadway musical, you don't want to put on weight before we do."

"I don't care," Emma said with a shrug. She dug into her salad with no interest and stopped eating when the voice coach came. She stayed for two hours and after that, Paige watched Emma take her bath, and then they spent another forty-five minutes going over her lines for the next day. She knew them flawlessly, although she was tired by then, and started to miss a few. She was drifting off to sleep as Paige stood looking at her for a moment and smiled as Emma's eyes fluttered closed. She was already sound asleep.

"Good night, my beautiful little star," she whispered and then closed the door softly behind her. Building an important career for her was a demanding, full-time job, but Paige never regretted it for a minute. Emma had made her dreams come true, and now she was going to do the same for her. She was going to give Emma dreams that she never even knew she had.

Chapter 2

Emma had a long shooting schedule the next day and was in every scene on the call list, but she knew all her lines. She met with Belinda, the teacher, during lunch to turn in her homework, and Belinda gave her a break and didn't assign her homework for that night, because she knew Emma would be tired at the end of the day. They had a flexible study schedule that accommodated her obligations on the set.

They finished shooting at four in the afternoon, after starting at seven A.M. Emma had been in hair and makeup at six-thirty, and had to learn a new, very emotional scene that the writers had added the night before. Paige had helped her learn her lines, as she always did. As soon as Emma came off the set, Paige drove her to Santa Monica for her hip-hop lesson. She would have canceled it, but she knew it was Emma's favorite activity. The traffic was terrible getting there, and the lesson ended at seven, which gave them just under an hour to pick up something for dinner and be back at their house in Beverly

Hills at eight o'clock to meet with Emma's drama coach, Marty Smith. He was an excellent drama coach for children, and he'd been working with Emma since she started on the show. She had learned a lot from him, he was a hard taskmaster, but known for his great results. He also didn't tolerate anyone being late, and Paige knew that if they didn't get there on time he was capable of leaving to make the point. She was trying to speed through heavy traffic, while Emma played on her iPad. Paige stopped at a 7-Eleven and picked up half a roast chicken for dinner when they got home, and she got Emma a blue Slurpee slush drink because she begged for it, and Paige didn't want to argue with her. They were both hungry and it was late, and they got back onto the freeway, and Paige groaned when she saw the traffic slow down up ahead. There was an accident, and she knew Marty would have a fit and might even leave if they were late. Emma's lips were blue from the dye in the drink by then, and Paige laughed when she saw her in the rearview mirror, and noticed then that Emma hadn't put her seatbelt back on yet after their stop at the 7-Eleven. She was going to remind her, but they were stopped in traffic. Emma was usually good about that, and always reminded her mother and told her not to text, which she sometimes did if they were very late. Paige always had her sit in the backseat, to be safe, and she was diligent about seatbelts, most of the time. But once in a while if she was too busy or rushed she forgot, even after the buzzer sounded three times before it stopped.

Whitney had had a long day too. It was her last day in the office before leaving on her trip. She was handing off all her regular patients to a psychiatrist who had covered for her before for the month of August. He taught at the medical school at UCLA, and her patients liked him. She'd seen her last patient that afternoon, and was going to finish packing that night. She had a stack of new bikinis and wraps for the trip, and a ticket for the flight to Paris at eight the next morning. She was flying straight to Charles de Gaulle airport, and had a two-hour layover until the flight to Nice at six A.M. local time. Three of the crew members from Chad's boat were meeting her, as they always did, and by eight A.M. local time, she'd be on his yacht. They planned to leave the dock immediately and head for Portofino, which was about a seven-hour trip by sea. By late afternoon, they would be in Portofino in time for dinner, and their vacation would have begun.

Chad liked to travel as far offshore as possible, and Whitney knew her cellphone wouldn't work then, so she wanted to call Paige and Emma that night, before she started traveling the next morning. Paige had all the Satcom numbers on the boat from previous trips, but Whitney had emailed them to her again. She wouldn't need to call, but it was good to have them, just in case. Whitney usually texted her a few times from the trip, but her vacations with Chad were the only time when she disconnected from all her responsibilities, and she could hardly wait. He was planning to have guests on board for a day or two in Sardinia, but for most of the three weeks, they would be alone. She loved her time with him, and being able to relax and forget life in L.A. completely.

Paige had rented a house in Malibu for the last two weeks of August so Emma could play on the beach. She wanted to stay close to home so Emma didn't miss any of her lessons during their brief hiatus. They would be off for August too, and Whitney would be back

23

from Europe halfway through their time in Malibu. She was planning to spend three weeks with Chad and a week on her own to get organized before she went back to work, as she always did. Whitney had promised to spend some time with Paige and Emma in Malibu then. Emma would still be having lessons. She never really got time off. Emma knew better than anyone that the road to stardom was hard work.

Traffic on the freeway started to speed up as they got closer to home. Emma had finished the Slurpee by then and was still playing on her iPad in the backseat when Paige looked at her watch and realized they were going to be late for Marty. And if he was in a bad mood, as he often was at the end of the day, she knew he wouldn't wait. He always said that he hated people wasting his time.

Paige grabbed her cellphone from the seat next to her, to send him a text, as Emma glanced up in the back with disapproval.

"Don't text and drive, Mommy!" she said sternly.

"I just want to tell Marty that we're running a few minutes late, but we're almost home. Otherwise, he'll leave before we get there." Paige started texting quickly, holding the steering wheel firm with one arm.

"You're not wearing your seatbelt!" Emma complained as Paige glanced at her and noticed that Emma still wasn't either. She'd heard the buzzer but forgotten again, worried about Marty leaving, and that he would charge them for the session.

"Neither are you," Paige said, distracted by the text she was writing. She'd been rushed and stressed all day.

"I forgot," Emma said and started to put it on, but it was caught in the door and she couldn't. She struggled to free it but it was stuck, and she told her mother.

"We'll be home in a minute," Paige said, and Emma's eyes grew wide as she saw a truck careening toward them from the left, which Paige didn't notice as she wrote the text. The truck hit them with immense force as Emma screamed. There was the sound of crushing metal as Paige's cellphone flew from her hand. Emma watched in horror as her mother's whole body shot through the windshield like a torpedo, careened through the air, and disappeared under the cars in front of them. Their car struck another, stopped abruptly, and Emma hit her head hard on the TV screen on the back of the front passenger seat. They were crushed in a tangle of other cars. The truck had forced them three lanes over. The driver lay inert with his head on the steering wheel as people rushed from their cars toward him, and several others ran toward Paige's car.

The door on Emma's side had flown open, and Emma lay unconscious on the freeway, her head, face, and arms covered with blood. People were calling 911, and a group of them were staring at Paige under the SUV where she had landed, covered with blood and broken glass from her exit through the windshield. Traffic was backed up as far as you could see behind them, and within minutes people could hear sirens in the distance as they surveyed the scene in shock. The driver of the truck was dead, and there was no sign of life under the car where Paige lay. No one dared touch Emma for fear of damaging her further, and they weren't sure if she was breathing. It didn't look like it, but there was so much blood everywhere, no one could see clearly.

Only one ambulance left the scene quickly with Emma. After that, it took time to move the truck, Paige's car, and the other disabled vehicles to the side of the road and to remove Paige's body and the truck driver's from the scene, and it was hours before traffic began moving again. In all, four people had been injured but none severely, except Emma. The paramedics had inserted a breathing tube as they left the scene with sirens shrieking and lights flashing and assessed her in critical condition. The police and paramedics had said Paige was dead on impact, when she hit the pavement.

The police found a pink backpack in the backseat of the car, with an ID badge from the studio with Emma's name on it, and Paige's purse with her driver's license was on the floor of the front passenger seat, alongside her cellphone with a shattered screen. She and Emma both carried a card that stated that their hospital of choice in an emergency was Cedars-Sinai.

Paige and the truck driver were taken to the morgue by the police, and there was nothing in Paige's purse listing next of kin or who to notify in an accident. They would have to get the information from the DMV, if it was listed. All they knew for now were their names.

The paramedics had assessed that Emma had a serious head injury, a broken arm, and probably internal injuries. The police had made due note that she hadn't been wearing her seatbelt. Neither of them would have fallen out of the car if they had been, or flown out, in Paige's case. All the police could deduce was that Paige hadn't seen the oncoming truck, and possibly had been on her cellphone or texting. Both were common causes of accidents and fatalities. Beyond that, they knew nothing, not even whether Emma would survive the accident. It had looked unlikely when they'd left the scene and headed at full speed to Cedars-Sinai.

Whitney sent some emails when she got home, took a bath, and washed her hair. She'd had a manicure and pedicure at lunchtime between patients. She closed her bags and called Paige. It went straight to voice mail. She tried again before she went to bed, knowing it would be too early to call them the next day before she left. She had to leave her house at five, to check in for her flight at LAX at six A.M., so she sent them a text, sending her love and promising to call or text from the boat. It was the best she could do, and she assumed that Paige was busy, or her cellphone might have run out of juice, which happened a lot when Paige ran around all day and forgot to charge it.

Whitney was in bed by midnight. Paige never called her back. She got up at four, left the house promptly at five in an Uber. Her flight to Paris was on time, and took off on schedule at eight A.M., and she settled back in her seat for breakfast and a movie. She wasn't worried about trying to reach Paige again. She had said goodbye to them the night before in her text. All she had to do was sit back and enjoy her vacation. Whitney was smiling as they flew over Los Angeles with the sun shining brightly. She was thinking of Chad and meeting him on the boat, and she fully intended to forget L.A., her work, and even her sister and niece for the next three weeks. This was her time, and she needed it badly. She would send Paige another text from Italy when they got there. They never stayed in constant contact anyway, even in L.A. They had their own busy lives in separate worlds. And once on vacation, Whitney didn't feel obliged to call. They would catch up on news in three weeks when she got back home.

Emma was unconscious when she got to Cedars-Sinai and was taken to the trauma unit, where the neurosurgeon on call examined her. She had a severe head injury from the impact and was in a coma. The debate was whether to operate on her brain or wait to see how severe the swelling was, if she even survived the next few hours. They had no next of kin to call, and the Highway Patrol and paramedics who'd brought her in informed them that the female driving was dead at the scene of the accident. They only had the information on Paige's driver's license, and Emma's name from her badge. They sent a squad car to the address on Paige's license and found no one home. The police were checking the DMV for next of kin, but had none by morning. They had the name of the TV studio to call, but had to wait until working hours to reach them. For now, Emma was alone in the world, and Whitney was on her way to France.

When Whitney arrived at Charles de Gaulle airport for her layover before the flight to Nice, she didn't turn her cellphone on, because she wasn't expecting any calls. It was four A.M. in France and too early to call Chad. It was seven in the evening in L.A. by then, nine hours earlier than Paris. It was almost twenty-four hours since the accident, and Emma's condition was unchanged. She remained in a coma, intubated, her life hanging by a thread.

The police had called Melvin Levy, the producer of the show, that morning. He was shocked to hear what had happened to Emma and of Paige's death. They had no light to shed on whom to call to notify relatives. They knew she had a sister, but didn't know her name or how to reach her. There was no record of a father to contact anywhere in Emma's files, nor the name of anyone to call in an emergency, other than her mother. The police had asked them to release nothing to the press until the family could be located and notified of the accident and Paige's death. Respecting the police request, no announcement was made to the cast, other than that Emma was out sick. They were shooting episodes for the fall, after the hiatus, and could shoot around her for several weeks and catch up later. She had just finished the school term with Belinda, so they had no work to do until September. Her absence was not a crisis for them yet, but it would be if she stayed out for too long.

The producer and director conferred quietly about the call from the police, hoping that Emma would survive, and wondering what would happen next. It was shocking to think that a child so young might die, and that her mother already had. Neither of them had any idea who to call. They knew that Paige was a single mother, and they vaguely recalled Paige saying that Emma's biological father had died around the time she was born. They assumed that some friend or relative would be with her. They called throughout the day for reports on Emma's condition and were told that no information could be released, but that her status was unchanged.

Whitney caught the first flight to Nice, as she'd planned to, and had been traveling for seventeen hours by then. Chad's strapping young, immaculately white-uniformed crew members met her at the Nice airport and whisked her and her luggage to their van. They drove her to Monaco, where Chad was waiting for her on deck in white jeans and a sky blue sweater, and a broad smile the moment he saw her. He already had a deep tan. She came up the passerelle, and he put his arms around her and held her as they basked in the warmth of each other's company for a moment.

"I've missed you," he said, beaming.

"I've missed you too," she said, with her arms around his waist. It felt so good to be there. In a way, being with him always felt like home, and at the same time whenever she saw him it always felt exciting and new. They saw each other infrequently enough to keep their relationship interesting.

"How was the flight?" he asked her casually.

"Long, but worth every minute of it," she said as they sat on a banquette, and a stewardess handed her a cup of coffee.

The boat was a hundred and eighty feet long, fifty-five meters, with a crew of fifteen. They had been waiting for her to arrive to set sail and were already casting off lines.

"We'll leave in a few minutes," Chad told her. It was a beautiful late July morning, the castle loomed over them, and the marina was full of yachts as large as Chad's and even larger, some of them quite well known. It was easy to get spoiled while sharing time with him. Her luggage had already disappeared to his cabin where a stewardess would unpack for her, and there was a pink marble bathroom and dressing room for her use next to his accommodations. She had given the crew her purse to take with her bags. There was nothing she needed now, it was the middle of the night in California, and she was in no rush to charge and turn on her cellphone. She was on vacation, and part of the beauty of being on the boat with him was that she could leave all her duties and obligations behind. She had none from late July to late August. Her time off had already begun.

They pulled out of the port, motoring slowly, and twenty minutes later the chef produced a sumptuous breakfast for them at the dining table on deck. As soon as they cleared the boats coming into port to dock, they turned the engines on full, picked up speed, and headed to the open sea where Chad preferred to cruise for the trip to Italy. They expected to anchor in Portofino in the late afternoon and go ashore for dinner at a small restaurant they knew and liked there.

They lay on deck chairs and chatted easily in the sea breeze, as Whitney dozed in the sun, and went down to Chad's cabin before lunch to change. Then they had a sumptuous meal on deck. It was a fairy-tale life being with him, and they held hands as they lay in deck chairs side by side after lunch and slept until they reached Portofino.

As Chad and Whitney watched the crew set anchor and tie up to a rock just outside the port of Portofino, Emma had been in a coma at Cedars-Sinai for thirty-six hours, since the accident. Her condition was still listed as critical. It was morning in L.A., and the police had obtained Whitney's name and cellphone number from Paige's DMV records in the computer system. She was listed as next of kin in an emergency. The police had been calling Whitney's phone for the past twelve hours but had been unable to reach her, and the producers of *The Clan* had been able to keep the story out of the news, since no family member had been contacted yet. For now, no one on the set needed to know the truth. Eventually, the writers would have to write her accident into the scripts, but that was weeks away, or after the hiatus. The producers had told the cast that she had mono, which would buy them some time, and everyone was sorry to hear it.

Whitney had gotten her cellphone out of her purse before she and Chad boarded the tender to go into the little port town and walk around for a while. She'd asked a stewardess to charge her phone and left it with her.

They wandered in and out of the little shops and stopped for a glass of wine at a restaurant with a terrace overlooking the port, enjoying each other. Their time together was always relaxing and uncomplicated. They were both people who appreciated life without drama, and they treasured their downtime together. It was the nature of their relationship, stress-free adult time.

They went back to the boat after an hour, and the stewardess returned Whitney's cellphone. She noticed that she had a slew of messages, which was unusual while she was on vacation. She glanced at them and saw that none of the numbers were familiar, and Paige hadn't called her. She was sure she was busy with Emma, with their long list of daily appointments and lessons that extended from morning to night year round. Whitney wondered if the calls were from patients, if they'd had trouble reaching her replacement, and decided to check before she went to Chad's cabin to dress for dinner on shore that night. Chad handed her a glass of champagne as she sat down to listen to her messages, and then he went downstairs to shower and change. Neither of them liked being interrupted by work unnecessarily when they were on vacation. Chad had strict rules about it at his office, and so did she.

"I won't be long," Whitney promised as she took a sip of the champagne and set it down on a table next to her, as he left her and she waited for the first message to play. She was surprised to hear that it was from a lieutenant of the LAPD. She couldn't imagine why he was calling her. She had three more from him and began to wonder if it was about one of her patients. Whitney dreaded hearing that one of them had been injured or worse, committed suicide. That hadn't happened in years. She pressed the number to return the call and asked for him by name when she reached the Los Angeles Police Department. The lieutenant came on the line quickly.

"We've been trying to reach you," he said when Whitney gave her name and sounded puzzled to be hearing from him.

"I'm sorry, I've been traveling. I'm calling from Italy. What can I do for you, Lieutenant?" She had on her official doctor's voice and waited for him to explain.

"I'm sorry to call you about this. We've gone to your home several times trying to locate you. There was an accident two days ago, involving your sister, Paige Watts, and her daughter, Emma." Whitney froze as he said it. She hadn't expected this, and now she wanted to know the rest of it quickly.

"What happened? Are they all right?" she asked, sounding hoarse. Suddenly she was shaking.

The lieutenant hesitated for a fraction of an instant. "No, I'm sorry," he said for the second time. "Your sister was ejected through the windshield of the car she was driving and was killed on impact when an out of control truck hit her car. It was probably too late to avoid it when she saw it."

"Oh my God." Whitney was deathly pale. Other than Emma, Paige was her only living relative. They had had their differences, but they loved each other, and now she was dead, at thirty-seven. "Where is she?"

"She's at the police morgue, where she's been while we were unable to get in touch with you."

"And my niece?" Whitney could hardly breathe now. What if Emma was dead too?

"She was unconscious at the scene. Neither of them were wearing seatbelts. The car came to a halt on impact with other vehicles, and your niece fell out of the car. She's been in a coma since the accident, with a head injury, at Cedars-Sinai. She's in critical condition, but she's alive." Whitney was trembling violently by then, thinking of Emma in a coma and Paige dead. "I can tell you who to speak to there," the police lieutenant said helpfully as Whitney grabbed a pen and pad and wrote down the names he gave her, of the pediatric neurologists in charge of her case at Cedars. "I told them to expect to hear from you as soon as we contacted you. Is there anyone you want to send over to be with her?"

"There's no one except me," Whitney said weakly. "The only relatives she has are her mother and me. She has no father." And now she had no mother either. Only Whitney.

"We spoke to the producer of the TV show she's on, to try and find out which relatives to locate. They've been very cooperative about not talking to the press until you were notified. You might want to speak to them." Whitney nodded, her mind racing about what to do next. She had to get back to Los Angeles immediately. She couldn't leave Emma alone in a hospital in a coma. And what if she died before Whitney could get there? She couldn't bear thinking about it, and Whitney was trying not to think of her sister dead in a morgue for the past two days while she was flying to France and getting on a boat to Italy. That was why she had never reached them. From the time of the accident the lieutenant had mentioned, Whitney could easily calculate that Paige had been dead before she'd left L.A.

She thanked the lieutenant and hung up and immediately called the doctors he'd mentioned at Cedars-Sinai. She was able to reach the second one within a few minutes, identified herself, and told him she was a physician. "How is she?" she inquired about Emma.

"There's been no change since she came in," he said simply. "There's frontal lobe damage with considerable swelling. We've avoided doing surgery until now. I'm still hoping the swelling will come down on its own. She's had several brain scans, a CT scan, and an MRI. We don't see damage or lesions, other than the swelling, but the fact is that she's in a coma, with no sign of her regaining consciousness since she's been here. She's had considerable trauma to her head, and she's young. There's no way to know yet what kind of damage that's going to leave her with, if any. There could be severe consequences or fully restored brain function after the trauma heals. As long as she's still comatose, there's no way to know how the trauma has affected her brain. We've intubated her and sedated her, but where it goes from here, we just don't know yet." Whitney felt sick as she listened. What had Paige been thinking? If they were on the freeway, why weren't they both wearing seatbelts? The image of her sister shooting through the windshield like a human torpedo was horrifying.

"There are no big decisions to be made right now," the doctor said quietly, "although there could be later. She has brain activity. How impacted she is, though, we just don't know, and we won't until she wakes up. *If* she does," he emphasized. "We need to see how the next few days go. Will you be coming in to see her?" the doctor asked.

"Of course. I'm in Italy," she told him again. "I have to get back to L.A. now as quickly as I can." She gave him her cellphone number and asked him to put it in Emma's chart as the family member to contact about any changes. "I'll be there as soon as I can get back," she said and hung up. After that, she called the producers of *The Clan* and explained the situation to them in greater detail than they'd heard from the police. She was grateful they'd been able to keep it out of the press. Whitney didn't want a feeding frenzy at the hospital, or anyone taking pictures of Emma, intubated in a coma. That would be awful.

Whitney looked like she was in shock when Chad came back up on deck a few minutes later and saw how pale she was.

"What happened? Is everything okay?" She shook her head as tears filled her eyes and she couldn't speak for a moment.

"My sister had an accident with Emma, my niece. Paige was killed at the scene two days ago, and Emma is in a coma at Cedars-Sinai with a serious head injury. It took them this long to find me." She felt guilty now for being so blithe about her absence, unaware that there was a problem.

"Oh my God, that's awful," he said, deeply sympathetic. "Who's with her?" He looked startled and shaken too. The news was so severe, with her sister killed and Whitney's niece critically injured.

"No one. I'm it now." The reality of it hit Whitney like an avalanche, and Chad looked stunned too.

"No father?"

Whitney shook her head. "He was just a friend of my sister's, a sperm donor. He died when Emma was a few months old. My sister wanted to have a baby on her own." He nodded, there was nothing he could say. "Chad, I'm so sorry, but I have to go back now, right away. I can't leave her there alone."

"Of course not." He had children and understood that. "You should meet with the doctors and see if there are any decisions that have to be made. You can come back in a few days, when you see how things are going." She stared at him as he said it and realized that he didn't understand the situation fully. She was not a concerned aunt now, she was Emma's only living relative, and her only stand-in parent. Emma had no one else in the world except Whitney, and she didn't even know yet that her mother was dead. If she came out of the coma, it would be Whitney who would have to tell her. She couldn't imagine herself coming back to the boat anytime soon, even if Emma made a miraculous recovery. And where was Emma going to live? The answer to that question was obvious too. And now Whitney had her sister's funeral to arrange.

"You'll make it back to the boat sometime in the next three weeks. I'll be waiting for you, Whitney. Please call me when you get there and tell me what's happening. Now, how are we going to get you home?" Chad rang for the purser and explained that Whitney had to get back to L.A. immediately. They had already unpacked her bags that afternoon on the way to Portofino, but they promised to pack her up again right away.

"Do you want to leave it all here?" Chad suggested, and Whitney shook her head. She didn't see how she could return to the boat.

Within minutes, they had arranged for a helicopter to pick her up and fly her back to Nice. It would be a much shorter trip than it had been by sea. They had tried for a flight out of Genoa too, but every seat was booked. They got a first-class ticket for her to Paris, and the first flight to Los Angeles a few hours after that. Twenty minutes later, Whitney was dressed in black jeans and a white shirt with a black cotton blazer over her arm. Her bags were packed and ready, and the helicopter arrived and landed on the upper deck landing pad ten minutes later. Chad pulled her into his arms for a long embrace.

"Call me. Let me know if there's anything I can do to help." She nodded, her eyes filled with tears.

"Thank you. I'm sorry to bail on you, Chad. There's nothing else I can do."

"Of course not. You'll be back in a few days," he said reassuringly, but she couldn't bring Emma with her with a head injury, nor abandon a nine-year-old child who had just lost her mother. Whitney's life was going to get complicated now. She just hoped that Emma would survive. Whitney didn't want to lose both of them. She couldn't. Chad kissed her gently on the lips and handed her into the helicopter. Her bags were already on it, and as they lifted off and headed toward Nice, Chad was standing on deck waving to her. He tried to look encouraging, but was sad for her. She couldn't help wonder when she would see him again. Probably no time soon. But that seemed unimportant. Her little sister was lying dead in the police morgue in L.A., and Emma was fighting for her life. Nothing else mattered now.

Chapter 3

It was a ten-hour flight from Paris to Los Angeles, with the additional flight from Nice before that, and a layover at Charles de
Gaulle airport. The flight took off from Paris at ten P.M., and with the
time difference, they landed at L.A. an hour later than the time they
took off from CDG. It was eight A.M. the next day in Paris by then, and
eleven P.M. in L.A. Whitney wasn't sure if Chad was up, so she texted
him that she had arrived safely, picked up her luggage at baggage
claim, cleared customs, and took a cab to her house to drop off her
bags. She just opened the front door and shoved them in, set the
alarm again, and ran back to the waiting cab and asked him to take
her to Cedars-Sinai. It was one A.M. She had dozed on the plane, but
only for a few minutes here and there. Whitney had too much on her
mind to get any rest. She was still trying to get her head around the
fact that her baby sister was dead. They had argued for most of their
childhood and been different all their lives. Paige had always frustrated her. Their thought processes were so opposite and conflicting

at times. Paige's ambitions had always seemed so skewed to Whitney, but she loved her and now she was dead.

Whitney couldn't understand why neither of them had their seatbelts on, according to the police. It seemed totally irresponsible to her. Was it an oversight, was Paige distracted, did she not care? She was usually so careful with Emma and treated her like a precious jewel. Why, this time, had she put her at risk, and herself as well? It was the kind of stupid, flaky thing Paige did at times that no one could explain.

Paige monitored a million unimportant details and left out the vital one that had cost her her life, and maybe Emma's. A head injury was a very serious thing. None of it made any sense. What was Paige doing when the truck hit them? Why didn't she see it coming? She wondered if the police lieutenant's guess was right and she had been texting, or talking on the phone. And what was Emma doing? Why was her seatbelt off? She knew better too. What was going to happen to Emma now? Whitney was her only relative, and Emma would have to live with her. She hadn't spelled it out to Chad before she'd left, but this was going to change Whitney's life radically. She was no longer a single woman with no children. She was a single woman who would be living with a nine-year-old niece, *if* she lived. And if she didn't, Whitney would be alone in the world, with no husband, no kids, no sister, and no Emma. She was overwhelmed with a sense of loneliness, loss, and fear as they pulled up in front of the hospital.

Whitney paid the cabdriver and gave him a big tip, then rushed into the emergency entrance of the hospital and asked for pediatric ICU, where they were monitoring Emma closely. There were no visiting hours at pediatric ICU, family could come at any time. Whitney got off the elevator and followed the signs. She went to the nurses' desk and glanced around at the cubicles where parents huddled with their desperately sick children. Whitney wondered which one Emma was in. The cubicles were dark since it was late at night, with monitors lit up, and nurses in hospital scrubs walked soundlessly in and out to check on a beeping monitor or the sound of an alarm.

"I'm Dr. Whitney Watts," she said quietly. "I'm looking for Emma Watts." The nurse at the desk nodded and got up and walked Whitney into one of the cubicles a few feet away. In the next one, you could hear a child crying, and a baby wailing down the hall. This wasn't a happy place, it was full of pain and fear, agonizing procedures, and parents' terror that their children might not survive.

Emma looked tiny lying on the bed, with a breathing tube in her mouth and tape attaching it to her face, while a nurse stood next to her, monitoring her vital signs. There was a huge bandage on her head, and electrodes poking out from under it recording an ongoing EEG to check her brain waves. Her face was black and blue, and her arm was in a cast. There was no sound in the room, except from the machines. The two nurses exchanged a look as Whitney approached the bed. Emma was covered with a thin blanket, and the nurse standing next to her whispered that she'd been spiking a fever since six o'clock that night.

"What does that mean?" Whitney asked, panicked.

"It can happen after an accident, or from the head injury. Her brain regulates her temperature and body heat, and it's deregulated right now. We're keeping an eye on it. The attending came in at ten o'clock. There's been no change." Whitney nodded, her eyes huge and swimming with tears as she gently touched Emma's delicate hand. It struck Whitney more than ever how much she looked like Paige. The two sisters didn't even look alike, Whitney was much taller, had long straight ebony-colored hair in contrast to Paige's blond wavy hair, although they both had their mother's sky blue eyes. Paige had always seemed more fragile, and Whitney calmer and stronger, although she didn't feel it now.

Whitney shuddered, thinking of her sister in the morgue. She didn't want Paige to be cold. She didn't want to leave her there, but she had to see Emma first. There was a narrow cot in the cubicle, if Whitney wanted to stay, and the nurse who had walked her in offered to make it up as a bed for her, but Whitney didn't want to sleep now, particularly if these were Emma's final hours. She wanted to stay close to her and sat down in the chair next to the bed. Emma had an IV in one arm, and Whitney tenderly took the other hand in her own.

"Hi, baby, it's Aunt Whit. I came back from France to see you. I love you so much. I'm right here with you. You're going to be okay." Whitney talked to her in soft, soothing tones without stopping for the next two hours, on the off chance that Emma could hear her. Medical reports were full of people who claimed that they had heard their loved ones speaking to them, even when they were in a coma. Whitney wasn't taking any chances. She wanted Emma to know she was there. She had been through a terrible trauma and been alone in the hospital for the past two days with no one familiar next to her.

Whitney sat next to her all night, and as the sun came up over Los Angeles, she gently laid her head down next to Emma and fell asleep. They left her there until the hospital neurologist came by to check Emma in the morning and saw Whitney sleeping there, her head close to Emma's.

"Who's that?" he whispered to the nurse. He knew that Emma's mother had been killed in the accident.

"Her aunt," the nurse whispered back. "She's a doctor." He nodded and left the room to add a notation to the chart that there had been no change.

Whitney woke up a few minutes later and went out into the hall to talk to the doctor.

"How is she?" Whitney looked as exhausted as she felt.

"About the same. Traumatic head injury. The monitors show that the swelling may be coming down a little, but not enough. She took a direct hit in the frontal lobe of her brain, and as a physician, you know what that means. Some of her major control centers are out of whack: swallowing, eating, body heat, speech, motor skills, reason, memory, the regulation of her heartbeat. Her pulse was one ninety for most of yesterday. It's a little like a major stroke in an adult, and we won't know exactly what functions have been affected until she wakes up. And there's no sign of that yet."

"Is she going to survive this?" Whitney asked him bluntly, and he hesitated.

"She might. There are no guarantees at this point. She's very badly shaken up. Kids are resilient, but she had a major blow to the head."

"Are we looking at permanent damage?" Whitney asked in a hoarse voice, afraid of what she'd hear, but she wanted to know the worst.

"Possibly. We just don't know. Even if she's severely injured, if she regains consciousness, she can begin to get back many of the abilities she's lost. With a lot of time and a lot of therapy, she could come out of this whole . . . or she might not. We just don't know yet." And then

43

he thought of something. "One of the nurses said she's a child actress. Is that true?" Whitney nodded.

"She's on a TV show." It seemed irrelevant to Whitney.

"We'd like to keep the press out of here," he said firmly. "I'm sure you would too. I'll put a warning on her chart. We don't want photographers showing up, upsetting everyone, and also violating the HIPAA privacy rights of other patients." Whitney knew protecting a patient's right to privacy was vitally important in hospitals, and press showing up would violate those rights for other patients as well as Emma. And the medical staff didn't want the disruption, nor did Whitney. She hadn't thought of that until now.

"Neither do I," Whitney said with a grim expression. She didn't want anything putting pressure on Emma now, or jeopardizing her recovery when she woke up. "Will she remember what happened?" This wasn't Whitney's area of expertise.

"I doubt it. At least not for a while, or maybe never. She may have holes in her memory for the rest of her life. This is going to be a huge shock for her to absorb." He looked at Whitney sympathetically then. "Try to get some rest. If she makes it, this is going to be a long haul." Whitney also knew from her neurology studies during her residency that Emma could be in a coma for the rest of her life and never regain consciousness. There was no guarantee that she'd wake up, or what kind of condition she'd be in if she did. But the fact that there was brain activity was a good sign. The only good news they'd had so far. The doctor went to see another patient then, and said he'd be back in a few hours, and Whitney went to speak to the nurse.

"Do you think it would be okay if I go home for a couple of hours? There are some things I need to take care of."

"Leave us your number," the nurse said kindly, "we'll call you if anything happens." Whitney nodded and left a few minutes later. She wanted to go home and take a shower, and she had to call a funeral home for Paige, and the producers of Emma's show. She wanted to take a quick look around Paige's house and see if there were any clues there about what had happened. She didn't know what they would be, but she wanted to go to their home. It was a way of feeling close to Paige too, almost as though she'd be there. Whitney knew she wouldn't be, but part of her wanted this not to be true. It was too cruel.

Whitney felt crushingly exhausted when she stumbled over her suitcases in the hall as she turned off the alarm at her own house. There was a small stack of mail that had already gathered since she'd left, which the cleaning woman had put on the hall table. Paige had promised to come and look at it for her once a week, and she wouldn't be doing that now.

Whitney made herself a cup of coffee and then went to take a shower. She stood with the hot water pelting down on her as she cried. It had been a terrible night since she'd heard the news about Paige and Emma. She put on jeans afterward and pulled her dark hair tightly back. Then she called the funeral parlor and the morgue. She assumed she would have to identify her sister and was dreading it.

The police sergeant in charge said that her face had been lacerated beyond recognition when she went through the windshield, and then slid along the pavement at sixty miles an hour. He said her dental records would suffice to identify her, and then the funeral home would pick her up.

Whitney called their dentist, who was heartbroken to hear what had happened, and said he'd take Paige's records to the morgue himself. She told the funeral home she wanted her sister to be cremated. She would decide what to do with the ashes later, and thought she'd bury them with their parents. Paige would have wanted to be with them. They had been her refuge and her idols all her life, and hadn't been for Whitney.

And then Whitney called the producer of the show again. He extended their condolences and then asked Whitney a battery of questions about Emma, wanting to know how bad it was.

"Is she disfigured?" Melvin Levy, the executive producer, asked her bluntly.

"No, she's not," Whitney said with a lump in her throat. "She has a head injury and she's in a coma, and we don't know how bad it is yet. We probably won't know until she wakes up."

"Kids are resilient," he said, sounding hopeful. "I've heard of cases where they've been in comas for months, and snap back when they wake up." Emma was neither waking up nor snapping back for the moment, although Whitney appreciated the optimism. "We want to keep her on the show."

"We have no idea what kind of shape she's going to be in, Mr. Levy," Whitney said.

"There will be a lot of sympathy for her after this. Especially after losing her mom. Will you be taking over for Paige?" he asked her directly, which shocked Whitney to the core. She didn't even know what that meant at the moment. Taking over what?

"I'm responsible for her now, if that's what you mean. I'm her only relative. But I have no idea what Emma will be capable of after this, or what she'll want."

"I hope she wants to come back to the show," he said with quiet determination as it became clear to Whitney how single-focused these people were. Paige would have been happy to hear it. Whitney wasn't. All Whitney wanted was for Emma to survive and come out of the coma as undamaged as possible. Her TV career was the least of their worries. But the producer had a hit show to protect. "We'd like to give a statement to the press today. *Entertainment Tonight, People, Us Weekly,* the major fan magazines, the network affiliates."

"What are you planning to tell them?" Whitney asked, feeling anxious about what he was saying.

"That Emma Watts was in an accident three days ago, in which her mother was tragically killed, and Emma is resting comfortably at Cedars-Sinai and will come back as soon as she can. Hopefully, right after the hiatus this summer. We're covered until then and for several episodes in the fall season. We've got some margin here before it becomes crucial for us to have her taping." He had thought of everything since the first call from the police.

"And if she's still in a coma when you run out of episodes she's already taped?" Whitney was shaken by the heartlessness of the business, and what mattered to them.

"Hopefully, she won't be in a coma by then," he said, as though wishing would make it true. "We could write the accident into the new season and even tape her in bed if we have to. We're willing to work around it, just not have her disappear off the air. Do you suppose we could get a shot of her today? It could look like she's just sleeping. It might reassure the fans to see her." He was thinking out loud, trying to work with what they had.

"She has a bandage on her head with EEG pads sticking out, her face is bruised, she has two black eyes and a breathing tube taped across her face. Is that the shot you had in mind?" Whitney was getting angry. She didn't want Emma exploited, or seen in the condition she was in. She was determined to protect her, no matter what Paige would have done. She didn't want to think about that now.

"Not really," he said, sounding embarrassed. "I guess she's not ready for a photo op." He tried to make light of it, but Whitney didn't laugh. She had just lost her sister, and might still lose her niece. "Well, let's stay in touch. We'll get the statement out to the press today about the accident and minimize the damage to her. We'll focus on her mother's death. Do you have a funeral planned?"

"Not yet," Whitney said softly.

"I'm sure there will be a tremendous amount of sympathy for Emma and her mom. This is really a tough break, for all of you." Whitney nodded as tears sprang to her eyes again. She couldn't answer. "Let us know if there's anything we can do."

"Pray," Whitney said in a choked voice.

"Of course . . . I'm sorry for your loss, Miss . . . er . . . Dr. Watts. We're going to miss your sister too. She was a trouper and a real pro." The truth was that Paige hadn't been a pro at anything except being a stage mother. She was a pro at that, but nothing else.

She drove over to Paige's house after the call and let herself in with the key Paige had given her. The house was slightly messy, as always, and there was a note under the door, signed Marty, saying he had waited half an hour for them, they were late, and to give him a call when they got home. She wondered if that was what they had been rushing home for when the truck hit them. Whitney wandered into Emma's bedroom and saw on her bed the teddy bear that she slept with every night. Whitney had given it to her when she was born. It was well-worn, and looked well-loved. Whitney picked it up and took it with her, to put next to Emma in her hospital bed. She wandered around the house feeling lost, missing her sister. The silence was oppressive, and she couldn't stand it after a few minutes. It was just too sad, and would be even more so if Emma died too. She didn't want to think about it.

Then she locked the house up again and drove back to Cedars-Sinai. She hurried to the pediatric ICU to make sure Emma was still alive, and the nurse at the desk told her nothing had changed. Whitney tucked the little teddy bear in next to Emma, and sat down to watch her, stroked her hand, and started talking to her again. Even seeing her in a coma was a relief, at least she was still there.

Three hours later, the nurse at the desk beckoned to her, and there was a security guard standing next to her in the hall outside Emma's cubicle. He explained that they were having a "situation" in the lobby. Throngs of people were leaving flowers and toys and balloons for Emma, and several of them were trying to force their way upstairs. It had just been on the news about the accident, and the reaction had been immediate. The hospital wanted to place a guard outside the ICU, and another near Emma's bed, and he asked if Whitney had any objection. She said on the contrary, she'd be grateful for it. It suddenly reminded her of her childhood, when she and Paige had to be spirited out of restaurants, hotels, and stores through a back entrance while photographers with flashing lights tried to take their pictures.

That was what Paige had wanted for Emma and what she had left her with.

When Whitney tried to walk through the lobby to see how bad it was, the paparazzi recognized her, leapt at her with their flashes in her face and questions about how Emma was. She rushed out without answering any questions, and got lost running through the basement of the hospital, trying to find her way to the right elevator bank to get back to the ICU, to make sure that Emma was all right. The security guard at the door was checking IDs before he let anyone through.

The accident was all over the news that night, with photographs of Emma beaming at them from her birthday party on the show when she'd turned nine a few months before. Reporters were adding a layer of angst and tragedy to the situation, and fans were reacting to it and leaving carloads of gifts in the lobby that had to be removed. Whitney requested that they be sent to be distributed in the children's ward and a homeless shelter across town.

Through it all, Emma remained in the coma, as doctors came and went to examine her, and study the scans of her brain that added no further information to what they already knew.

Chad called her a few days later, and she told him there had been no change. He hadn't wanted to disturb her before that and asked Whitney when she thought she could come back to the boat. She was startled by the question, given Emma's condition, and said she had absolutely no idea. She didn't see how she could come back at all. He seemed surprised and disappointed to hear it and ended the call quickly.

Her office knew she was back in town by then, but she told them she wouldn't be returning to work any earlier than planned. Her life was on hold until something changed with Emma.

Two weeks after the accident, nothing had. Whitney felt like she was on a never-ending treadmill. She only went back to her house every day to shower and change clothes and pick up her mail. She was sleeping in Emma's cubicle in the ICU. The hospital was letting her come and go through the staff entrance, so she could avoid the paparazzi permanently camped out in the lobby, lying in wait for her, and begging for news.

It was beginning to look to Whitney like Emma was never going to come out of the coma, and the MRIs and CT scans hadn't changed in weeks.

Whitney had been sitting in Emma's room, thinking about Paige. She had decided not to plan a funeral for her. She could have a memorial service for her later, and the funeral home was holding her ashes. She couldn't handle a funeral for Paige and being with Emma day and night. Whitney just hoped it wouldn't be a service for both of them. She was wondering what to do about Emma if she remained in the coma, when she heard a slight stirring next to her and glanced at her niece to make sure she was all right. They had lightened the sedation they were giving her a few days before, but that had had no effect either, and when Whitney turned to look at her, she saw Emma open her eyes and stare at her. Whitney could feel her heart pounding in her chest. There was no recognition in Emma's eyes, but they were definitely open, and she looked as though she was trying to guess where she was. Emma reached for the breathing tube, and Whitney stopped her and rang for the nurse, who came immediately and saw what had happened. They sent for the doctor, and Whitney and the ICU nurse spoke soothingly to Emma as tears rolled slowly down her bruised cheeks and she made a grunting noise as they held her hands so she didn't try to remove the tube. She obviously wanted it out so she could talk.

"They're going to come and take it out in a minute," Whitney reassured her, and showed her that her teddy bear was next to her. Emma's eyes were full of questions, and Whitney was sure she wanted her mother. She was dreading having to tell her what had happened. It was a moment of truth that neither of them was ready for but would have to be faced now that she was awake. They had waited nearly three weeks for this since the accident, and now that it had come, Whitney was terrified about what to say to her. It was going to be the worst news of Emma's life. But at least she was finally awake!

The doctor removed the breathing tube when he arrived and examined Emma as her eyes drifted closed again. She didn't speak once the tube was out. She slept for a few minutes as Whitney wondered if she would slip back into the coma, but she didn't. She opened her eyes again with a vague look, and no apparent recognition of Whitney. She looked around the room and seemed confused.

"Let her get oriented for a while," the doctor said gently. He spoke to Emma for a few minutes and told her she was in a hospital. The tube was out, but she hadn't spoken or voiced any of the questions that Whitney was sure were plaguing her. When she woke again, she made a series of unintelligible sounds, as though she was trying to speak to them but couldn't remember the right words. Whitney glanced at the doctor and he nodded. "Her speech center is affected," he explained. "That's not unusual with frontal lobe trauma. She'll get the hang of it again." He asked Emma if she remembered her name, and she shook her head and then said something in her own language again. It sounded like the garbled gurgling of a two-year-old. He asked her then if anything hurt, and she nodded, and then pointed to her head and said the word "Ow," which made sense. He asked her several more questions, and she didn't answer, and then, looking exhausted, she went back to sleep. It was two hours later when she woke again, and Whitney was alone with her. She bent down to kiss her cheek, and Emma looked surprised. Whitney had the feeling that Emma didn't remember her, and then she made the garbled sounds again, as though she had returned from the coma with her own language. She looked irritated when Whitney didn't understand.

"It's going to take a while to get used to things again," Whitney said, trying to reassure her, as Emma turned her head away and cried. The nurse tried speaking to her when she came in with some juice and a straw. Emma took it from her and drank it, and then threw the plastic cup on the floor. The doctor came back later and told Whitney that everything Emma was experiencing was to be expected with a traumatic brain injury. She was liable to be confused and frustrated for a while, and even hostile at times.

"I don't think she recognizes me," Whitney said, looking worried.

"She may not. It's going to take her time to sort things out. Like language, for instance. So far, from what I can see, her speech center has been the most affected."

"How long is that going to take to return to normal?" Whitney asked him.

"She may have to learn everything all over again, or some of it may come back gradually. For now, she seems to have lost speech." He had already made note of it on the chart, and Whitney tried not to look panicked. Now they were beginning to face the results of the accident and Emma's brain injury. She could no longer speak to them, which was going to make communication difficult. Her large motor skills seemed unaffected, the doctor thought she could walk, sit, and stand when she was strong enough. But her ability to speak coherently was gone.

"Do you remember who I am, Em?" Whitney asked when she was back in the room with her again, and Emma looked blank, with no response.

"I'm Whitney. I'm your aunt. And you're Emma." She pointed to herself as she said her own name, and then pointed to her niece, while Emma looked at her with no comprehension, and then shook her head. She said a few more words in her own language, which sounded like nothing to any of them. It bore no resemblance to normal speech, and sounded like caveman grunts or animal sounds, and then she let out a screech as though she was in pain. The nurse asked if she could hear them talking to her, and Emma gave no sign of it. Her hearing had been affected too, which was also not unusual, given the nature of her injury. It was frightening to realize how many of her faculties had been impacted.

The nurse offered to take her for a stroll in the wheelchair and pointed to it, and Emma fought them not to get into it and looked terrified. She didn't understand what they were trying to do. Everything was suddenly new to her, nothing was familiar or made sense. Not their words or their actions, or her own words when she spoke to them, or even the sight of her aunt's face. By the end of the day, Emma was exhausted and fell asleep clutching her teddy bear as Whitney watched her sleep and wondered how they would communicate with her, and if it would last forever. She was like a feral child who had returned from the wild into the midst of strangers. She hadn't asked for her mother, at least not in a language anyone understood.

For the next week, Whitney and the nurses fought to understand what Emma was saying and got nowhere. Her small motor skills had been affected, her speech, her vision, and her hearing. The doctor had done some simple vision tests on her and was certain her vision was blurred. And from some equally simple tests with loud noises, he determined that Emma was deaf. She was living in isolation, and the language she was speaking made no sense except to her. She had only said one intelligible word so far when she first woke up, "ow."

The attending neurologist suggested bringing in two specialists he frequently worked with on brain injury cases, Drs. Bailey Turner and Amy Clarke. He said that none of what Emma was experiencing was unusual or unexpected, but they needed to make a plan as to how to deal with it, especially once Emma went home. She wasn't there yet, but the day would come, and for now, she was severely brain damaged from the physical trauma of the accident. The emotional trauma was impossible to measure, but was an important factor too. He told Whitney that Dr. Bailey Turner was an experienced pediatric neurologist, and Dr. Amy Clarke was better with adults but made creative suggestions, and the two often worked as a team.

Melvin Levy called Whitney, wanting to set up a photo op and even an interview with Emma, which was unimaginable in the condition she was in. Whitney didn't want to admit the details to him of how damaged she was, but said that an interview was unthinkable. Emma was out of the coma, but she bore no resemblance to the child she had been before the accident. They would have been terrified if they'd seen her, and there was no way she could return to the show in her current state, which Whitney chose not to explain to him. She didn't want it appearing on the news that Emma Watts was now severely brain damaged, possibly forever. She didn't want anyone saying that about her, and it was too soon to know how much of the damage would last, and for how long.

The two specialists who came to see her, Drs. Turner and Clarke, were slightly older than Whitney, serious clinicians who shared a practice. They were gentle and sympathetic and explained the effects of the accident in detail. As the referring neurologist had said, Whitney found Bailey Turner warm and easy to talk to, Amy Clarke more matter of fact, but both were intelligent, kind, and helpful. Bailey Turner was more optimistic and hopeful, and particularly nice to Whitney. They reassured her that everything Emma was experiencing was normal, even if upsetting. Whitney's big question was how long it was likely to stay that way, and if Emma would eventually recover normal speech and hearing. There were no answers to those questions. Only time would tell, Emma was constantly frustrated when no one understood her, and often would throw things and have tantrums as a result.

"Can we teach her to speak again?" Whitney asked Dr. Turner after his initial evaluation. She was looking desperate, and he tried to reassure her. He was impressed by her devotion to her niece.

"Yes, but not this soon. We need to give her brain a chance to settle down, before we begin stimulating it. If we start too soon, we'll only confuse her more." He was a smart, sensible person with a kind manner. Nothing presenting in the case surprised him or indicated to him that Emma could not improve over time. How much time no one knew. He tried to break the news as gently as he could, while Whitney ignored how attractive he was. She couldn't think about that now. He was a fellow physician and she needed his help. He was tall and athletic looking, with dark brown eyes and hair as dark as hers. Amy Clarke was a pretty, petite blonde.

"Do you think she can read?" Whitney wanted to know. They tried some experiments with paper and pen, and Emma had no idea what they were doing. Another eye exam confirmed that she had blurred vision, and she clearly had no memory of how to read or what the letters were. It was obvious that she couldn't hear them. Emma had returned to the land of the living, but she had come back in a hermetically sealed world which included no language anyone but Emma herself understood, no ability to hear them or read simple phrases, and she didn't recognize Whitney. Her mind was a slate that had been wiped clean and everything familiar to her was gone. It left Whitney feeling panicked and heartbroken for her. If it stayed that way, it would be a tragedy. The bright, bold, clever, brilliant little precocious child who had dazzled everyone who met her and had been the star of a TV show no longer existed. In her place was one very frightened, lonely, isolated, brain-damaged little girl.

Whitney cried when she told Chad about it, when he called again. He was back in San Francisco by then, and he felt desperately sorry for both of them, the woman he knew and the little girl who was trapped in a silent world without words or language or the ability to hear. He offered to come to L.A. to spend a weekend with her, and Whitney explained to him that much as she'd like that, she had no time to see him right now. She couldn't leave Emma alone for a minute. Emma was the limit of her world. Whitney hadn't gone back to work yet, and she lived in a sea of CT scans, MRIs, and EEGs and felt like she was drowning. She had no time for anything else. Whatever Paige had done that night had cost her her life, and nearly Emma's, and now Whitney's life was altered forever. She hated her sister for it at times and cried for her at others. Her own emotions seemed as confused as Emma's, and as conflicted.

She wondered if she and Chad would ever see each other again, and he wondered the same thing as he hung up after their call. She had become exactly what they both knew he couldn't handle and didn't want, a woman with deep family attachments and obligations. She spent all her time at the hospital, in the private room they had moved Emma to from the ICU. It felt like a prison cell. Whitney felt like she was trapped on a desert island, and it looked like she and Emma were going to be there forever. It was too soon for her to go home, and she wasn't ready for rehab.

It was terrifying, as they sat in Emma's room, staring at each other in silence, tears rolling down their cheeks, as nurses came and went to check on her. Whitney went to Emma and put her arms around her, trying to comfort her, and Emma slapped Whitney across the face as hard as she could with a look of fury in her eyes. It was the only thing she knew to do. The Emma Whitney knew was gone now, and the one that was left was trapped in lonely isolation in a silent world. Whitney's cheek was still stinging as she left the room to go for a walk and get some air, while a nurse stayed with Emma. When she came back, they'd try again until some form of communication finally got through. It was all Whitney could do, as tears of frustration rolled down her cheeks again. The future was looking very bleak.

Emma turned her face to the wall and cried with a look of rage on her face. The nurses warned Whitney that Emma could become dangerous as a result of the brain injury. That was typical from frontal lobe damage too. They said that psychotic behaviors were normal, as a result of losing her inhibitions from the injury. No part of the original Emma remained from before the accident. A stranger had taken her place. Whitney had to make the best of it, no matter how hard, upsetting, and frightening it was. There was no way she could explain it to Chad. She knew he wouldn't want to hear it. She had never felt so alone in her life.

Chapter 4

Four weeks after the accident, on the date Whitney had been planning to return anyway, it was a relief when she went back to her practice. The big difference was that she only went back part-time. She resumed seeing her most seriously ill patients and her long-term ones, but she had to ask the psychiatrist who had taken over her practice in August to continue seeing the others. She didn't want to leave Emma for too many hours, and tried to be back at the hospital by two P.M. every day. She was also acutely aware that they couldn't leave Emma in a hospital forever once her body recovered, which it hadn't fully yet.

Whitney had to refuse to take any new patients for the time being. She was trying to reduce her time in the office by half and spend the rest of it with Emma. She spent hours with her every day and was still sleeping with her at night, or lying awake and worrying about her. Whitney hadn't had a full night's sleep in just over a month, since the accident.

Emma's private room was still adjacent to the ICU, but the hospital neurologist in charge of her case reminded Whitney that they would have to make other arrangements for her eventually. The physical damage from the accident was severe, but none of it was life threatening now except for the occasional deregulation of her heart, which was also less acute. What they were left with was the evidence of the brain injury, which hadn't abated yet, the lack of speech, the obvious memory lapses which were still huge, her inability to hear or communicate. Her arm was healing, the bruises on her face were gone, but her brain was continuing to refuse to function normally. Her reactions were still those of a three-year-old, and not a warm cuddly one. Emma was angry, aggressive, and acting out most of the time. She had rages and tantrums, tried to hurt people, and had knocked several of the nurses down. In her madness, she was strong, unusually so for her size, and it sometimes took two adults to control her.

"Do you think it's frustration from not being able to speak that leads to her outbursts?" Whitney asked Bailey Turner when he dropped by. He was her chief interpreter of what they were seeing, most of which was a mystery to Whitney. He spent hours explaining it all to her, with endless patience. He said most of Emma's violent reactions were a result of the frontal lobe damage she had sustained, and typical of her injury too. It made caring for Emma that much more difficult, and she had injured Whitney several times. Whitney had bruises on her face and cuts and scratches on her hands and arms from the many times Emma had hit her with her fists or assaulted her with an object near at hand. She hit Whitney whenever she could, and sometimes drew blood. Whitney was patient with her but it was upsetting and disheartening. She lashed out at the nurses too and was a handful to manage. It made the prospect of taking her home frightening. Whitney wasn't sure how she would manage and was in no rush to try. She was afraid to be alone with her. The ICU nurses were there to help her, but once home alone with her, Whitney knew that Emma could injure her aunt, or herself. Whitney was no match for the tiny elfin child when she was acting out and at her worst.

"You can't do it alone," Bailey Turner said quietly. He was the constant deliverer of bad news with as much grace and compassion as he could muster. His work partner, Amy Clarke, tended to be harsher and more blunt, although Whitney liked her too. Amy never sugarcoated anything, and often told Whitney the harsh truth, more so than Bailey, who had a softer heart and liked Whitney.

They were using three different kinds of sedation to calm Emma in the hospital, but they didn't want to turn her into a zombie either, at home or in the ICU, and the right dosage was still in question. "You can't keep her in the hospital forever either. This isn't a holding tank for brain injured kids. You could put her in a rehab for a while," Bailey said, watching the despair in Whitney's eyes. She wanted to be there for Emma, but there was also only so much she could do, and some days, despite her own experience as a physician, Whitney was overwhelmed. Putting her in a rehab facility felt like a defeat to Whitney and there was always the risk of exposure to the press.

Bailey Turner was trying to help Whitney devise a living plan that would work for her, in their circumstances. She needed to be able to keep Emma safe if she was going to bring her home, and the violence she was demonstrating was making the future even more complicated. "We can continue to sedate her to a moderate degree when she goes home, but you don't want her sleeping all the time either.

Let's try to stabilize her further before we talk about her going home," Bailey suggested and Whitney nodded, slightly relieved at the reprieve, and wondering when that would be. So far, there was no immediate plan for her to leave the hospital, and she still had many obstacles to overcome before she did, things like hearing and speech. But what if all her faculties never returned? Emma was nine years old now and a lot smaller than Whitney, but what would happen at twelve and fourteen and eighteen, when her violent outbursts, if she was still having them, would pose a real threat?

"Let's not get ahead of ourselves," Bailey would say simply when Whitney brought up the distant future. "We're not there yet. Right now she's a nine-year-old kid who was in a car accident four weeks ago. A lot can change in the next few months, or even weeks." His partner, Amy Clarke, agreed with him, although she was less optimistic than Bailey. She wanted Whitney to be prepared for the possibility that Emma might not improve at all, and might never regain her full faculties or memory. But both specialists thought it was unlikely that she would stay as severe as she was now. "You're seeing the worst of it. And the restoration of language will help a lot." For now, whenever Whitney or the nurses didn't understand Emma's garbled speech, she eventually got frustrated and tried to hit someone, usually her aunt. Whitney had bruises everywhere to show for it and had been bitten several times. Bailey was very kind and patient with Emma about it, and Whitney assumed he must have children of his own. She asked him about it once, and he said he had figured out years before that his feeling for children was clinical not personal. He had never wanted kids, but he loved his work.

Emma hadn't asked for her mother yet, or if she had, they hadn't understood it, and all her anger seemed to focus on her aunt, as though it was Whitney's fault that Emma's private language was impossible to decipher.

She was having a particularly bad day, and had bitten one of the nurses, when Melvin Levy called Whitney on her cellphone and she left the room to talk to him. The show was about to start filming again after their summer hiatus, and he needed to know where things stood, so they could adjust the scripts accordingly and figure out when she could start filming again. He expected them to know by now. They hadn't spoken in two weeks, and if anything, as she got stronger, Emma seemed to be worse. She was regressing in age and her brain was still severely impaired. Whitney tried to find the right words to tell him, without being too explicit.

"How is she now?" he asked with a tone of deep concern. They were all worried about her, and heartbroken over what had happened, but he had a hit show to keep on the air, ratings to worry about, and sponsors and a network to satisfy. "We can shoot around her for a while longer," he explained to Whitney, "but we can't do it forever. It all depends on how long she'll be out. We can keep the fans happy with some interviews and write her absence into the show. But we can't make it work for a whole season." Emma was in the first few episodes of the new season, but after that they would be stuck, particularly if she was still a long way from being able to come back. "Can we shoot some videos of her now and get them on social media, to keep everyone happy?" he asked hopefully as Whitney tried to decide how much to tell him. She didn't want Emma labeled as brain damaged forever, particularly if she recovered eventually. This wasn't about her career, it was about her life.

"I'm sorry, Melvin, you can't video her, or photograph her." Emma didn't even look the same, her expressions had changed, and she either seemed angry or blank, which altered the look of her features. "There's no way that she could handle it. She's still too injured from the accident. She's got a long way to go."

"I was afraid of that," he said sadly. "I was hoping she had youth on her side."

"She does, but she has a brain injury and has suffered trauma to some very important functions. At best, she won't be able to work for months," if she ever can again, or should, she didn't add. Even if Emma recovered, Whitney couldn't see the wisdom of letting her overtax herself. And for now it was out of the question. She couldn't even speak intelligibly, let alone act on a show or do an interview. She was going to have to learn to speak all over again, which could take months or even years. And for now, she was no longer mentally nine years old, let alone the whiz kid she'd been before.

"We're going to have a meeting about it tomorrow," Melvin told her in a subdued voice. "I'll get back to you with what the network decides. We'd like to come and visit her. The whole cast feels terrible about what happened."

"I appreciate it," Whitney said sadly. "It's not possible to visit her yet." Whitney didn't want them seeing her in the condition she was in, deaf, unable to speak, violent with frustration much of the time. It wasn't fair to Emma to let them come, and she wouldn't recognize them.

"I understand," he said, but he didn't. How could he? How could anyone imagine the difference between what she had been barely more than a month before and what she was now? It was shocking.

"You don't think you're being overprotective, do you?" he asked, clutching at a last ray of hope, and Whitney's voice was raw with emotion when she answered.

"No, I'm not. I wish I were."

"We could shoot her on a reduced schedule until she recovers fully," he offered.

"She still has a long way to go," Whitney said softly, and he hesitated for a moment.

"Tell me honestly, just between us and not officially, is she going to be okay? In the long run, I mean." Whitney wasn't sure what to answer, the truth was too terrifying.

"I don't know. I want to think so. I don't think anyone can tell yet. She could get there eventually, but she may not. The brain is a delicate mechanism, it's impossible to say how far she can come, if at all."

He had tears in his eyes when he nodded. "It's going to be a tragedy if that little girl doesn't recover fully. You do everything you can for her," he said in a gruff voice. "We're all rooting for her."

"So am I," Whitney promised him, "believe me, so am I." She had never been a fan of Emma's career, but she agreed with the producer, if Emma stayed like this, it would be a tragedy, he was right.

"I'll call you when I know something," he promised. "And let me know if there's anything we can do for her. Anything she wants."

A huge bunch of heart-shaped balloons arrived for her that afternoon with a giant card signed by the entire cast and crew, with photographs of them glued to the card. Emma loved the balloons, but she looked blank when Whitney pointed to the names and photographs on the card, as though she hadn't seen any of them before. Whitney tied the bouquet to the foot of her bed, and Emma lay there, staring at them for hours. Whitney wondered what was going through her head but there was no way to know. There was no clue in her eyes.

Melvin Levy didn't call Whitney back for three days. The meetings they'd had, trying to decide what to do about Emma, had been arduous and painful for everyone. Their final decision, with the network's insistence, was to write her out of the show. They couldn't wait any longer, and they bitterly regretted the outcome after everything she had gone through. Melvin was in tears over it when he called Whitney back. They were offering her a settlement that would have knocked Paige right out of her chair if she'd been alive to hear it. It would pay for Emma's college education many times over and provide a comfortable life for her for a long time, while she recovered. They were offering it in gratitude for her outstanding performances on the show, and out of sympathy for all she'd lost.

"That's incredibly generous," Whitney said with tears in her eyes too. "My sister would have been deeply grateful."

"I wish she were still alive," he said sadly. "I wish they'd had their seatbelts on. I don't know what happened or why they didn't," he added, moved to tears again.

"We'll never know," Whitney said quietly. She had her own issues about it and waves of anger at Paige. The thought haunted her constantly, every night. Why were neither of them wearing seatbelts?

"Emma hasn't said anything to you about the accident? Does she remember it?" he asked, concerned.

"She doesn't speak of it," Whitney said simply, not willing to tell him that Emma couldn't speak at all.

"I'll send you the paperwork," he said somberly. "Legal will draw it up in a day or two. I really hate to see them write her off the show. I put up a good argument, but maybe it's better for her this way, to heal from the accident and start fresh when she's ready to go back to work, on another show. We'll miss her. Give her our love," he said, and Whitney hung up and contemplated the vast amount they were going to pay Emma as compensation for losing her place on *The Clan.* Paige had managed Emma's trust account from the show responsibly, and still had some of their parents' money left, but it was nothing compared to what Emma would have now. She would have real security one day, and Whitney wondered if she would ever be well enough to use it. It made Whitney sad thinking about it, and she was profoundly moved by how generous they had been. Their main sponsor had even added a sizable bonus in gratitude and as a gesture of goodwill. Whitney was still mulling it over when Chad called her later that day to check in. He'd been good about it since he got back, and made an effort to call her. He said he was coming to L.A. for meetings and wanted to have lunch with Whitney.

"I can't stay, but I'd love to see you before I fly back to San Francisco." He sounded serious and sympathetic. "How are you holding up?"

"I'm doing what I have to. I'm still at the hospital with Emma every night."

"When do you think she'll be going home? She must be better by now."

Whitney sighed deeply, she didn't want to lie to him or raise false hopes. "Unfortunately, she's not. This is a big deal. I don't know when she'll get better, or if she will."

"I guess you won't be able to keep her at home then, when she leaves the hospital. There must be rehabs for brain injured kids. She can probably go straight there." He was speaking purely practically, without considering the emotional issues involved, and the fact that Emma was only nine years old and had lost her mother, had no father, and only her aunt now. "I was hoping we could catch a weekend in New York in a few weeks, since we got shortchanged on the boat this summer. How does that sound?"

"Wonderful, and like a page in someone else's life, not mine. I can't leave her, Chad. She's still too sick, and she's my responsibility now. I can't walk away from that."

"Even for a weekend?" He sounded shocked. "She's not your child, Whitney. No one expects you to give up your life for her."

"And if I don't, who will? I'm all she's got." That was her reality now, not weekends in New York.

"That's crazy, Whitney. She's your niece, not your daughter, and even if she were, you can't be expected to dump your whole life for her. You need to get her into a good rehab as soon as you can. We can talk about New York over lunch." But she already knew he didn't understand. He had always admitted to her that he had been an inattentive father in order to pursue his astounding success. There was no way he was going to understand her sense of duty to her niece, especially in these circumstances. He would have understood her starting a new business, but not sacrificing herself for a brain injured child. And he had left out one element completely, the fact that Whitney loved her. That hadn't occurred to him at all. His suggestions were all about convenience, not love.

*   *   *

Whitney had lunch with him two days later when he came to L.A. They met at La Scala, which she had always loved. She enjoyed the Old Hollywood feeling it had, and she was happy to see him. He held her in his arms for a minute as he smiled down at her, and then they sat down, and he took her hand in his own.

"I've missed you, Whitney. Italy wasn't the same without you, and I was beginning to feel like I'd never see you again. Why don't you come up to San Francisco next weekend? We can go to the Napa Valley or Tahoe. It would do you good." He was startled by how pale she was, how thin and tired she looked. She'd had a rough time for the last month, worse than he had realized, or understood.

"I'd love to but I can't," Whitney said quietly, and he looked puzzled.

"Why not? They've got great doctors at Cedars, and she's getting everything she needs from the ICU nurses, I'm sure. You don't have to be there with her every minute. What you're doing has been an impressive gesture of respect for your sister, but you've got to know where to draw the line."

"And where is that?" Whitney asked, watching his eyes. They were cold and calculating, and always had been, she realized now. He felt sorry for her, and Emma, but he wanted time with her now. He thought he had been patient for long enough.

"Bottom line, she's not your kid. She's someone else's."

"And if that someone else is gone now? Then what?"

"You write a check to a good rehab hospital every month," he said with a hard look in his eyes. He was a great businessman, but not a warm father. "You don't take care of her yourself. That's above and beyond the call." He was definite about it.

71

"And if I do take care of her myself, then what?" She met his eyes squarely and he didn't answer for a minute.

"You'll miss out on having a life. You don't have to do that. You don't owe that to your sister or her child. You've never wanted kids of your own. Why get tangled up in this mess now? You had a great life before this happened, just the way you wanted it. Why give all that up now?" He didn't understand the choice she was making, or the fact that she felt she had no choice.

"I don't think I have an option, Chad. Sometimes things happen that you never expected, and all you can do is step up to the plate." It was what she was doing and wanted to do for Emma, and Paige.

"Or write a check to ease your conscience if you need to do that. She'll be well taken care of, and I assume your sister had decent insurance, and probably some money put aside."

"That's not the point. This isn't about money." It was all about love for Whitney.

"You always told me you had no maternal instincts. I love that about you, Whit. It keeps everything so simple. I'd hate to see you complicate things with us now."

"My sister did that for me when she failed to put on her seatbelt, whatever the reason, and didn't notice the truck coming toward them from the left. And now here we are." Her eyes were bottomless pools of sadness. She had never looked more beautiful and didn't know it.

"It doesn't have to be like this," he reminded her, "and to be honest, it can't be like this for me, Whitney. I can't wait around to see you while you play Florence Nightingale to your brain injured niece. I need more of you than that. My kids are grown, you don't have any, we're both adults with no encumbrances. It's not going to work with us if you take this on." He was being honest with her, and not making any bones about it.

"Is that what you came to L.A. to tell me?" She looked sad as she said it, but she wasn't really surprised. After five years, she knew who he was, and he had told her right from the beginning that he didn't date women with children. Now she had crossed that line, and with a brain injured child on top of it. But fate had dealt her this hand, and she was going to play it, not run away and abandon Emma to strangers.

"I guess it is," he said simply in answer to her question. "I wanted you to know where I stand on this. I'm not good at waiting in the wings. I need you to be available when I have time. It's worked pretty well for us so far, but it won't if you take on this incredible burden and play Mother Teresa to a severely injured niece. You could have come back to the boat," he said reproachfully. "You didn't have to be here with her the whole time."

"Actually, I did," Whitney said quietly. "She was in a coma for the first two weeks I was back."

"Then you could have come after she woke up. Don't blow what we have, Whit. It works great for both of us," he reminded her.

"It did, as long as everything was fine. Now I'm dealing with a tough situation, and I'm not going to run out on her so I can take a trip with you once a month. I have a responsibility now, Chad, and I'm not going to walk away from it. And I get your drift. If I take care of my niece, you're out of the picture from here on. Do I read you correctly?" Her voice was cold as she asked him, and he nodded. She was disappointed more than angry. He was less of a human being than she'd hoped.

"I think you do," Chad said as he gazed at her regretfully. "I can't take this on, Whitney, and I don't want to. I can't be there for you if you want to be the stand-in parent for a nine-year-old, brain injured kid. You need a different kind of guy, if that's what you want to do. We're lovers, Whit, that's all we ever wanted to be. I'm not married to you. You can't expect me to share this with you, when I don't think you should be doing it yourself. You're a shrink, for God's sake. You have a terrific career. We both do. You don't need to take this agony on. Get out of it now before it's too late and you get even more deeply involved."

"I already am, Chad," Whitney said as she stood up and looked at him. They'd had some good times together in the past five years, but in the end, that wasn't enough. After five years, she needed more, especially now. And he didn't want to be more. "Life is messy sometimes. Love is messy. People get hurt, they die, they leave a trail of problems behind them. And I'm not going to walk away from the mess my sister left because it's inconvenient for you." She patted his shoulder then, as he looked at her coldly, and made no move to touch her hand. He was colder than she'd ever realized. "Take care of yourself," was all she said to him, and walked away from the table as he signaled the waiter for the check. He had done what he'd come to do. He'd wanted to give her fair warning that unless she stepped away from Emma now, there was no room in his life for her. She had heard him loud and clear and instead of making her feel closer to him, he had severed the slim tie they had. Whitney walked out into the late afternoon sunshine and felt as though she could hear a door closing behind her. It was the door to her old life and the fun she'd had with him. She had a new life now. She had Emma to take care of, and whether Chad understood it or not, suddenly Whitney did. She loved Emma with all her heart, and somehow, whatever it took, and no matter how hard it was, they were going to get through this. A new era in her life had begun. She owed it to her little sister, and to Emma, and she wasn't going to let either of them down.

Chad had written her out of the show now too. It hurt, but they didn't love each other. It had been easy and convenient for both of them for a long time. Nothing about her life was either one now. But she realized that she didn't love Chad any more than he loved her. She loved Emma, and that was enough. And as it turned out, she was a mother of sorts after all. It was a major realization, and she smiled as she drove away from lunch. Her life would be less glamorous without him and the trappings of his life, but it would be infinitely more real, and that was what she wanted now. He had wanted Whitney to make a choice between him and Emma and she had. It was Emma, hands down. She had no regrets and knew she'd never look back. Her life was about her and Emma now. Chad was history.

Chapter 5

The announcement that Emma would no longer be part of the series *The Clan* was handled with all the discretion and poignancy that Melvin had promised. And it was met with all the grief and heartbreak of Emma's millions of fans. It was explained that Emma needed all her time and energy for her recovery now, from the accident that had nearly killed her and claimed the life of her mother. All the major fan magazines ran tribute articles about it, with photographs from her two years on the show. The writers of *The Clan* killed Emma's character in a riding accident, which happened off camera, and had all their viewers sobbing and in mourning the night it was shown. Whitney debated about letting Emma see the magazines, but then decided it was too soon to do so. But eventually, she wanted to try and jog her memory by showing her DVDs of the show. She had to try to remember someday, just not yet.

There was a flood of articles online and in the press about her, talking about her accident in real life and how much she would be missed. The paperwork had come from the producers of the show by then along with the huge severance settlement that Whitney put into a trust account for her and invested with a major brokerage firm. It would give her a real nest egg one day, which might be useful if she could never work again, even as an adult, which was possible. There was no way to know how far her recovery would go.

By mid-September, Emma had been in the hospital for about six weeks. Her improvements had been minimal so far, and her progress was slow. She was steady on her legs, and her motor skills had improved. But her speech and hearing had gone nowhere. Her frustration over her inability to communicate seemed to be getting worse, and led to more violence against Whitney and the nurses. She began to have night terrors, which led her to scream for hours in the middle of the night, and all Whitney could do to calm her was hold her tightly in her arms and wait until they passed. It was impossible to soothe or reason with her when she had them. Whitney wondered if Emma was reliving the accident, or pining for her mother, and Emma had no way to ask questions about Paige in a language all her own. Whitney still hadn't told her that Paige was dead. It seemed too cruel to do so when she couldn't talk about it, or express anything she felt. Emma was trapped in a silent tomb of her own.

Whitney hadn't heard from Chad again after their lunch at La Scala. She had no regrets about the choice she'd made and had lost all respect and affection for him, which made losing him easier, even after five years. He didn't seem to be missing her either. The only support she was getting was from the two neurologists, Bailey Turner and Amy Clarke, who were guiding her through the difficult process of helping Emma through her recovery from the accident. She still showed marked effects from her frontal lobe injury, all of which affected her ability to communicate. And with impaired vision, she seemed unable to read and focus on the books they showed her, even those for a much younger child. There were so many things she could no longer do that used to be second nature to her. The contrast between then and now was shocking and very sad.

And at the end of September, the neurologist who had taken care of her at Cedars since the accident was suggesting to Whitney that it was time to put Emma in a rehab facility or take her home. The rest of the progress she still had to make would take months or even years, and she couldn't stay in the hospital for the remainder of her recovery. Whitney discussed it with Bailey when he came to check on Emma one afternoon. He stopped by almost daily, and it was comforting when he appeared. Even Emma seemed to brighten a little when she saw him.

"How am I going to manage her at home?" Whitney asked him in the hallway when they stepped out of the room. She was feeling breathless at the prospect. Sometimes waves of panic washed over her at what she would be facing on her own.

"You don't have to take her home," he said gently. He was three years older than Whitney, and had gone to the same medical school at UCLA. He respected Whitney's courage and her sensible decisions. He had sent her a patient for a psychiatric evaluation a few weeks before, and had been impressed by her report. She was managing to do her work effectively despite the strain she was under in her personal life. "You could put Emma in a facility. There's one I would recommend for a child her age, although I'll admit it's not ideal. She might make better progress at home, with individual therapists and personal care, but she's not your daughter, and from what you've said, you're not set up for kids at your house."

"She can't hear me, she hasn't regained her language skills yet, she has night terrors, and she gets violent when she can't communicate. I have no one to take care of her when I go to work. It's a lot to take on." Whitney expressed her concerns to him. It had been much easier having her in the ICU at Cedars.

"I understand." He smiled at Whitney to reassure her. "No one's pushing her out the door. The medical staff just think that they've done as much as they can for her here, and the rest needs to happen at home if she's going to make progress, which isn't a sure thing by any means. For one thing, you'd have to hire experienced nurses to take care of her. Two or three nurses, so they can have time off. I don't think you should try to take care of her on your own. And besides, you have your practice." He had been honest with her so far, and she was grateful for it. She liked the way he related to Emma. His associate, Amy, was better with adults, as Whitney had been told from the first. But Whitney liked talking to her more clinically. She liked them both. Bailey was more casual and warmer. "Why don't you start by interviewing some nurses through an agency, and see what turns up?" It seemed a sensible approach, and she called an agency he recommended the next day.

They sent six women to Whitney's office, and she hated them all. Even though all of them had worked in homes with brain injured patients, mostly from strokes, none had experience with pediatric trauma patients, and they seemed dreary and too old. In some ways, dealing with Emma now was like taking care of a toddler, with her limited skills. She was not the easy, sunny child she had been only two months before, able to entertain herself, almost like a small adult. She had the physical independence of a nine-year-old, and the brain of a much younger child since the accident, and she might act like a three-year-old forever, even once she was an adult. Most of the time, trying to figure out how to deal with her, Whitney felt like she was flying blind, straight into a wall.

The agency sent four more candidates the following week, two of whom seemed like reasonable possibilities when she discussed them with Bailey. One was an older woman who had taken care of a brain injured young woman for seven years until her family finally institutionalized her when she got too aggressive in her late twenties. She sounded enthusiastic about working with Emma. And the other candidate who appealed to Whitney was four years out of nursing school, and had worked with learning-delayed children at a residential facility for two years, and she had an upbeat positive outlook that Whitney liked. She was unfazed by Whitney's description of Emma's violent spells when no one could understand the language she was speaking.

Whitney was still debating about hiring both of them, when she went to the ICU to visit Emma one afternoon and discovered a new nurse on the floor posing for a selfie with her, to show her friends. Her excuse to Whitney when she walked in on her was that she and her mother were fans of the show Emma had been on, and she was taking the photo for her. But taking a selfie with her violated the confidentiality of Emma's situation as a patient, victimizing her in Whitney's opinion, or exploiting her helpless situation, and was exactly what Whitney wanted to avoid. She reported the incident to the head of the ICU immediately, and that night Whitney realized that it was time to go home, no matter how much it scared her or how unprepared she was. This was all new territory for her.

They had been at the hospital for long enough, and it served no therapeutic purpose now to keep her there. Emma needed a home environment. She needed to get out, live a more normal life, and get some air. The next day, Whitney hired both of the nurses she had liked and spent the weekend trying to figure out how to adapt her house for Emma. She decided to turn her guest room into a bedroom for her, and went to Paige's house to decide what to bring over. There were books she could no longer read and toys and games she couldn't play with, like Clue and Monopoly, her chess set, and a backgammon game she'd been learning to play and was good at before. She had dozens of dolls lined up on a shelf. There were photographs of her with the cast of the show and her mother, some posters that Whitney had gotten her, of favorite movie stars and from other shows.

Whitney packed as much of it as she could in boxes and drove it to her house, along with the bedspread from Emma's bed. She went to IKEA to buy a bookcase and by Sunday night, Emma had a room waiting for her at Whitney's house. She had briefly considered moving into Paige's home, for Emma. But she realized that it was Emma's past and her aunt's house was her future. So she packed Emma's favorite possessions and prepared to start a new life with her at her own home. It was where they lived now.

Whitney realized too that she had a job to do at Paige's. She needed to get rid of her sister's furniture and clothes, and put the house on the market. She hadn't had time to deal with it since July, but she knew that it was time. There was no point keeping the house.

Even if Emma recovered, she couldn't live alone for many, many years. Whitney was giving her a home.

Whitney had a meeting with a hospital neurologist and Bailey to decide how to manage Emma's care at home, and when to make the move. They agreed that the following weekend would be as good a time as any, and for the rest of the week, Whitney lay awake next to Emma every night in her room near the ICU, panicked about how it would go.

Eileen, the older, more experienced nurse, was going to start them off. She had agreed to work four days a week as a live-in. She said she didn't mind twenty-four-hour duty. And Whitney would be there to help at night. Brett, the younger nurse, would work for three days a week, starting on Friday mornings, and through the weekend. She already had plans about where she was going to take Emma during her days with her, the park, the zoo. They were going to do art projects. And Whitney had bought a new station wagon so the nurses could drive her places if Emma was comfortable going with them and didn't act out in public, which remained to be seen. So far, she hadn't ventured past the safe confines of the ICU, and Whitney didn't want them taking Emma anywhere without her at first, until she saw how they interacted with her, and how Emma responded to them. She still had flare-ups of violent behavior whenever she was frustrated.

Whitney had consulted with Bailey about photographs she had of Paige around the house. She didn't want to upset Emma, but they also agreed that it might be helpful to jog her memory, and see how she reacted to the images of her mother. At some point, Whitney still had to tackle the terrible news of Paige's death, whenever Emma was ready for it. Bailey thought it was a good idea to leave the photographs in place. Emma's new bedroom at her aunt's house was filled with familiar things, which might jog her memory as well. Whitney wanted her to feel at home, and had filled her bedroom with her favorite things.

Eileen, the older nurse, met them at the hospital the morning they were to leave. Emma could sense that something was happening, but Whitney couldn't explain it to her, or reassure her. She got her dressed in a pair of pink leggings she'd brought from home and a pink sweater, and Emma stared at them as though they reminded her of something, but she wasn't sure what, and then she let Whitney put them on her as Eileen watched and smiled encouragement. Three of the ICU nurses came and went as Whitney put Emma's long blond hair in braids. She'd been wearing hospital pajamas and nightgowns for the past two and a half months, and now she was ready to go home. Whitney's hands were shaking as she did her hair. They packed up all her stuffed animals and cozy blankets from home, with the cards the cast of the show and some of the fans had sent her. There was more than Whitney had realized, and Eileen helped her carry it downstairs to the car. Then they went back upstairs to get Emma. Whitney tried to get her into a wheelchair, and Emma bolted across the room and hid behind the bed, looking terrified. She had no idea where she was going, or why. Whitney was never sure if Emma recognized her from before, but she was a familiar figure now, since she slept in Emma's room every night.

Whitney spoke to her soothingly, which she couldn't hear, stroking her face and her hair, which she understood, and Whitney put her arms around her to hold her and could feel Emma shaking in terror. The hospital was the only home she remembered now. Everything before that had disappeared from her mind the night of the accident, and when Whitney tried to get her in the wheelchair again, Emma hauled off and slapped her in the face hard, as Whitney tried not to react. She glanced up at the nurses, who suggested that maybe they should let Emma walk downstairs if she was willing. She was wearing little pink ballet shoes with sparkling hearts on them, and she was carrying the teddy bear she slept with and clutching it to her chest, as Whitney took her other hand and walked her out of the room she had slept and spent her days in since she had come out of the coma. They walked past the nurses' desk, as all the nurses on duty waved, and tears filled Emma's eyes as she looked at Whitney and spoke rapidly in the non-language that was familiar to them now, although they understood none of the words. She sounded like a Martian.

"We're going home," Whitney said gently even though Emma couldn't hear her. She said it over and over as they continued walking to the elevator, and Whitney pointed to the button so she could push it, but she wouldn't, as the security guard watched them. He was still there to protect Emma from fans, although the crowds in the lobby had thinned since the announcement had been made that Emma had left the show in order to speed her recovery.

Emma hesitated for a long time before she got into the elevator holding tightly to Whitney's hand. She acted as though she'd never seen one. She gave a start when the doors closed, and a moment later, they were at the level of the emergency entrance where Whitney had left the car with Emma's belongings in it. She recognized them in the back of the car, and turned to Whitney with a look of panic, and then shrank back against the hospital wall, looking like she was about to bolt and run. It was easy to guess that seeing the car was bringing back some subliminal memory of the accident, and she was pulling Whitney away from the car with all her strength.

Whitney put her arms around her to comfort her and tried edging her toward the station wagon as Emma hid her face and pummeled her as hard as she could and started screaming so people in the parking area were looking at them, wondering what was going on.

"Would you like me to put her in the car, ma'am?" the security guard offered and could have done it easily. Whitney shook her head. She didn't want anything to happen to Emma by force.

"I'd rather she get in on her own," Whitney said and handed the car keys to Eileen, who seemed patient as she waited for Whitney to handle the situation. "I'll sit in the back with her," Whitney said to Eileen as Emma continued to fight her and swung at her face again, but this time Whitney saw it coming and dodged. They stood there together for nearly an hour, as Whitney tried to inch Emma toward the car, and finally she gently pulled her in with her, sat her down on the seat and buckled the seatbelt, as Emma screamed at the top of her lungs. The security guard closed the door, and Whitney held her close as Emma continued to scream. Eileen pulled out, and they drove home with Emma shrieking and swinging wildly at her aunt. She looked like they were trying to kidnap her, and Whitney was unnerved as they pulled into her driveway in Beverly Hills, and Eileen turned off the engine. For a minute, Emma stopped screaming and glanced around. Whitney could tell that something about the house was familiar to her, but she wasn't sure what. Emma stared at Whitney with a puzzled expression, her face still red from crying. Whitney gently unbuckled the seatbelt, and Eileen opened the door to let her out. Her first car ride since the accident had been traumatic for all of them, but they had made it home in one piece. Eileen helped her out, and Whitney got out right behind her, walked to the front door, unlocked it, and turned off the alarm. Emma still looked confused, as though something about her surroundings had struck a chord of memory but she had no idea why. Whitney took her hand and led Emma into the house, where she looked around the living room she had seen dozens of times before, and had even spent Christmas in several times. She walked from room to room, checking things out, looking at photographs, picking things up and putting them down. She walked into the kitchen and stopped there for a minute, and then Whitney beckoned her to come upstairs, and they walked to the bedroom she had set up for her, next to her own. Emma looked around and smiled, and Whitney could tell she had recognized her belongings, she stared at the posters on the wall, touched the dolls and stuffed animals, and rubbed her face in the cozy bedspread and lay on the bed, gazing at her aunt.

"Welcome home, Em," she said as she smiled at her, relieved to see her happy and not terrified as she had been in the car. Then Eileen went to the kitchen to make them lunch, and Whitney was pleased that she had appeared calm in the storm while leaving the hospital, which had been much more traumatic than Whitney had anticipated.

Emma left her bedroom to check out Whitney's room next to hers and then came back and lay on her bed until Whitney heard Eileen call them downstairs for lunch, and Whitney took Emma's hand and led her downstairs. She let her aunt settle her on a chair at the kitchen table, and they ate the sandwiches Eileen had made for them, and Emma ate the potato chips thoughtfully, looking around the room, as though still trying to remember it. When she'd finished eating, she went back to the living room and looked around some more.

She stopped in front of a photograph of her mother and stared at it for a long time, but she never looked at Whitney or seemed to question it. She picked it up and set it down and walked away, and it was obvious that she didn't remember her mother yet or she would have reacted to it, and she didn't. It was disappointing in terms of her memory loss but also a relief in some ways. After the agony of getting her home from the hospital, Whitney wasn't eager to deal with another crisis quite so soon.

Emma curled up on the couch with a cashmere blanket and drifted off to sleep after the emotions of the morning, and Eileen came to check on her, and said she'd watch her while Whitney went upstairs. She had realized that it was going to be much harder keeping track of Emma here than at the hospital. There were more rooms for her to roam around in, places to hide if she wanted to, a garden just outside the house, and a pool beyond it, which could be dangerous for her, since she probably didn't remember how to swim either. They would have to keep careful track of her to make sure she didn't leave the house or get lost. Whitney was thinking about it when the phone rang, it was Bailey asking how the trip home had gone.

"It was an event," she said, sounding exhausted. "She was terrified as soon as she saw the car. It took us an hour to get in it, and she screamed all the way home. I don't know if she remembered the accident, or just the feeling it gave her when she saw the car."

"What happened when you got home?"

"I think something about the place looks familiar to her, but she isn't sure what. She looked at a photograph of her mother, but she didn't react to it. She just stared at it and then walked away. But she recognized her toys in the bedroom I set up for her. She loved it." Whitney smiled as she said it.

"It sounds like you're off to a good start." He sounded pleased. These were all things that he and Whitney had discussed when planning Emma's homecoming, and he was in favor of trying to provoke Emma's memory with some gentle prodding and familiar objects, even the photograph of her mother. Sooner or later, it would be better for her to remember than to lose her memory forever, even if reaching back into the past would be painful for her. "How's the nurse doing?"

"She seems fine. She didn't freak out when Emma was screaming on the way home. She's competent and professional and very nice. Emma doesn't appear to care one way or another."

"Where's Emma now?" he asked gently.

"Downstairs, asleep on the couch. We're going to have to watch her closely. I don't want her getting lost in the house, or letting herself out and falling into the pool."

"No, that would not be good," he agreed. "Call me if you need anything." Whitney had the sedatives they used whenever Emma got too aggressive, but she was hoping she wouldn't need them now that they were home. She was also hoping that Emma would settle in and feel comfortable there, but she had brought her brain injury home from the hospital with her, and the problems were not solved yet by any means. In some ways, they were just beginning. This was the next phase of her recovery. "I'll check in with you tomorrow," he promised.

When Whitney went downstairs a little while later, Emma was still asleep. She slept for most of the afternoon, after the upheaval of the morning, and Whitney had a chance to return some calls and answer emails, sitting near Emma on the couch. She smiled at her when

Emma opened her eyes and looked around. She still had that puzzled expression, which suggested to Whitney that she remembered something but didn't know what. She went back upstairs to her room then, found the bathroom and used it, and was playing with her old dolls when Whitney walked into the room to check on her. She nodded at her to reassure her, and Emma smiled her old familiar smile that made Whitney's heart sing just looking at her. She looked better. She just couldn't think better yet.

They had dinner together in the kitchen with Eileen, and then Whitney bathed her in her big marble bathtub, and Emma splashed happily and chattered in her gibberish but didn't seem to expect Whitney to respond. Then Whitney put her to bed. She had been tense for a good part of the day, fearing something would go wrong, but on the whole, she thought it had gone well. It was stressful having Emma home and being responsible for her on her own, but it also seemed more natural to be there.

Everything was peaceful until two in the morning when Whitney heard a bloodcurdling scream and rushed into the next bedroom, and found Emma hysterical with one of her night terrors. Nothing Whitney could do would console her. She just continued to scream with her eyes wide open, until she finally wore herself out two hours later, curled up in a ball, and went to sleep, and Whitney went back to her own room, and lay awake for a long time, wondering if life would ever be normal again, and if Emma would ever recover from the accident and the injury to her brain. She had no more answers to the question now that they were at home. All she could do was wait and hope.

Chapter 6

T he next morning on her way to breakfast in her nightgown, Emma stopped in the living room and stood in front of the framed photograph of her mother again. She picked it up and walked into the kitchen with it, and sat it in front of her plate where she could look at it intently. She made no sound and didn't look at Whitney. She just kept looking at the photograph of Paige in a bathing suit and a big sunhat on the beach at Malibu, at a house she'd rented two years before.

Emma ate her breakfast, sitting next to Whitney, and took the photograph with her when she left the kitchen and went back to her room. Eileen was doing the dishes to be helpful when Whitney went back upstairs to dress and checked on Emma in her bedroom. She was standing in the middle of the room, staring at the photograph, and suddenly her eyes flew wide and she looked at Whitney and pointed at the image with a desperate expression. Whitney knew instantly that she had remembered who the woman was, and now she wanted to know the answer to the question Whitney had feared for almost three months. She pointed to the photograph again and again and held it up to Whitney's face, making grunting sounds and speaking in the language that had no meaning.

Whitney nodded to show her she had understood.

"I know, baby, I know . . . that's your mom." She knew that Emma couldn't hear her, but the expression on Whitney's face showed that she knew, as she put her arms around her and held her, wanting to give her whatever comfort she could, even without words.

Emma pulled away from her and put the photograph back in Whitney's face, with a frantic look that expressed what she wanted to know. She remembered Paige now and wanted to know where she was. Whitney could feel her pain viscerally. Neither of them needed words to express what they felt. Emma was beginning to make small shrieking sounds, as Whitney nodded. Emma's grunts grew louder and more insistent, and suddenly their eyes met and Whitney shook her head, which conveyed to Emma what she couldn't say in words. She just kept shaking her head and holding her, and then she made a gesture as though saying that Paige was asleep. And as soon as she did, Emma let out an anguished scream. She had understood Whitney's meaning and collapsed to the floor at her feet, rocking back and forth and clutching the photograph to her as she threw her head back and cried inconsolably. Whitney sank onto the floor with her, and this time Emma let her hold her as they rocked back and forth on the floor, and after a while, Emma just lay there crying silently, too exhausted to move. They were both crying, and Whitney felt as though her sister had just died all over again. Emma lay there for a long time, and didn't attempt to move, still holding the photograph. Whitney was still with her when Eileen came to tell her that Dr. Turner was on the phone. She asked her to have him call her cellphone, which he did a minute later. She didn't want to leave Emma alone, not now after she had just learned that her mother had not survived the accident.

"Good morning, how did last night go?" Bailey asked in a cheerful voice that seemed too loud in her ears, even though Emma couldn't hear it. She was crooning softly at the photograph, and still lying on the floor.

"Okay, I guess," Whitney responded. "She had a night terror. And I think we had a breakthrough just now, and not an easy one," Whitney said as she kept an eye on Emma next to her.

"What happened?" He sounded concerned but not panicked, since Whitney sounded calm.

"She's been walking around with her mother's picture all morning. She brought it to the breakfast table and set it in front of her. I don't think she recognized it, but there must have been something familiar about it, and all of a sudden, when we got back to her room, it clicked. She started looking frantic, and kept staring at me, and I understood, and shook my head a bunch of times and showed her by resting my head on my hands that Paige was sleeping. She let out a hideous scream, and she's been crying for the last half hour. She's better now. She's lying next to me at my feet, holding the photograph. I think she understands now that Paige is dead." It was the moment Whitney had dreaded since the accident, and now Emma knew what had happened, and that Paige was never coming back.

"That's liable to unblock some other things. It's a biggie. I'm relieved it happened now that you're home. I think she was ready for it, which is why her mind let her recognize her mother. How does she seem now?"

"Exhausted. And to be honest, so am I."

"I'd like to come by and observe her today for a while, if that's all right with you. I want to see if any of her other behaviors have progressed as a result. This really is a major breakthrough for her, and we might be able to build on this in some way." It made sense to Whitney as a clinician herself, but the moment had been agonizing and she felt drained.

"You can come over whenever you want," she said, sounding tired.

"I'd like to see if we can unlock some other doors for her, though not too fast. She went over a big hurdle today. It sounds like you handled it perfectly." He was always generous with his praise, and impressed by Whitney's mothering skills, especially for a woman with no children, dealing with an extremely difficult situation.

"I don't know how you figure that, I'm flying blind most of the time," Whitney said humbly.

"You do a lot better than you realize. This is an almost textbook case of frontal lobe brain injury, with nearly every symptom it presents, and you've handled it perfectly every step of the way." She had the advantage of being a doctor, but he could tell this came straight from the heart. In his opinion, you couldn't fake good parenting.

"Well, she's not talking yet, and she's still speaking her own language. She can't read and she can't hear me, so I'm not sure what part of this you think I'm handling so well."

"The night terrors, the aggressive outbursts. You just managed to convey to her that her mother is dead when her memory loosened up. You got her home in one piece. You've hung in for three months of an incredibly stressful situation with a child who isn't your own. Give yourself some credit. No one said this was going to be easy. She's come a long way and so have you."

"I feel like she's not even halfway there yet, there is so much progress she still needs to make." Whitney sounded discouraged. It had been a hard morning.

"Give it time. When she starts speaking again, everything will be a lot easier."

"How long do you think that will take?" Whitney wanted answers and there were none.

"No one knows. We just have to wait and see. If it's okay with you, I'll come by this afternoon."

"That's fine. I think we're just going to stick around here today. I don't want to traumatize her with another ride in the car."

"No, I wouldn't," he agreed with her. "I'll come by around three." They hung up then and when Whitney looked down at Emma again, she was asleep on the floor, cradling the photograph of her mother in her arms, with Paige's face in the image close to hers. It was a heart-rending sight, watching Emma there. She understood now what she had lost, and for the thousandth time, her aunt's heart went out to her. Whitney had never loved anyone so much in her life, not even Paige when she was alive.

Emma was playing in her room when Bailey came by to see them that afternoon. He stopped and watched her from the doorway and

Emma ignored him. He was a familiar sight by now, part of the furniture in the hospital, as far as she was concerned, and she didn't seem surprised to see him at home, nor appear to care.

Whitney said she had been subdued all day after her discovery of the morning about her mother. She had gone all over the house, looking at other photographs, and found three more of her mother and had taken them to her room, and set them on the table next to her bed, where she could see them. It was obvious that she remembered who her mother was now. And she had pointed at Whitney when she found photographs of her and Whitney nodded. Emma had done very little speaking in her own language that afternoon. She had been mostly silent and had reorganized the photographs of Paige several times, until she had them the way she wanted them.

Whitney and Bailey were speaking quietly in the doorway to Emma's room, when she turned to them with an intense look, as though she had something important to say to them. They stopped talking and waited while Emma pursed her lips together and pressed hard as though it took a superhuman effort, and with all the strength she had she let out a sound and she almost shouted the word "Mom," and then repeated it again and again. . . . "Mom . . . Mom! . . . Mom! . . . MOM! MOMMMM!" She couldn't stop saying it once she started, and there were tears running down Whitney's cheeks as she nodded and spoke to her.

"That's right. . . . That's your mom. . . . Mom," Whitney said as Emma continued to repeat it, and Whitney looked at Bailey. "Oh my God, she spoke . . . she said a word." He was beaming and Whitney laughed through her tears.

"You had two major breakthroughs today. She remembered her

mother, and she said a word. I think you had a very good day. She's starting to come through it, Whitney. This is just the beginning. She may regress for a while after this, but she's headed in the right direction. She's not going to recover in a straight line, it's a bumpy process."

"Thank you," Whitney whispered to him, and he nodded. It was one of the most interesting cases he'd ever had, and the victories weren't over yet. They had only just begun.

Whitney invited Bailey to stay for dinner that night. He had spent several hours watching Emma play with her dolls and toys, and then going to look at her mother's photographs. She said the word "Mom" again every time she did, and it seemed to get easier for her each time. She was saying it more smoothly by the time they went downstairs for dinner, and Bailey thanked Whitney for letting him stay. It helped him to watch Emma eat her dinner too. She wasn't a messy eater and picked at her food. Her appetite still wasn't great, which was part of the brain trauma too. He had warned Whitney in the hospital that some brain injury patients tended to overeat or eat erratically, or want the same foods again and again, and others barely seemed to eat enough to survive and had no interest in food. Emma had to be cajoled, and Whitney had been tempting her with treats for three months in the ICU, but she was still looking very thin. Whitney had lost weight too. Bailey had noticed but didn't comment.

Emma seemed to be lost in her own world as she sat at the table, but she had faced an important memory that morning, and spoken intelligibly for the second time. The first time she had said "Ow." She seemed to have retreated into a private space afterward, as though to find some relief after the effort she had made, and the unhappy discovery about her mother.

Bailey had suggested that Whitney put on a DVD of Emma's old TV show the next day. He wanted to provide as much stimulus for her brain as they could without going too far and putting her on overload.

"If she's not ready for it, she won't identify with it," he told her. "It will be interesting to see how she responds. Now that she's confronted the memory of her mother, she'll be able to open other doors. It all fits together like a puzzle." After he said it, Emma wandered away from the table halfway through the meal and went back to her room. She seemed to find comfort there, and feel safe among her familiar things. Eileen said she'd keep an eye on her, and Bailey and Whitney sat at the table for a while, finishing their meal. She had picked up a roast chicken for them, and made a salad to go with it, and it was nice just sitting and talking with another adult. For the past three months she had done nothing but work and spend every waking moment with Emma. And with Chad out of her life now, she had no one to talk to and unwind with. Bailey was curious about her.

"What do you do for fun?" he asked her as she poured coffee for them and served him a bowl of ice cream. She laughed at the question.

"You mean when I'm not seeing patients and hanging out at the ICU with my niece?" He nodded in response. "I used to travel, but I guess I won't be doing that anymore, or not for a while. I love art galleries, museums, movies, the theater, ballet. I enjoy going to Lake Tahoe. I was on vacation in Italy on a friend's boat when the accident happened. I came back the same day I arrived, and something tells me I won't be able to leave Emma for a long time." She looked serious as she said it, and he didn't disagree with her.

"You're going to need to make time for yourself too. Everything can't be about Emma or you'll wear yourself out."

"There's no one else to pass the baton to. I'm it now. What about you? What do you do for fun?" she asked him to get the focus off herself.

"Write, read, hike, run, ski, play tennis. I ride horses when I can. I write a lot of papers for medical journals about brain trauma. There's so much we all need to learn on the subject. It's fascinating."

"I have to admit, if Emma weren't my niece I'd be fascinated too. But it's a little close to home for me right now, and very intense."

"We should write a joint paper about it when this is over," he suggested. "You bring a lot to the table with your psychiatric background. I've always thought that with brain injuries, the two disciplines should be combined, psychiatry and neurology."

"That's an interesting point of view." She liked talking to him. It was different sitting in her kitchen than consulting with him in the ICU. That had been strictly professional, but this was more relaxed now that they were home, and she enjoyed his company, as an extremely competent physician.

"Amy Clarke and I want to write a book together, but we haven't gotten around to it yet."

"I want to write a layman's guide to family therapy, or maybe one on sociopaths," Whitney commented. "Same problem. I never have the time," and now she had even less. She had none at all.

"Maybe you'll have time to write about Emma when this is over," he said thoughtfully. "Do you suppose she'll go back to acting when she recovers?" He was curious about it, and Whitney was skeptical.

"That was her mother's obsession. It wouldn't be mine. I don't think it's a good life for a child. Emma hasn't been to a normal school in two years. She had a tutor on the set. It's not a healthy life. Her mother thought it was great. I never did. We grew up around Hollywood and a lot of famous people. All I wanted was to get away from show business as fast as I could, and do something entirely different. Paige was desperate to have a piece of it. Our mother was an actress, and our father was an agent. I hated everything I saw about it. It ate my mother up. She died at fifty-four." He looked surprised.

"I'm sorry. What did she die of?"

"Early onset Alzheimer's. Elizabeth Winston." He looked shocked when she said it.

"Good Lord, she was a major star." Whitney nodded and smiled, still proud of her.

"Paige wanted Emma to be just like her. I won't stop her if that's really what she wants, but I'd rather see her lead a nice normal life when she gets better. She can always go back to acting twenty years from now. We'll see how it goes, if she even has the option to go back." He nodded, impressed by what she'd shared with him. She was a very modest person, and there had been nothing to suggest that she was the daughter of a major film star, although Whitney was beautiful too. "Paige wanted Emma to win an Oscar one day. She's a good little actress, but it's so much pressure for a kid. I see a lot of patients from the film world, they're all so unhappy and their lives are so screwed up."

He helped her clear the dishes away then, and he left a little while later, without disturbing Emma again. He thanked Whitney for the evening and said he'd call her in a day or two to see how Emma was doing, and Whitney walked upstairs after he left. Emma was lying on her bed, playing with her dolls. She looked happy and peaceful, and if Whitney hadn't known about her brain injury, she wouldn't have guessed, looking at her. It made her wish that their life could be normal again, and her sister were still alive.

It had been nice having Bailey over for dinner. He seemed like a good person, and she thought his specialty was interesting. It was just nice talking to another adult, and having a new friend. Now that Emma was living with her, she didn't have time for more than that, and probably never would again if Emma didn't recover.

The next day she followed Bailey's advice and put on a DVD of one of the episodes of *The Clan*. Emma walked past several times while she was on the screen, but didn't react. It was as though she didn't recognize herself.

Whitney tried it again a few days later, and this time Emma stopped with a puzzled expression and stood there for a long time, and then turned to Whitney with a quizzical glance. Whitney nodded and pointed to her and then to the screen.

"That's you," she said. Emma hadn't spoken again since the time she'd said "Mom," but after Whitney pointed to her, she continued to stare at the screen, as though trying to understand what she was doing on the show. Then she shrugged and walked away. It didn't seem to jog her memory or interest her at all. And as Bailey had predicted, after the big breakthrough about her mother, Emma regressed for several days. She spoke in her gibberish again, and she had night terrors almost every night. Whitney heard her start one of them one night, and then she stopped before Whitney could go in to her, so she assumed that Emma had gone back to sleep. And ten minutes later, she decided to check on her anyway. Eileen was standing over Emma's bed when Whitney walked in on bare feet, and saw the nurse restraining her with her full force, with a hand clamped over Emma's mouth so she couldn't scream, as she looked wild eyed at the overpowering woman who was holding her down. Whitney flew across the room, grabbed her, and pulled her away from Emma with a look of outrage.

"What are you doing?" Whitney shouted at her. Eileen looked panicked when she saw her.

"I'm calming her down," she said with a guilty look.

"No, you're not, you're restraining her. Get away from her right now. You're leaving immediately."

"It's the only way to deal with night terrors," Eileen said with a vicious look on her face, furious to have been caught. But Emma wasn't screaming, she was watching the looks on their faces, and Whitney picked her up and held her and told Eileen to pack her bags, call a cab, and leave, and not come back. She was shaking as she held Emma. What if she hadn't come in to check on her? Emma was at the mercy now of anyone who took care of her.

"I'm sorry," she said to Emma again and again, even though she couldn't hear her, but she could see Whitney's face. "I'm sorry, baby," she said and lay her down gently on the bed, as Emma pursed her lips with that intense look again, trying to force out a word, as Whitney waited, and Emma finally exploded with another single sound.

"Bitch!" she shouted as Whitney stared at her, and then Emma sat down on the bed, grinning, pleased with herself. "Bitch! Bitch! Bitch! Bitch!" Emma repeated with determination, and Whitney started to laugh. They had just had another breakthrough, and any word was fine with her! She nodded at Emma, gave her a thumbs-up, and Emma gave her a high five. She had just remembered another word. It was another victory for their team. Whitney couldn't wait to repeat it to Bailey the next day. At least they could share a good laugh. Emma looked at Whitney gratefully. She had saved her again.

Chapter 7

After Whitney found Eileen the nurse restraining Emma, with a hand over her mouth, and fired her on the spot, she contacted Brett, the younger nurse she was planning to use three days a week. She asked her if she would consider working a five-day week, and Whitney was going to take care of Emma herself without nursing help on the weekends. Brett was thrilled with the extra two days of work, didn't mind living in, and on her first day with Emma, Whitney found them baking cookies, while Brett showed Emma how to apply the colored sprinkles. She didn't need language to figure out how to do it, and Brett was patient as she demonstrated it to her, and then waved Emma toward the pans she had spread out on the kitchen counter. Emma looked very pleased with herself when they were finished. Brett had a million ideas for projects she wanted to do with her, and they were off to a good start. Whitney felt like she was running a school now, and in a way she was.

Whitney reported to Bailey about the incident with Eileen holding

Emma down with a hand over her mouth, and firing her on the spot, and Emma managing to say another word, which happened to be "bitch." Bailey laughed out loud.

"That's very common with frontal lobe injuries," he said to Whitney and had warned her about it before. "It disinhibits them, and we get some very interesting language from the adults, and even some kids, depending on what they've heard at home. We hear everything from racial slurs to propositions. Some of the old guys get really salty and hit on the nurses."

"Emma was very pleased with herself after she said it. My sister was pretty liberal with her mouth around Emma. We may hear something worse if she really starts talking," she said, and they both laughed. Then he thanked her for dinner the night before.

"That was fun. Let's do it again. I'll bring you food next time," he offered, and she liked the feeling that they had become friends. The only adults she talked to these days were her patients, and she couldn't let her hair down with them.

She enjoyed Amy Clarke's visits too. She was a little more serious and intellectual than Bailey, who was warmer and more informal. He was still amazed that Whitney and her late sister's mother was Elizabeth Winston. She had been a legend, an icon, and it seemed tragic that she had died so young, and of such an unfortunate illness. Now Paige had died young too. Bailey was impressed that Whitney was carrying all the burdens of Emma's situation on her own shoulders. She was doing a great job with her niece, encouraging Emma's recovery in every way she could. It was her mission in life now, the way Paige's had been Emma's TV career. Whitney just wanted to get Emma healthy again and her brain functioning normally, whatever it took.

She had begun reading about brain injuries in the medical journals she subscribed to and was becoming very knowledgeable on the subject. She had serious questions about what part of the damage was psychiatric from trauma and which component was purely physical. There were conflicting opinions on the subject among professionals in the field. Whitney had a theory that Emma's inability to speak was as much due to the psychological trauma she'd been through as the damage to the frontal lobe of her brain. She wondered if Emma would eventually recall the accident itself, and if she did, would she then be able to speak again? She was convinced the two were related. But Emma still had no recollection of it. It led Whitney to believe that she must have lost consciousness very quickly when she hit her head, so it was anyone's guess as to what she had seen, how traumatic it had been, and precisely what her silence was due to. Whitney was still trying to unlock that door, particularly after Emma had said her first two words. But Emma was still speaking gibberish all the time, as though it were a real language.

As soon as Emma appeared to be comfortable with Brett, Whitney decided to confront the task of emptying Paige's house. She took three days off from work to go through everything Paige had left behind. She wasn't a tidy housekeeper, and there were closets full of old albums, clippings about their mother, fan mail to Emma from the show, and letters from old friends, including several from Emma's biological father, which Whitney thought she might want one day. She boxed up all the papers and sent them to a storage unit she had had since her father's death. It was filled with boxes of her mother's contracts, and those of some of his other famous clients. She sent Paige's papers to the same place.

She packed up Paige's clothes to send to a resale store, including some of their mother's old furs, which were very glamorous and nothing Whitney would ever use. Paige had saved them to wear to award ceremonies she attended, and she intended to wear one of their mother's old white mink coats if Emma was ever nominated for an Emmy, or even an Oscar one day. Paige was sentimental about that kind of thing, and Whitney was always more discreet and simply dressed. She didn't have the grandiose pretensions of her younger sister, or the taste for reincarnating Old Hollywood. Paige wanted everyone to know she was Liz Winston's daughter. Whitney usually tried to hide it, and avoided bringing attention to herself.

She had a local auction house come out and look at Paige's furniture, none of which was of any value. She donated all the kitchen equipment, the pots and pans she didn't need herself. Whitney didn't like her sister's taste in art, so she gave that to the auction house too, and she gave away Emma's baby toys and equipment, like a broken high chair and the stroller Emma hadn't used in years.

By the end of three days, the house had been stripped, and she had signed a listing agreement with a realtor. Paige had left no will, but Whitney was going to put the proceeds from the house and anything else in Emma's trust account, along with the salary she had made, and the recent payment from the producers and the network when they'd bought her out of her contract for the show. Emma would have a very respectable amount in her account when she was old enough to have access to it, and hopefully the amount would have grown from the investments in her portfolio by then. The only things that Whitney kept of her sister's were a sapphire bracelet and ring that had been their mother's. She was going to give them to Emma one day.

As she looked around the house once it was empty, Whitney felt a wave of sadness wash over her. It was all such a waste. If Paige had paid attention and driven more carefully with her seatbelt on, and Emma's in the backseat, none of this would have been necessary. She would have been alive to continue driving Emma's career, whatever Whitney thought of it, and Emma wouldn't have a brain injury that might hamper her forever and destroy the future Paige had wanted so badly for her. It made Whitney angry all over again as she drove away.

An industrial cleaning service was coming the next day, and then a stager to put in generic rented furniture to make the house sell better than it would have with Paige's slightly battered mismatched pieces. Whitney had agreed on a price with the realtor. It was a cute house, with two bedrooms and a sunny kitchen that needed new appliances, but was otherwise okay. Paige had bought it when their father died, two years before she had Emma, who had lived there all nine years of her life. Whitney wondered if Emma would miss it, if she remembered it one day. But she didn't want to wait to sell it. It made no sense to keep it for Emma to use later. She was better off having the money invested. Paige hadn't been in love with the house either. It was just convenient, on a street at the edge of Beverly Hills, and had been a good buy at the time, since it was part of an old lady's estate, whose children didn't want it either. Paige had always talked about fixing it up, but she never did. She didn't really care, and decorating wasn't her thing.

When she got home, Whitney found Brett and Emma doing an art project on Whitney's smoked glass dining room table. Emma was drawing tall trees with birds and butterflies in them, and children playing underneath. She seemed to be enjoying herself. Brett was very creative with her, and she was letting Emma use her iPad. Emma handled it hesitantly at first, and then seemed to be remembering how to use it, as Brett pointed to it and reminded her each step of the way. It gave Whitney an idea as she watched them, and she spoke to Brett as she put away the art supplies that she had brought with her.

"Why can't we teach her sign language, since she can't hear or speak? She could communicate with us that way." Emma was still having trouble reading, and remembering how to do it. It seemed to take a great deal of concentration and sometimes she just looked baffled, put the iPad down, and walked away. Brett had used applications on the iPad for young children that were all pictures instead of text, including some fashion options that Emma had caught on to quickly. Both Whitney and Brett kept trying to find ways to reach out to Emma.

"Sign language might be a little too stimulating for her brain at first, but we can try it," Brett said thoughtfully. "It would be fantastic if we could find a way for her to communicate with us."

"There's a school for the deaf. I'll call them," Whitney said and then went to take a bath, after clearing Paige's house all day. She was still angry at her sister for being negligent with her daughter's safety. It was so typical of Paige to do something stupid, and this time it had cost her her life and her daughter's future, which made it the ultimate stupidity, and no one could undo it. At least not so far.

She felt better when she put on clean jeans and a T-shirt, and had dinner with Emma and Brett a little while later. She'd worked hard clearing Paige's house, and it gave her a sense of closure. It reminded her that she still had to bury her ashes at her parents' grave site at the cemetery. She hadn't felt up to dealing with it yet, but she was planning to. Brett went to her room after she put Emma to bed, and Whitney went to bed herself with a book about children and traumatic brain injuries that Bailey had given her. The house was quiet and peaceful, and Whitney was surprised when Bailey called her. She told him she was reading the book and they agreed that it was excellent.

"You really do your homework, don't you?" he said admiringly.

"I try. I want Emma to have the best chance I can give her for a full recovery."

"You're already doing that," he said gently. He didn't know any other parent who had worked harder at it.

"How did you get into this field?" Whitney asked him. It was nice hearing a friendly adult voice at the end of the day. She missed talking to Chad occasionally but would never have called him. Their last conversation had been final for her.

He hesitated before he answered, he didn't usually talk about his personal history, but she was a doctor, they were becoming friends, and he wanted to invite her to the next brain injury conference sponsored by UCLA. "My younger brother, David, nearly drowned in a neighbor's pool when he was three. He never recovered from it, and he was seriously damaged. My parents never got over it. They each blamed the other for not watching him. I was five years older and I blamed myself. I always promised myself I'd become a doctor one day, and help children like David. My parents got divorced two years later, and he was institutionalized. Neither of them could deal with what had happened. He died at fourteen of pneumonia. His respiratory system had been badly compromised along with his brain. He was a very severe case. Neither of my parents ever remarried or had more kids. His accident ruined their lives, and his. My mother was depressed for the rest of her life, and my father drank himself to death after the divorce. The guilt was too much for them. It's not a happy story. But I wanted to make a difference after that.

"I'm not sure I have, though. I met Amy Clarke during my residency, and she had a sister who died pretty much of the same thing. She was in a coma for two years before they took her off life support. We met at a brain injury conference, consulted jointly on a few patients after that, and decided we liked working together. We combined our practices and it worked out well. Maybe our similar histories gave us a common bond as friends and work partners. There are more stories like this than you think. One careless moment, and lives are changed forever. At least for you, Emma's situation is clean. There's nothing you did wrong, or could have done differently, so you don't need to feel guilty. I know my brother is why I never wanted kids. It was such a heavy responsibility, and such a tragedy for the whole family, I never wanted to risk it. These cases destroy everyone's life, not just the victim's. I'd much rather try to save the victims than have a child of my own." It seemed sad to Whitney.

"I've been pretty angry at my sister," she admitted, impressed by what Bailey had told her, and deeply touched. "She was always irresponsible when we were kids. She let our dog out of the house once, and he got run over. She got in a couple of car accidents when we were in our teens, and I don't know what she did this time, but some part of it must have been her fault. If she really was texting as the police think, it was unforgivable." Whitney sounded harsh as she said it. But she was haunted by what had happened and the price Emma was paying for it. "I just wish I could turn the clock back for Emma, so it comes out differently. She doesn't deserve to suffer for her mother's mistake and carelessness."

"In Emma's case, I think she'll recover. It'll take time, but when she regains some of her memory, and we get her speaking again, I think her initial IQ will play in her favor. She may not be perfect, but she can be highly functional." Whitney told him about her idea then to teach Emma sign language so she could communicate with them, despite her lack of language and hearing.

"It's worth a try," he said, impressed by her ingenuity. No one had ever suggested that to him before. But it might work.

"I'm going to call the school for the deaf tomorrow and see what they think. Maybe they can send someone over to teach her. Brett and I can learn too." They talked for a while longer and then hung up, and when Whitney turned the light off she couldn't sleep. She kept thinking of Paige's house stripped bare, eventually with strangers in it. It all seemed like such a waste.

After tossing and turning for an hour, Whitney turned on the light again. She was thinking about Bailey's little brother and what a waste that had been too, and how it had destroyed his parents' lives, and impacted him, but inspired him to embark on a medical career. Her mother's high-powered Hollywood life, and her father running everything and treating her like a beautiful puppet while he pulled the strings, had done that for her. Medicine had seemed an ideal place to hide and look for a more meaningful life.

She clicked on the TV with the remote, and turned on the movie channels to see what she could find, until she came to an old film of Anne Bancroft's called *The Miracle Worker,* where she had played Annie Sullivan, the woman who had taught Helen Keller to communicate. The story had always fascinated her, about a time when no one was trying to save children like Helen Keller, and had locked them away in mental institutions. Whitney became engrossed in the movie, and was mesmerized by it as the story unfolded. Some of Keller's early behaviors reminded Whitney of the condition Emma was in now, particularly when she attacked Annie Sullivan physically, and Annie Sullivan forced her to learn to sign in the palm of her hand. It was what brought Helen Keller into the world as a sane, rational, functional person. It reinforced Whitney's idea about teaching Emma sign language. Emma could see, her vision had cleared again after the accident, even if she couldn't hear or speak now, and Whitney wanted to teach her to read again, since she had apparently forgotten that too ever since her injury.

There were tears running down Whitney's cheeks when the movie ended, and she slept peacefully that night. There was a glint in Whitney's eyes when she met Emma at the breakfast table the next day, while Brett put a bowl of cereal in front of Emma. As soon as they had finished eating, she hurried off to call the school for the deaf. They agreed to send one of their teachers out to meet Whitney and Emma the next day. They said they had never taught sign language to anyone with a brain injury, but they thought it was an intriguing idea, although they wanted to meet Emma first to see how cooperative she would be, and how capable she was of learning the basics. One of their teachers would come to the house to do an assessment.

Whitney was waiting for Samuel Bond when he drove up to the

house the next day. He was an attractive, pleasant African American man somewhere in his mid-thirties, and he looked very serious as Whitney led him into the house, walked him into the living room, and invited him to sit down. As soon as he started speaking with a slight impediment, she realized that he had a hearing problem. She noticed that he was wearing hearing aids, and he explained that he had been deaf most of his life as a result of chicken pox when he was a child. He had been teaching at the school for the deaf for many years, and he thought teaching Emma would be an interesting challenge. He seemed warm and kind, and Whitney liked him and hoped Emma would too.

Whitney went upstairs to find Emma then, and beckoned her to come downstairs, which she did with considerable suspicion, and she looked shy and uncomfortable as soon as she saw Sam. He signed hello to her, and Emma looked from him to Whitney, as though baffled by what he was doing. Whitney explained to him that she and Emma's nurse wanted to learn to sign too, since their whole goal was to communicate with Emma in case she never regained the ability to speak, or at least in the meantime. They agreed to a series of a dozen lessons, and he promised to return the next day with the books they needed to learn the symbols. He was enthusiastic about the project, and Emma didn't know what they'd agreed to, but she looked angry when she went back to her room. She was having a bad day, which still happened frequently, and she didn't like new people around.

Some days she was just bored and out of sorts, and frustrated. She'd been trying to talk to Brett in her own language, and Brett hadn't understood a word she'd said. And she still acted out occasionally. She did that night when Whitney set a dinner down in front of her that she didn't like. Before Whitney could protect herself, Emma took a swing at her, and cuffed her on the ear, which set off a ringing in Whitney's head. Whitney grabbed Emma's wrist firmly, as Annie Sullivan might have done, looked Emma in the eye, and shook her head.

"No, don't do that. It hurts," she said, rubbing her ear, and Emma ran out of the kitchen and upstairs to her room. Whitney left her alone for a while, put Emma's dinner aside, went upstairs to check on her when she'd finished, and sat down on Emma's bed. Emma wouldn't look at her, and Whitney was reminded of Helen Keller all over again. She leaned over and kissed Emma, who stroked Whitney's ear apologetically, and said something garbled in her gibberish. Whitney could tell she was sorry that she'd hit her. It went with the territory, but it was unpleasant anyway. And then Whitney went downstairs with her and sat with Emma while she ate dinner after Whitney reheated it. Emma was docile this time, and kissed Whitney on the ear to make it better.

Emma looked angry again when Sam Bond showed up for their group lesson the next day. He set up his charts in the kitchen, they sat down at the kitchen table, and two minutes later, Emma ran away.

"Why don't we start without her," Whitney suggested. "Brett and I can learn it first." She knew there was no point forcing the issue when Emma was frustrated and in a bad mood. Sam agreed to start without her, but he said that she would have to participate in the class eventually, and Whitney promised that she would.

She and Brett were diligent students, although they each made several mistakes. He laughed at them more than once, and translated what they had actually said. It was easy to make mistakes at first, but he was an intelligent, patient man, who admired what Whitney was trying to do, and hoped it would work as a means of communication with Whitney's niece.

The next time he came, Brett got Emma to join them. She made a few halfhearted signs, and Sam nodded his approval at her, and then she disappeared again. She wasn't a willing student, and watching him gave Whitney an idea. She called Belinda Marshall that night, the teacher on the set of *The Clan*. She asked how Emma was doing, and Whitney said she was making progress, but she still had a long way to go.

"Everyone misses her on the show," Belinda said sadly. They hadn't replaced her when they wrote her out. Fans were still mourning her, and begging the producers to bring her back, which they couldn't now. It wasn't possible in the plot of the show, nor in the condition Emma was still in. And they had paid handsomely to release her.

"Belinda, I've had an idea and I need your help," Whitney said and Belinda was intrigued. She explained to her about wanting to teach Emma sign language so she could communicate with them.

"She can't speak at all?" Belinda was shocked. She hadn't heard that before, but it explained why Emma had to leave the show. The producers had been very closemouthed about it, according to the confidentiality agreement they'd signed, to avoid gossip about Emma in the press.

"She's forgotten all language. She speaks in some kind of talk that makes sense to her and no one else. Sign language might bridge that gap. We have a teacher, but I don't think Emma likes him. She loves you, and if she remembers you, she might be willing to work with you. Her reading skills are sketchy now too, but I was wondering if you could try to get her to use an iPad? She has an app with pictures, but for now she's trapped in a silent world until she learns to speak again, and that could take a long time. They don't want us pushing speech therapy on her too soon. So what do you think?" Belinda was stunned by the offer, but also very touched.

"I learned some sign language in college. My best friend was hearing challenged. I've forgotten most of it, but I can learn again. Why don't we give it a try?" Whitney told her when the next lesson was, and Belinda said she'd be there. She wanted to do everything she could to help, and promised not to discuss it on the set. She was eager to get started, now that she knew the limitations Emma was facing.

When Belinda rang the doorbell the next time Sam Bond was due to arrive, Emma was standing behind Whitney when she opened the door, and she couldn't see who it was at first. As soon as she saw Belinda, she stood very still, as though digging through her memory, and unable to find what she was looking for. And then suddenly she let out a scream and flew into Belinda's arms. Belinda stood there hugging her and fighting back tears.

"She remembers you," Whitney said gently, watching Emma hug Belinda and beam up at her. Sam Bond arrived minutes later and their lesson went much better this time. Belinda remembered most of the signs, and showed Emma how to make them with her hands, as Sam watched them. He was vastly impressed with the young teacher, and in awe of her elegant Ethiopian grace and beauty, and he praised her for being so patient with Emma. The lesson went smoothly, and afterward, Belinda let Emma play on the iPad she'd brought with her. She had an application with big letters to teach toddlers to read, and

Emma was studying it carefully. They were opening doors for Emma that night. Before Belinda left, she talked to Whitney with tears in her eyes.

"I had no idea she was this impacted by the accident. I should have known when she left the show. I didn't want to intrude on you and call. Is she going to be okay?"

"I hope so," Whitney said quietly. "I really appreciate your help."

"I'll do whatever I can to make communication easier for her, and get her reading again." The difference between what Emma was capable of now and what she'd been able to do before had shocked Belinda profoundly. She had regressed to the stage of a five-year-old, which was an improvement from where she'd been right after the accident, when she first came out of the coma.

Sam offered Belinda a ride when she left, and in the car she explained to him what Emma had been like on the show, how bright and alert and precocious she was. It was heartbreaking to see how much ground she'd lost, and they both hoped that learning to sign would help her communicate, even though she was doing surprisingly well with no words at all, and a language all her own.

"Her aunt is an amazing woman," Sam said as he drove Belinda to her apartment in West Hollywood, and he thought the same about her. He'd been impressed by what he'd seen Belinda do during the lesson. And he couldn't help but notice that she was a beautiful woman. "I think Whitney is going to do everything she can to get that little girl talking again. If anyone can do it, I think she can. And maybe so can we," he said hopefully. He dropped Belinda off a little while later, and said he'd see her at the next lesson. She waved as he drove away, and walked up the stairs to her apartment, thinking of

Emma, and how happy she'd been to see her again, and how heart-breaking the effects of the accident were. She had enjoyed meeting Sam too. He was a very appealing man, and he thought exactly the same thing about her.

Emma looked exhausted when she sat down at dinner that night. The lesson had worn her out, and she was angry at Whitney for push-ing her. She didn't want to learn their stupid language, even if it meant she could see Belinda again, and she was having trouble work-ing the iPad. It all felt like too much, and as Whitney bent over her to set her dinner down in front of her, Emma looked at her with an evil glint in her eye, and with no warning, she hauled off and punched Whitney, hitting her squarely on the chin. It sent Whitney reeling backward for a minute, as Brett reached out to steady her. Then she ran to get a plastic bag filled with ice for her. Whitney put it on her chin and sat down. Her knees were shaking. She hadn't seen it com-ing. It was the second time Emma had hit her recently. Her eyes were smarting from the pain in her chin, and she looked at Emma ruefully.

"You've got a mean right hook for a nine-year-old," she said to Emma, as she got up from the table without touching her dinner, and slunk upstairs to her room, looking embarrassed. She hadn't meant to hurt her aunt again, but sometimes she couldn't help herself and she did it anyway. She lay on her bed with tears in her eyes, and Whitney came up a few minutes later, and took her in her arms and held her, as tears slid down Emma's cheeks.

"It's okay, baby, don't cry," she whispered to her. "It's going to be all right," she said, kissing the top of her head and stroking her hair. She just hoped it was true. Until then, it would be like *The Miracle Worker*. Her new role model in life was Annie Sullivan. If she could do it, so could they. And one day, the doors would open, and Emma would be back again. They were doing all they could. As Whitney sat holding her, Emma reached up and kissed her on the chin where she'd hit her, and Whitney smiled at her. This time, Whitney didn't let herself think about how angry she was at Paige, or wonder why the accident had happened. There was no point looking back. All they could do now was go forward until they reached better days. Emma sat clinging to her like the baby she had become, and whatever Whitney had wanted or hadn't, or planned for her life, like it or not, she was a mother now, and she smiled as she rubbed the growing bruise on her chin. The price of motherhood was higher than she'd expected, but hopefully worth it in the end.

Chapter 8

Within a few weeks, they settled into a routine, with Brett's help. Whitney went to her office to see patients every weekday, while Brett kept Emma busy with projects around the house. They baked cookies and made things. Brett showed her how to make a little cloth doll with button eyes and an embroidered mouth. She helped her on the iPad, and Brett practiced signing with her. Emma still made mistakes but it was the only way she could communicate other than pointing at what she wanted or pushing it away. She still lashed out occasionally, and Brett and Whitney had the bruises to show for it. Brett was a good sport about it, and on one occasion Emma had given her a black eye. They were learning to dodge her flailing fists whenever necessary. Bailey and Amy assured them that Emma would calm down eventually, as the damage to her brain began to heal, if it ever did. If not, they would have to live with the way she was now.

Emma continued speaking in her own unintelligible language, and got angry and frustrated when they couldn't understand her. It was obvious that the sounds meant something to her, but to no one else. And she had added no new words to her vocabulary, except those she learned to sign, which were simple and basic, like food, lunch, dinner, dress, shoes, bath, time for bed, which was a message she never liked. It was November, three and a half months after the accident, and they were managing as best they could. Bailey and Amy evaluated Emma weekly, and reported to the neurologist at Cedars-Sinai. All three doctors still believed that further improvement was possible, but there were no solid signs of it yet. And if it didn't happen, Whitney knew she would have to make their current systems work.

There was no way Emma could attend school the way she was now, but she seemed happy and healthy a lot of the time. She still stared longingly at the photographs of her mother, and followed Whitney around the house as soon as she got home from work. Emma's mental age now was closer to five than nine.

Whitney was still seeing half her normal caseload, and had taken on no new patients since September. She had enough on her plate as it was, but she was grateful things weren't worse. Brett was a godsend for her. She had grown attached to Emma, and was deeply committed to helping her try to relearn all the things she had lost.

Whitney was seeing a patient when a red light flashed on the desk in her office near Melrose Place. It meant that there was an emergency of some kind and she had to interrupt the session. She was seeing a seventeen-year-old boy who had suicidal tendencies and had just left the hospital after a month's stay. He was doing better, and they were focusing on his current plans, when Whitney apologized and picked up the phone to speak to her secretary at the desk outside.

"Yes, Rosie?" Whitney asked in a calm voice. She assumed there was another patient in distress holding on an outside line, which happened from time to time. Her secretary sounded breathless when she answered.

"It's Brett, at the house. You'd better talk to her right away." Whitney asked no other questions, pressed a button, and picked up the line. Brett was crying when she answered.

"It's Emma, I can't find her. I went upstairs to get her a sweater so we could go outside, and I couldn't find her when I got back. She wasn't upset or angry or anything. She was playing with the iPad. It was on the floor and the back door was open when I got back. I couldn't find her anywhere. She's gone. I'm so sorry. I ran up and down the block and asked everyone. No one has seen her."

"Did you check the pool?" Whitney asked with her heart in her throat. She lived in constant terror that Emma would fall in and drown, since she no longer remembered how to swim and her balance still wasn't perfect. Whitney had had an automatic cover installed, but sometimes the pool cleaners forgot to close it.

"It was the first place I looked," Brett said, choking on a sob. "Should I call the police?" If someone picked her up off a street, or Emma were lost, she wouldn't be able to tell anyone where she lived or even her name. Whitney had tried leaving little slips of paper in her pockets with her name and address, but Emma threw them away.

"I'll be home in ten minutes," Whitney said in a tense voice. "Let's drive around the neighborhood first." Whitney glanced at her patient with an apologetic look as she hung up the phone. "Charlie, I'm really sorry. I have an emergency at home." It was the first time she had ever said anything like it to him and he looked surprised. Whitney's home life never intruded on her work, and in fact, he knew nothing personal about her, not even if she was married or had kids herself. He smiled as they both stood up. He liked knowing that she was human after all, and he wasn't the only one with problems. His life was a constant battle with his parents, and he hated the school he went to. He said he had no friends there, but his parents liked its social status. He had done everything he could think of to get kicked out. His parents' large donations to the school had kept him there so far, but he was working on it.

"It sounds like you have a kid who ran away," he said, curious about her, and Whitney sighed.

"Not really. She may have wandered off. My niece lives with me. She was in an accident last summer, she has a brain injury, and she can't be out on her own. She lost her memory and can't speak." It was as simply as she could put it, without dragging him through the details.

"That sounds sad," he said, looking sympathetic. "Is she going to be okay?"

"I hope so. She's probably walking around the neighborhood. She's nine. I've got to go home and help find her. I'm really sorry. Can we reschedule for tomorrow?" He nodded. "Your mom should be back in a few minutes," she said, as she put on her jacket, thanked him for his understanding, and hurried toward the door.

"I hope you find her!" he called after her, and stood at the window as he watched Whitney get in her car. He liked her. She was a lot nicer and more reasonable than his parents, whom he hadn't gotten along with since he turned fourteen. He broke all their rules, and smoked joints in his bedroom when they were out. They went nuts when they found evidence of it later. He watched Whitney's car drive away as fast as she dared, and sat down to wait for his mother to pick him up, thinking about the injured niece that Whitney had described. It was a surprise to him to realize that his psychiatrist had problems and a life.

The house was ten minutes from Whitney's office, and she pulled into her driveway a few minutes later. Brett was waiting outside, looking frantic.

"Any sign of her?" Whitney asked, looking worried and fighting panic as Brett shook her head.

"I drove all around the neighborhood before I called you. No one's seen her." Whitney's new station wagon was parked at the curb. It was the car she had Brett drive for errands, or when they had to take Emma to the doctor. She still hated riding in the car, so Whitney knew she wouldn't get into a stranger's car easily, but she was a nine-year-old child, and delicate for her age, and it wouldn't be difficult to pick her up and abduct her. She was a beautiful little girl.

"I'll head north, you go south," Whitney instructed her. "Call me if you see anything. We can call the police as soon as we get back. I'll meet you back here in twenty minutes, if we don't find her first."

"What if we don't?" Brett said with tears brimming in her eyes.

"Then the police will find her," Whitney said with a look of iron determination. "You checked every place in the house?" Brett nodded, and Whitney made a quick run-through before she got back in her car. She noticed that one of the photographs of Paige was missing from next to Emma's bed, and Whitney wondered if Emma had gone looking for her somewhere, and then she sped off. She had an idea. Brett had shown Whitney the iPad she'd been playing with before she left. There was a picture of a house on the screen, which looked a little like Paige's home, except that the one on the iPad had roses in front of it, a family with two children and a dog, and the word under it in bold letters said "Home." But Whitney knew that Emma wouldn't be able to find her way back to her old house. It was about two miles away, across several big streets.

Paige's house had sold almost immediately. They'd had an offer on it a week after Whitney had listed it, because of the reasonable asking price. It was in escrow now, and the sale was due to close in two weeks. Whitney just wanted to get rid of it, and the stager had already removed the rented furniture since the deal had been made. The buyers were thrilled with their new home, and had already gone through it with an architect planning some changes. Whitney wondered now if the image of the iPad had reminded Emma of it, unlocked another door in her brain, and she was trying to find her old home. Whitney looked carefully down every street she drove through. She saw mothers pushing babies in strollers, deliveries being made to houses, a two-year-old on a little plastic tricycle with his mother, and then she saw Emma, sitting on someone's front lawn with her arms around a black Lab, looking forlorn and lost. Whitney slowed down, and pulled over to the curb. Her heart was pounding, but Emma looked unharmed and the dog wagged its tail as Whitney approached and sat down next to Emma on the lawn. She could see that she was holding the framed photograph of her mother in her hand. Whitney gently leaned over and kissed her, and Emma looked away, and seemed disappointed to have been found. Whitney signed to her then.

"Where are you going?" Emma didn't answer her for a long time, and struggled with a word instead of signing. She had to push out the word like she was giving birth to it, but finally made a sound that tore at Whitney's heart.

"Home . . ." she said clearly, and then added one of the other words she had mastered. "Mommmm . . . Home . . . Mom . . ." she repeated several times. How could Whitney explain to her that both were gone now, her old house and her mother? Emma knew that Paige was gone, but there was no way to explain to her about the house, and Whitney didn't want to. It was too complicated to tell her the house had been sold, and all the reasons why. Instead, she sat there with her arm around her, and nodded, and then slowly she stood up, and Emma did too. They walked to Whitney's car, and the black Lab tried to follow. Whitney opened the back door of her car, and Emma slipped onto the backseat. She didn't try to resist this time, and Whitney knew what she had to do now. Emma was still clutching the photograph of her mother as Whitney fastened her seatbelt, and then got into the car and turned on the ignition. She texted Brett that she had found Emma before putting the car in gear. She didn't have the keys to Emma's house with her, but even if they couldn't go inside, at least Emma could see it. Maybe it would release some memories that would open other doors for her and remind her of all she had forgotten and was trying to remember. All her old memories were still out of reach.

Whitney drove the remaining distance, and the familiar house came into view a few minutes later. The for sale sign had been removed since it was in escrow, and Whitney noticed, as the buyers had, that it was in need of paint, but it was a sweet house, and Emma nearly jumped out of her seat when she saw it, nodded frantically at Whitney, and pounded her on the shoulder. Her guess had been right. Emma had been trying to find her old house.

"Home!" she shouted. "Home! Mom!" The words didn't come easily as Whitney pulled into the driveway and stopped the car. She wondered if Emma thought she would find Paige then.

"I know, baby . . . I know. . . ." Whitney said softly, and how could she explain to her that they didn't live there anymore, or even own it, or not for much longer?

Emma ran to the front door, and tried to open it, and looked at Whitney expectantly as she walked up to it, and shook her head, and gestured that she couldn't open it. Emma nodded frantically, pounded on the door then, and rang the doorbell, and no one answered. Whitney shook her head and then signed to her. "Mommy isn't here anymore" was the best explanation she could think of, as Emma continued to nod and then started to cry, and then sank down on the front steps, looking defeated. Whitney sat down next to her, and signed, "I'm sorry."

They sat there for a long time, as though expecting someone to come and meet them, or Paige to show up and not be dead after all. And then Emma got up and tried to look in the windows. With an aching heart, Whitney held her up, so she could see that the inside of the house was empty. She looked at Whitney with desperation. She was wondering where everything had gone but didn't know how to ask it, or even sign it. Whitney shook her head again, and Emma was sobbing as her aunt led her back to the car and they got in. They were going home now, but not to the one Emma remembered. That home was gone forever. But at least Emma had remembered it, which Whitney thought was a good sign. The doors of the past were unlocking slowly, even if facing the memories was painful for Emma.

Brett saw them as soon as they drove up, she had been pacing on the front lawn waiting for them, and threw her arms around Emma as soon as she saw her. She looked at Whitney. "Where was she?"

"She was trying to get to her old house. She was heading in the right direction, but she had a long way to go." Emma walked into the house looking dejected and still holding her mother's photograph. She went up to her room and set it on the night table with the others, and then sat there, staring into space for a long time. She already knew her mother wasn't coming back, or Whitney assumed she did, but she looked as though she had lost her all over again after seeing the house.

Whitney called Bailey and Amy and told them about it that afternoon after Emma had settled down. They both got on the phone.

"That's pretty amazing," Bailey said, impressed. "She remembered the house and tried to find it. Maybe she thought she'd find her mother there. But either way, that's very enterprising, and she even recalled which direction to go. I think we're having another breakthrough." And she had retrieved one of her lost words when she said "Home," but it was a small consolation, seeing how unhappy she was.

"It's going to be hard for her when she remembers things," Amy reminded both of them. "This isn't an easy process for her. She lost her mother, their home, her job on the TV show, all her friends on the show. She's going to have a lot to face as her memory comes back.

There's no good news in it for her, and when she remembers the accident that's going to be the toughest memory of all. But she can't heal fully until she remembers everything, and faces it, and after that she can go forward. For now, she's still digging in the past for the answers. She tried to find one of them today." They all agreed that it was an important step, even if not a happy one, and Bailey promised to come and see Emma later. She was uncommunicative when he did, and Whitney looked troubled too.

"Do you think I'm wrong to try and keep her at home?" she asked him honestly. "Is it too dangerous for her? It never occurred to me that she might try to run away. What if someone had found her and kidnapped her today? Maybe I'm being crazy since I can't protect her here." She'd been thinking about it all day, ever since Brett called her at the office and said Emma was lost.

"You mean institutionalize her?" Whitney hesitated and then nodded, and Bailey was shocked. He didn't think Whitney would have been open to that idea even though many people would have preferred that option rather than trying to bring Emma back, inch by inch, themselves. "She didn't run away today," he reminded her. "She was trying to find something, the house she lived in with her mother. That's a very ambitious project for her. I'd say that's more of a positive than a negative and it shows she's fighting to come back, not run away."

"What if I don't know enough to do this safely for her?" Whitney asked, worried. "I'm just groping around, trying to find answers for her, but maybe she'd be better off with professionals taking care of her, full-time. She could have gotten hurt today, kidnapped or injured, or run over by a car while crossing the street. She's just a little kid, and now she's brain injured and vulnerable."

"She's a very resourceful little kid, if you ask me," he said with a tone of admiration. "And to answer your question, no, I don't think she'd be better off in an institution of some kind. She wouldn't make as much progress there and they wouldn't try as hard as you do. She might not even make any progress there at all."

"She might not make progress here either. Maybe I have to face that." It was something she had been avoiding since the accident, the fact that Emma might stay the way she was. Whitney hadn't wanted to confront that or accept it, but she wondered if maybe now she had to.

"She already is progressing." Bailey pled Emma's case. "She still has a long way to go, and she hasn't gotten language back yet, but her memory is obviously waking up. We saw evidence of that today. So, if you're asking for my opinion, I don't think she belongs in an institution, at least not yet. We can always reassess that later, but for now, I think there's still hope, even if she hasn't unlocked all the doors yet. I think she will." It was easy for him to say, he didn't live with her, and he hadn't almost lost her today when she ran away, whatever her reason for doing it. What if she had gotten hurt as a result? It had been a sobering experience for Emma and for all of them.

Bailey could tell how badly Whitney was shaken by it. He came by that afternoon to check on them and reassured Brett too. And after that he stopped by every day without fail.

It was several days before Whitney had calmed down again, and

Brett as well. By the weekend, when Whitney was alone with Emma, she felt more confident again.

Bailey dropped by to see them on his way to play tennis with a friend and Whitney was calmer than she had been earlier in the week.

"Feeling better?" he asked her, concerned. It had been a hard week. Every week was hard. There were no easy gains.

"A little." She smiled at him. "She scared the hell out of me when she disappeared. I think she understands the house is gone now, but that's another loss for her, and there have been so many."

"And positives too," he reminded her.

"Like what?" Whitney couldn't imagine them.

"You. She lost her mother, but you've stepped into her shoes. It's not the same, but you haven't let her down for a minute in the last four months. And from what you've said to me, I'm not even sure her mother would have been as dedicated. This is not an easy path you're on. Not everyone could do it."

"I was beginning to think I couldn't either," she said. "I don't want to make things worse for her, or slow down her progress by trying to keep her here."

"You aren't. How's she doing with her signing lessons?" He thought it was a brilliant idea.

It was an interesting experiment, and Belinda and Sam were still coming twice a week. "It depends on the day. Sometimes she signs perfectly, and at other times she can't remember any of it. That's what's happening with her reading too. Sometimes you can see that she's not interested and it makes no sense to her, and then the next time, she's fascinated and reads simple things for a while. None of it happens in a straight line or goes smoothly every day."

"That's how brain injuries are," Bailey explained again. "People make significant advances, and then regress and lose ground. Eventually, she'll get there, but it's going to take time. How's the aggression?"

"That depends on the day too. When she's frustrated, she takes it out on me, but at least she feels bad now when she hurts me. She can't stop herself when she gets upset." He nodded, and then she thought of something she'd been meaning to ask him. She wasn't sure how appropriate it was. She knew Bailey had no family and he didn't seem to have a big social life. He was always happy to visit them, and had free time at night. Amy seemed busier and had a serious boyfriend from what she said, and family she visited in Colorado. Bailey appeared to be more solitary. "What are you doing for Thanksgiving? If you have nothing to do, we're having a turkey here. I've always done it. My sister wasn't much of a cook, and since my father died, it's just been the three of us. Brett's having Thanksgiving with us, she doesn't want to go home to Salt Lake." She knew Bailey had no family to be with either, since he had no siblings and his parents were dead, but she wasn't sure he'd want to spend the holiday with her and Emma. They were patients, but slowly becoming friends. She knew Amy was going to her future in-laws' in San Francisco, but Whitney wondered if Bailey was going to be alone, or maybe going to friends. She decided to ask him anyway.

"I'd love sharing it with you. I'm not big on holidays which are family events, since my parents are gone. I usually volunteer at a soup kitchen or a homeless shelter, which at least turns it into a useful event, but I'd love to spend it with you and Emma." He knew it would be a hard holiday for both of them this year. He looked touched to be asked, and really pleased.

"We just do a simple lunch, nothing elaborate."

"That sounds just right. Holidays like Thanksgiving and Christmas always make one feel like such a loser if you're not married and don't have kids," he admitted. Whitney laughed and nodded her head.

"Actually, they've always made me feel grateful I wasn't married and didn't have kids." She laughed. "And now I've kind of backed into it. I want to make it as nice as I can for Emma. She's going to miss her mother now that she remembers her. It'll be nice having you here," she said warmly. "I never figured I'd have a child of my own, and never felt ready to take that on, and now I've got Emma." It made her think of Chad briefly. She hadn't heard from him in two months, and knew she wouldn't again. She missed the fun trips with him, but not who he turned out to be when Emma got hurt. He was a cold, selfish man, and she saw that now. She no longer had time to travel with him anyway. Her whole life had changed.

"Thank you for inviting me," Bailey said again, and then left to play tennis, and he offered to come by with some Thai food the next day. Whitney was planning to spend a quiet weekend with Emma, and do some things around the house. She was trying to teach her to play chess again, but she hadn't mastered her old skills, and was better at Monopoly and Clue, which they played loosely, ignoring the rules so they were easier for her. And Belinda had left her some new games on the iPad, which kept Emma busy for hours as she struggled to master them. She played several of them with Bailey when he came back with dinner on Sunday night, and then beat him at a game of gin, which impressed him. Her abilities were spotty and irregular, and some were better than others.

"What did she do? Deal blackjack in Vegas in a past life?" he said after she beat him at gin several times. "I think she may have been cheating, but either way she beat me. You have to be smart to cheat too." He laughed. "She is one very bright little girl." Whitney laughed too, and Emma looked pleased. Bailey had been a good addition to their life, as a doctor and a friend. They had medicine as their common ground. He told Whitney about the brain injury conference he would be chairing in a few weeks. He still wanted her to speak there, and Whitney wasn't sure, although the meetings sounded interesting.

"I don't know enough about it to sound intelligent," she said modestly. "Brain injuries are new to me."

"They're new to a lot of neurologists in the field too. New information is published every year. Think about it. I want you as a guest speaker. You can talk about what you've been through with Emma. She's taught me several things too, and every case is different. Her IQ must have been incredible before the accident." Whitney had lent him some of the DVDs of the episodes of *The Clan,* and he was impressed by Emma's performance, and her strength in delivering her lines on a very emotional dramatic show. Whitney had played a few of them for Emma, but she seemed to have no interest in them, and no recollection that the actress on the screen was her. Her role on the series hadn't emerged from her dormant memory bank yet, and there was no way of knowing if it ever would. There were other things they thought she needed to remember first, like the accident that had killed her mother. That was the real nucleus of the trauma and was the memory most likely to open up the rest. But there had been no recent breakthroughs since she went to find her old house, and she was content to play games and try new apps on the iPad.

Belinda and Sam joined them on Thanksgiving too, since neither had local family to be with, and they were a congenial group. Whitney prepared a delicious meal. Bailey helped carve the turkey, and Brett and Emma had made all the pies from recipes Brett had gotten from her mother in Salt Lake. Whitney had learned by then that Brett was the youngest of nine children and had twenty-nine nieces and nephews, which explained why she was so good with kids, along with her nursing skills.

Emma signed several times during lunch, and joined the conversation, and as soon as the meal was over, she went upstairs to her room and lay down on the bed. Whitney was sure she was thinking about her mother, and it saddened Whitney too that her sister wasn't there with them. It was hard to believe that she was gone forever, and that it had only been four months since the accident.

"Is she okay?" Bailey asked Whitney when she came back downstairs after checking on Emma, and she nodded.

"I think she misses her mother. I think the things she does remember are hard for her. Maybe all that she's forgotten is a mercy for her. At least she doesn't need to feel sad about it. You can't miss what you don't remember," she said with a sigh.

"Are you doing okay?" Bailey asked her gently and she smiled.

"I guess I'm like Emma that way. It depends on the day."

"Have you given any more thought to the conference?" She hesitated, not sure what to say. "You've still got time to decide. You have a lot of good firsthand information to share, about living with a brain injured child, and the psychiatric aspects of it."

"Maybe." She wasn't convinced yet, although medically she readily admitted the subject was fascinating. But her personal experiences were too close to home, and she didn't want to violate Emma's privacy.

All in all, it was a surprisingly nice Thanksgiving, better than she had expected. She was startled when Emma's agent, Robert Jones, called the next day.

"How's our girl doing?" he asked with interest. Whitney didn't particularly like him, although she knew her sister had, and thought he was great for Emma's career. "I've been getting a lot of calls recently, asking when she'll be ready to go back to work. I've had some inquiries for other series, and a Disney movie, and some product endorsements. Whenever you think she's ready, the work is there. She's still a hot property, more so than ever with the sympathy factor. No one has forgotten her yet."

"She's not ready," Whitney said firmly without going into detail. His comments smacked of exploitation to Whitney and made her angry.

"Don't let it sit too long," he warned her, "we don't want producers to lose interest. She's still a valuable commodity." That wasn't how Whitney viewed her, although she knew her sister had.

"She's a little girl, Robert. She's got a lifetime in show business ahead of her, if that's what she wants."

"She must miss the show," he said in a wheedling tone that made Whitney's skin crawl. He was the epitome of everything she hated about Hollywood. Her father had been a cut above him, and of a much higher caliber as an agent, but the theories were all the same, as far as she was concerned, and she wasn't going to let him take advantage of Emma. He couldn't anyway, since she couldn't even talk, which he didn't know and Whitney wasn't about to tell him. He had a big mouth. "Well, keep in touch. I'll send you some scripts after the holidays," he said hopefully, and Whitney couldn't wait to hang up. She wanted to keep people like him as far away from Emma as she could. Whatever Paige's views had been on the subject, Whitney was never going to let anyone exploit Emma again. Paige had given her a career as a child star, and Whitney wanted to give her the life of a child. What Emma would want one day when she recovered remained to be seen. As long as Whitney was in charge, those decisions would be up to Emma, and no one else.

Chapter 9

D espite their different interests and philosophies about life, the one thing that Paige and Whitney had always agreed on was their love of the holidays. Christmas had always been a big event in their family, with elaborate decorations and lots of presents, an enormous tree lit up on the front lawn, and another one in the living room. When they were children, their family had celebrated on Christmas Eve with a black tie dinner, and their mother had always worn a glamorous evening gown, with a new piece of jewelry their father had given her. Even after she was gone, the girls had helped their father maintain their family traditions. After his death, Whitney put up a tree every year and Paige and Emma had come to dinner, wearing pretty dresses, and they had exchanged gifts on Christmas Eve after dinner, and met again for lunch the next day. Their celebrations were less formal once their parents were gone, but the sisters had spent Christmas together every year.

Whitney had always spent several days decorating a tree she could barely get into the house, with an elaborate angel sitting on top, and beautiful ornaments Whitney had collected for years. She was determined that this year should be no different. She wanted Emma to have a wonderful Christmas, even if they were going to be alone. Their family had shrunk dramatically, and the memories would be overwhelming for Whitney, remembering her parents and her childhood and now her sister, but she was planning to decorate a tree in her living room, as she always did. And she bought a new red velvet dress for Emma to wear on Christmas Eve. She clapped her hands when she saw it and Whitney tried it on her. It fit perfectly. Four days before Christmas, she took Emma with her to pick out a tree and had it delivered to the house.

Whitney had brought several boxes of decorations from Paige's house, and planned to use them, so they'd look familiar to Emma. She had also brought a collection of music boxes that Paige had put on her mantel every year. Her favorite had been an antique one with an angel in it, and a crèche with baby Jesus. It played "Silent Night." Whitney set them all on the mantel carefully, and Emma paid no attention to them. They didn't seem to be familiar to her, and she watched with fascination as Whitney stood on a ladder hanging ornaments on the tree. Brett even got Emma to hang a few on the lower branches, and she smiled and chattered in gibberish as she did it. Whether she remembered their earlier Christmases or not, she enjoyed the process and how pretty the house looked once the decorating was complete. The night she finished the tree, Whitney turned all the lights off, plugged in the tree, and the effect was magical. She and Emma sat on the couch and admired the result.

On Christmas Eve, she and Emma had dinner together, and Emma wore her new red dress. Whitney gave her a pretty gold bracelet, and high-top pink Converse that Emma put on immediately with her velvet dress. Then Whitney tucked her into bed in her pajamas so she could fill the stockings, and pile up the gifts from Santa that she'd been hiding downstairs. Emma had believed in Santa Claus the previous year, and presumably still did. Whitney scurried around the house after taking off her dress and putting on a pink cashmere dressing gown.

She could hardly wait for Emma to open her gifts from Santa in the morning. When everything was set up in the living room, Whitney sat down on the couch and enjoyed the sight of all of it. Emma was already sound asleep, and in a moment of nostalgia, Whitney got up and wound her sister's favorite music box, and it began playing "Silent Night," just as Whitney remembered. She sat listening to it with tears in her eyes in the darkened house, and suddenly she heard a scream and a dark flash shot past her, shrieking, and Emma began attacking the Christmas tree, using all her strength to try and knock it down, while shouting "No!" as loud as she could.

Whitney couldn't understand what was happening. She rushed forward to stop Emma before she knocked over the ten-foot tree and injured herself. The tree was teetering precariously, as Emma screamed and flailed wildly as she hit Whitney, with the music box playing in the background. Emma stood there distraught, dwarfed by the tree with her hands over her ears, as Whitney finally dragged her away, breathless, as she forced her to sit on the couch before she did any more damage. Then Emma rushed to the mantel, grabbed the music box, and threw it to the ground, where it broke in a million pieces at her feet and the familiar Christmas carol finally stopped. It looked like a bomb had hit the room. Some of the gifts were crushed where Emma had trampled them, and the enormous tree stood at an angle in the stand, as Whitney tried to understand what had happened and what had set her off.

"No!" Emma was still shouting again and again, and as she did, Whitney had a sudden realization. Emma had come from upstairs, and she had heard the sound of the music box. She was shaking as she looked at Whitney.

"No song! No song!" she screamed at her as Whitney realized what had happened. Emma's hearing had returned. She had heard the music box playing "Silent Night," and it brought back too many memories and too much pain. The cloud had lifted over her hearing. She could hear Whitney now, which was a huge leap forward, the biggest one of all so far.

"You heard the music box?" Whitney asked her intently, and Emma nodded and spoke more softly this time.

"No song . . . No Mom . . ."

"It was your mom's favorite song, wasn't it?" Whitney asked sadly, and Emma nodded. "No song . . . No Mommy."

"Emma, you can hear me, can't you?" Emma nodded again. Whitney suddenly wondered if Emma had been hearing for a while, or if this was new. Five months after the accident, her hearing had returned. It was huge.

Whitney led her gently upstairs back to bed and tucked her in, and then went downstairs to clean up the debris. The music box was smashed beyond repair. Whitney put what was left of it in the trash, wrestled with the tree to straighten it, and put the room back in order. And if Emma inquired why the gifts were there that night, she was going to say that Santa had already come by when Emma was asleep. But she had been so upset about the music box playing "Silent Night" that she hadn't even noticed them.

Whitney also realized that things would be different now if Emma could hear. She would be able to communicate with her without signing. Whitney stopped to gaze at Emma sleeping when she got back upstairs. She looked peaceful and there was no night terror that night. Whitney lay in bed awake for a long time, wondering what would happen next, if Emma would be able to talk now that she could hear. But in the morning when Emma woke up, she didn't speak. She signed to Whitney as though nothing had changed. Whitney didn't sign to her, she spoke to her.

They opened their gifts. Emma was subdued and went back upstairs immediately, carrying as many of her presents as she could. Whitney called Bailey on his cellphone when Emma went to her room. He had gone skiing with friends over Christmas and she wanted to share the news with him.

"She can hear," she said, sounding stunned. She described what happened the night before. "I don't know if it just started last night when she heard the music box or if she's been hearing for a while. She acts like she can't hear me today, but I think she can." Now that her hearing had returned, Whitney assumed that it would stay, and Bailey thought so too.

"It probably frightened her if it happened all at once. Did the song have any particular meaning for her?" He was excited by everything Whitney had to say.

"It was Paige's favorite, 'Silent Night,' and she loved the music box. Maybe Emma was angry that Paige wasn't there for Christmas. She seems very withdrawn today."

"She needs time to adjust, and she obviously remembered the music box, so her memory is coming back, along with her hearing. I think speech will be next. Just let her do what she wants today. I want her hearing tested after the holiday. This is a big step, Whitney." She knew it too, and it gave her hope for further recovery in the future. Hopefully soon.

"I know," she said, still sounding shaken by the events of the night before. "I know it sounds crazy, but this is the first big sign of improvement we've had."

"It is," he agreed. "She may regress for a while after this. These gains are frightening for her. It's like being carried along by a river. She has no control over the memories that come back to her. She needs to move at her own pace. How is Christmas otherwise?" he asked and Whitney sighed.

"There is no 'otherwise,' this is all there is in our life now, her progress and her recovery and her setbacks. Her hearing again is so huge. How's your ski trip?" She was hungry to hear about normal life. Hers hadn't been normal for five months, and she wondered if it ever would be again.

"Fantastic, but not as exciting as your news. 'Silent Night' must have reminded her of her mother in some unbearably painful way." Whitney agreed. She wondered if it had brought back some memory of the accident, but she didn't want to ask her and upset her again. Emma spent most of Christmas Day in her room, playing with her new toys, and seemed very quiet, which in some ways was a relief. Whitney felt drained too after the shock and emotions of the night before. She called Brett in Salt Lake to tell her about Emma's hearing, and she was thrilled. The noise of children in the background was so loud that she could barely hear Whitney.

Whitney went to check on Emma again after she and Brett hung up. She was eager to get back to see Emma now that she could hear. Whitney stood watching Emma from the doorway, she was looking at one of the photographs of her mother, and then she glanced at Whitney.

"She loved you very much, Em," she said softly.

"No," Emma said harshly, her voice too loud in the room. "She went away." She was speaking again too, Whitney tried not to look startled, and treat it as a normal event.

"She didn't want to leave you, Emma. She never would have done that to you. She loved you."

"No!" Emma shouted at her again. "She didn't love me. She went away," and then she looked at Whitney with despair and pantomimed her mother texting, just as the police had guessed about the accident. Emma kept texting to show Whitney what had happened. Emma was remembering the accident, or what had come right before. She looked broken and angry as she pretended to text again and again. But she was speaking, and she could hear, and her memory was coming back. Whitney's heart sank as she saw Emma pretend to text with her hands. That was obviously how it had happened. It was clear now. Paige had been texting and driving, and just like Emma, Whitney felt rage at her sister wash over her again like a tsunami. How could she do something so dangerous? It had been so stupid of her, and was such an incredible waste. And now Whitney knew for sure because Emma had remembered her mother texting.

"I told her no," Emma said as tears rolled down her cheeks. It had taken five months, but now they knew the truth.

After that, for the rest of the day, Emma didn't speak again, and pretended not to hear Whitney when she spoke to her. She would only sign, and retreated back into her silent world. Whitney was haunted by what she had said. "She didn't love me . . . I told her no." Emma had taken giant leaps forward, and now several steps back, as she lapsed into silence again. . . . But the words "I told her no" cut through Whitney like a knife.

Chapter 10

Bailey took them out to dinner when he got back from his ski trip, but like Whitney, he found Emma shut down. She wouldn't look at him or talk to him. She answered none of his questions and pretended not to hear anything he said. She had retreated back to a safe place, where the memories couldn't touch her again. He didn't force the issue personally, but the next day he sent her for a hearing test. The technicians cajoled her into cooperating with them by playing games with her, and the results came back that her hearing was acute. She could hear everything said to her, whether she acknowledged it or not. And as soon as she got home, she chose not to again. She preferred silence to talking about painful subjects, or questions they might ask about the accident.

Bailey stayed for dinner after coming to tell Whitney the test results and neither of them was surprised. Emma was showing no signs of her newly recaptured skills, and she pointedly ignored Bailey whenever he spoke to her, so he directed his conversation at Whitney, and took no notice of Emma, on purpose, so she wouldn't feel threatened or cornered. Now that she could hear, she had nowhere to retreat to get away from them. So they gave her space.

He brought up the subject of TV shows with Whitney, and ignored Emma while they chatted about it, and suddenly out of the blue, she spoke up with her newfound words, which had waited five months to be released, like pent-up birds.

"I was on TV," Emma commented, and Bailey turned to her in surprise.

"Really? How interesting. Did you like it?" She thought about it for a minute and then nodded cautiously.

"Sometimes. My mom wanted me to." He and Whitney exchanged a look.

"It must have been hard to remember all those lines," he said in a relaxed tone, and Emma shook her head to indicate it wasn't.

"I sing too. My mom wanted me to be in a musical." It was more information than they'd had for five months, and Whitney hadn't heard about the Broadway show Emma had auditioned for. Her sister hadn't had the chance to tell her before the accident.

"I'd love to hear you sing sometime," Bailey said casually, and Emma shrugged, and then seemed to withdraw again, and a little while later she went upstairs to her room, having communicated enough for one night. Her words were back, but using them appeared to wear her out. It seemed to be a major effort for her to speak, but at least she was able to now, when she chose.

"I wish I understood better what happened on Christmas Eve," Whitney said thoughtfully. "Has she remembered things that have broken through the trauma, so now she can speak again, or is her brain healing physically, which allows her to speak and hear again? I never totally understand what part of this is physical, and what part is psychological," Whitney said, musing about the changes of the past few days.

"I don't think you can separate the two, they're so closely connected," Bailey responded. "I think they go hand in hand. Brain injuries aren't just about physical damage, the trauma at the outset is intimately connected to it." Whitney agreed with him, it was her feeling about it too.

"What happens to her memory now? Does it come back, or is everything erased by the accident?" Whitney wondered about that.

"That's hard to predict. She already remembers some things from right before it happened. How much more comes back in the end remains to be seen. She may always have memory lapses. Or it may all come back. She can only remember what she saw before she became unconscious. And we don't know what she remembers of her life with her mother. She may have lost memory of some of that too. It may take years for her to retrieve that, and it'll be painful to remember," he said quietly as Whitney thought about it. "She lost part of her history. We just don't know how much of it, or if it's gone forever."

Belinda was impressed by Emma's progress too when she came to visit her. She was still having trouble reading and said her eyes hurt, and it gave her a headache when she struggled with it for too long, which Bailey didn't want her to do. They didn't want to overstimulate her brain, or cause flare-ups and more memory lapses. There had been no incidents of frustration or violence since she had started to speak again. And the gibberish had disappeared. She hadn't had a night terror since Christmas Eve and seemed much calmer now.

It brought up the question of school, which Bailey said was still months away. She wasn't ready for that yet, or to go back to her career, which Whitney was still leery of. The final decision on that would be Emma's, if she wanted to pursue the acting career her mother had fostered since she was six years old. Whitney realized that it might be important for her. She didn't want to deprive her of it, or push her into it, as Paige had done. And her skills weren't solid enough yet for work or school.

She thought about it that night, alone in her room, and played a DVD of episodes of Emma's series on her TV. In the months since the accident, Whitney had been so worried about Emma's survival and the damage to her brain that she had forgotten how challenging some of her performances were. She hadn't had an easy role on *The Clan* and Whitney was stunned as she watched, remembering how talented Emma was, how smooth her delivery. It really was in her blood, and Whitney could see now what Paige had seen in her child, and why she had encouraged her with all the lessons and coaches. Emma had a gift, and at the end of the episode she could also see how different Emma still was now, how stilted and halting her speech and what a struggle for her it was at times. She had come a long way in the past five months, but seeing the DVD made it clear how far she still had to go. There were subtle differences in her abilities and her personality. The exuberance she'd had only six months before was gone, the sharpness of her memory to learn extensive lines, the complexity of her ability to play chess against adults. She had come out of the mists, and the coma after the accident, but there were many subtleties of her brain function that Emma hadn't regained yet, and perhaps never would again. It made Whitney want to help her even more, and suddenly her participation in Bailey's brain injury conference made sense, and she felt she had something to contribute to it, using Emma as a living example of what a person with a brain injury had to deal with every day and how those who loved them and cared for them could help.

She called Bailey the next day and told him that she would speak at the conference. He was thrilled, and she had two weeks to prepare. There was so much they all still needed to learn about the brain, particularly after traumatic injury. She worked on her presentation every night after Emma went to bed, and she hoped she could do the subject justice. It was all new to her, except what she had learned through experience with Emma in the past six months, and she had so much more to learn.

As she started preparing her presentation, she thought of Chad briefly. This was the time of year she'd gone to the Caribbean with him on his boat for the past five years. It had been exciting and fun and luxurious. Now she'd been catapulted into parenthood with a brain injured child, and there were no trips on yachts in her future. She felt like a whole different person, but it did cross her mind once after Christmas.

She was working on her speech for the conference when Amy Clarke contacted her and asked her to see another patient for her. It was a child with encephalitis, some of whose symptoms resembled Emma's. The cause of the child's damaged brain was different, but there were clinical similarities, which Whitney found fascinating. She consulted with Amy and Bailey after she saw the patient, who was a thirteen-year-old girl. Whitney thoroughly enjoyed working with them, and she found the addition of neurological evaluations to her practice added depth and substance to her work life. She told them how much she enjoyed the cases they referred to her, and they fully agreed with her diagnosis of the patient. She found that she liked working with Amy as much as she appreciated Bailey's help with Emma. Amy was cooler and more clinical, which Whitney found stimulating, and she thanked both of them for the opportunity to consult on their patients. Their faith in her was flattering, and the cases challenging.

"Be careful, or we'll be dragging you into the practice with us," Bailey warned her, and Whitney laughed at the suggestion, thinking he didn't mean it. They were already an efficient team.

"I'd love that," Whitney commented. "The neurology cases are much more complex than what I see in my practice with straight psychiatry. This adds a whole additional element I find fascinating."

"We need your psychiatric expertise at times. You can't ignore the psych side of brain injury," Amy persisted. "I've been saying that for years, although there is some real resistance to it in neurology circles, particularly around brain injury cases." It was the essence of what Whitney was planning to present at the seminar Bailey had invited her to, and she felt as though she was heading in an important direction. It had added some real excitement to her work, and she and Bailey talked about it for hours, whenever he dropped by to see Emma, or have dinner with them. And Amy was respectful of Whitney's perspective too.

"What are you doing for yourself these days, by the way?" Bailey asked her one night and she looked blank.

"What do you mean?"

"That's my point. You're with Emma all the time, or at work, or working on your research paper. When was the last time you went out to dinner or saw a movie, or did something you enjoy doing?"

She looked startled at the question. "I don't know. I haven't done anything since before the accident, I guess." She hadn't even had a manicure since July. "I really don't have time now that I've got Emma to take care of." It reminded her again of her trips on Chad's yacht, which were ancient history now. She had no regrets.

"You have you to take care of too. Try not to forget that," he said gently. His concern for her took Whitney by surprise. They were allies in Emma's recovery, but she didn't expect him to think about her, and her need to relax and have entertainment.

"I've got too much on my plate right now to think of anything else except Emma, my patients, and your seminar." She smiled at him. It was the truth.

"When was the last time you had a vacation?" She smiled at that.

"The day of the accident. I was back in twenty-four hours. I used to go away at least once a month with a man I was dating. We used to go to Saint Barts in the winter, and Italy in the summer on his boat. It was a nice, easy, self-indulgent life. That's why I always said I never wanted kids. But I've got Emma now and all of that has changed. No time, no desire, no one to travel with. No more yachts in my life, borrowed or otherwise." She sounded matter of fact about it, and didn't miss it.

"What happened to him?" Bailey felt like he knew her well enough now to ask, and he could see that there were no diversions in her life, not that he could detect anyway. She was all about duty and responsibility, her work and her sister's child. She was the most unselfish person he'd ever met.

155

"He took a hike, or maybe I sent him on one when I told him I wasn't going to institutionalize Emma to get her off my hands. He doesn't do kids. He has four grown ones of his own that he never enjoyed much. He wants a trouble-free, responsibility-free adult relationship with a single woman and no kids. I no longer qualify. So that was that."

"That's a little cold, isn't it?" Bailey said, looking shocked.

"I guess so. I thought so, but he was honest about it. He never pretended to want anything different. And as I pointed out to him, love is messy sometimes. It doesn't come all wrapped up in a neat little package. You can't control everything in life. My sister taught me that in spades. I thought she was crazy when she decided to have a baby with a friend and no partner. You couldn't have paid me to do that. But maybe she was right. I don't like the way she exploited Emma and became the stage mother of all time, but maybe she gave Emma something wonderful in the process. She helped her develop her talent, and she loved Emma passionately. Maybe that's what love is about, doing something crazy with all the energy and passion you've got. Until the night she screwed it all up and didn't put her seatbelt on, I don't think there was any doubt how much she loved her daughter, for better or worse. So I don't mind at all that I'm not having vacations on yachts right now, or going to the ballet, or to Italy in the summer. My life may be a mess at the moment, I don't even have time to go to the hairdresser right now, but so what? Emma and I love each other, and she's better than any fancy vacation or adult relationship I might have had. I'm not hurting, Bailey. I'm happier than I've been in a long time. Maybe my flaky, slightly crazy sister was right, and I was the one missing the boat in life, until now."

He could see that she meant it, and seemed satisfied with her life. There was no question how much she loved Emma, and was willing to sacrifice for her.

"You don't sound angry at your sister anymore," he said with interest.

"I still am sometimes. Every time I see Emma struggle or suffer. She's the one paying the price for her mother's mistake, and it makes me mad. But I'm fine. I don't miss anything I've given up. I just wish she'd put their goddamn seatbelts on, but who knows why she didn't. Careless, tired, busy, distracted. Oddly, I'm not even as angry at my father anymore either. I never wanted to marry because I hated the way he ran my mother's life and controlled everything. It looked like a nightmare to me, and I never wanted some guy doing the same thing to me, telling me what to do. I always thought that was why my mother died so young. But now I wonder if she was happy and she enjoyed it. She had a fabulous career, thanks to him, and maybe having a ball till she got sick at fifty-two was enough for her. We all have to decide how we want to lead our lives and what love means to us. Love always looked too difficult to me, like you had to pay too high a price for it. Right now, love means a nine-year-old child to me, even if she's got a brain injury and may never recover fully from it. We'll manage somehow, and if it's messy and I don't have time to get my hair done, that's okay. I think Emma's worth it."

"It's funny, I always felt the same way. My parents' lives were so destroyed when my little brother almost drowned that I never wanted kids of my own after that, as I told you on the phone that night. It looked too painful to me, and it was for them. I wanted to help other children like him, but I never wanted to take a risk with a child of my own, or get married. But watching you with Emma, I realize that the only way to live is with your whole heart, despite the dangers and the risks. I admire you for taking it on, and doing everything you can for her. Suddenly having kids and taking a chance on love doesn't look so scary. It's a lot scarier being forty-two years old and never having had the guts to take a chance on love. Just working isn't enough." He said it as though it were a recent revelation for him.

"No, it's not," she agreed. She had figured that out too. "We're a lot alike in some ways. Too scared to take a risk, and then suddenly, you're in the thick of it, and it's not so bad." She smiled at him.

"So one of these days, will you have dinner with me, without Emma, when you feel like you can leave her with Brett—and not in your kitchen, with one eye on Emma? Let's go have some fun one of these days, and do something silly. Go to a movie, go bowling, go to the beach or go windsurfing, whatever sounds like fun to you. We both have a lot of time to make up for. We've both been working too hard for a lot of years."

"Paige used to say that to me too. I thought she was silly and frivolous, but she was right. I was always the serious one. I don't want to be that serious anymore. Not all the time at least. Life's hard enough. It's good to take a break sometimes."

"Good. Let's go be silly together. Although I have to admit, your yacht vacations sound pretty damn cool," he said with envy, and she laughed.

"There are no yachts in my future, Dr. Turner. A small rowboat maybe, or even a tiny sailboat. But I'm afraid the fancy boat trips are history for me now. Although I'd be happy to introduce you to my ex-boyfriend if you like boats," she said, and he laughed.

"I'm probably not his type."

"Neither am I now," but the prospect of spending time with Bailey was very appealing to her. They had their work in common, and they had both spent a lot of years being responsible and building their medical careers, and they had both been careful to avoid deep emotional relationships, which Whitney thought now had been a mistake. She had finally realized that she needed more than that. Paige and Emma had taught Whitney that, and she was showing it by example to Bailey. Just watching her was teaching him about relationships and life, seeing all she gave to her niece.

"We'll talk about this after the seminar," Bailey promised. "And I'm not letting you off the hook for dinner."

"That's a deal." The idea of a real date with him sounded like fun. It had taken months to occur to her but now that it had and he had mentioned it, she liked the idea, and wondered why they hadn't thought of it sooner.

Her presentation to the brain injury seminar was a knockout, even better than Bailey had hoped when he'd invited her to do it. She started by showing a film clip of Emma on her TV program seven months before. She chose an astoundingly sensitive scene where her performance reduced nearly everyone in the room to tears. And then she described the accident, the results, and Emma as she was now. She talked about all the things she could do again, the things that still eluded her now, even things as simple as reading a first-grade book, compared to the scripts she used to learn and never miss a line. She talked about the doctors' hopes for her, and the statistical likelihood of her recovery. Everything she described illustrated the complicated and conflicting symptoms of brain injury, and the range of how severe and how minor some of the cases were. Whitney said that in many ways, Emma had been lucky, and she was functioning surprisingly well given the trauma she had sustained. But she described her memory as something akin to Swiss cheese now, some of it was solid, and the rest was full of holes no one could explain. Whitney described the violence and the aggression that were typical with frontal lobe injuries, and the minor injuries she had sustained while caring for her, from a child who would never have laid a hand on her, or anyone else, before. Then she posed a long list of questions that neither psychiatry nor neurology had easy answers to, and questioned which side of the illness should be treated first and by whom. Her conclusion at the end of it was that they needed better interdisciplinary cooperation, better research, and better protocols to treat brain injury patients, which addressed the full spectrum of symptoms, not just some, or the physical issues. They had to deal with the psychological and emotional ones too. They were all part of the picture.

At the end, she expressed what their hopes were for Emma, and what encouraging signs there had been so far. She pointed out that the medical field was making some real progress in the area of traumatic brain injury, but there was room for more. And then she thanked them and stepped down, and the entire room got to their feet to give her a standing ovation, and there were tears in Bailey's eyes when he hugged her. Even Amy Clarke looked deeply moved, and she was usually less emotional than Bailey. Her eyes were damp when she hugged Whitney.

"You were fantastic. I knew you would be," Bailey whispered when he took the podium over again to thank her for her presentation, and then they broke for lunch. And she joined him and Amy and four other neurologists who praised her again for what she'd said.

"We're trying to get her to give up psychiatry and come and work with us on brain injury cases," Amy said, and everyone agreed on what rewarding work it would be. Whitney said she was thinking about it, but she liked the work she did too, and was considering finding a way to do both, which was an intriguing idea, and would add variety to her practice.

She had a wonderful day at the seminar with Bailey, and was happy to see Emma when she got home. She was reading aloud from the iPad with Belinda. It was a simple book for a five- or six-year-old, and way below her previous level of reading ability, but she was speaking clearly, and bigger chunks of language had returned. As Whitney had said in her speech, Emma had come a long way, and had a long way to go, and how far she would get down the path to full recovery remained to be seen. Others had done it before her, and some hadn't gotten as far. It was a step-by-step process. Along with the first-grade reader, she was learning to play chess again. It was a checkerboard pattern of recovery for the brain.

Bailey dropped by to see Whitney later that night, after the seminar ended and he had wrapped it up. He wanted to come by and thank her again. Her presentation had been the highlight of the conference, and humanized some of the issues for them.

"So when are we going bowling?" he whispered as he put his arms around her. They didn't want to wake Emma, who was asleep upstairs. Brett's room was at the other end of the house, and she never re-emerged once she went to her room at night.

"How far the mighty have fallen," she said, laughing, "from yachts to bowling nights. How about a movie instead?"

"Don't be such a snob, just because your mother was a big movie star," he teased her, "and your niece was the star of a hit TV show."

"I'm just a lowly Beverly Hills shrink," she reminded him, but she was a lot more than that, and so was he, they were both stars in their fields, and there was an undeniable attraction between them that neither could ignore anymore and didn't want to.

"How about roller-skating at Venice Beach?" It sounded like fun to her. She nodded and he pulled her closer into his arms and kissed her, and then looked down at her with a smile. "I've never gone out with the mothers of any of my patients," he commented with a mild look of concern, but it wasn't enough to stop him.

"You're off the hook. I'm just her aunt," she whispered back, and he kissed her again. The future seemed particularly bright to both of them. Things were looking up. There was fun in their future, and possibly some work together, if they could figure out how to do it. He left a few minutes later, and Whitney smiled thinking of roller-skating at Venice Beach with him. Her life had suddenly gotten very real. Emma was an important part of it, and so was Bailey now. She didn't feel quite so serious as she thought of his arms around her. Suddenly there was something to look forward to, more than just Emma's recovery. She felt like a woman again. It was a very nice feeling indeed.

Chapter 11

The long road to recovery continued in the erratic pattern that Amy and Bailey had warned Whitney it would, without rhyme or reason. Emma was speaking again, intelligibly, but sometimes familiar words eluded her. At other times, she had to struggle for every word, or her thoughts came out in a rush. Her memory was still spotty. She remembered some sequences of events perfectly, or parts of the scripts she had learned and diligently worked on. At other times, she couldn't remember what she'd had for lunch. She could sing all the words to a song, but couldn't say them. She remembered her singing lessons, but insisted she had never had dance lessons. Although Whitney told her she had taken tap, hip-hop, and ballet, Emma didn't believe her.

Although she had never mentioned it again, she remembered her mother texting right before the accident, and telling her to stop. But she remembered nothing past that moment, which Whitney said was a blessing. She and Bailey assumed she'd been unconscious after that. She had a thousand memories of her mother, but none of the accident itself, or the first weeks in the hospital.

In March, she started speech therapy, which she found arduous and tiresome. It made her struggle to find words she could no longer remember. And in April, Whitney discussed her acting career with her.

"What do you want to do, Em?" Whitney had been avoiding her agent until they made a decision. Emma had missed the other child actors she worked with. Adam Weiss and Virginia Parker were still on the show. Emma had never watched it after she'd left it. And both of her fellow child actors had wanted to visit her in the hospital, but she was in no condition for visits then, and they had eventually stopped asking. When Emma wrote to them after she was speaking again, they didn't answer her. It had been nine months since the accident, too long for most people to sustain their interest. Nine months was an eternity to most people. Life moved on. Emma's feelings were hurt by it, and Whitney tried to explain to her that the actors she knew on the show were busy with their own lives by then. Emma had had no friends except the people she had worked with. She hadn't been to a normal school in three years, two while she was on the show, and one since the accident.

"Your agent has been calling," Whitney told her. "He says there's work out there if you want it. Maybe even on another show," although Bailey had said it was too soon for Emma to go back to work as an actress. It would be too stressful for her and liable to cause an increase in memory lapses and other symptoms. She still had holes in her memory, and might for several years.

"I want to go to regular school," Emma said in a small voice, as though she should apologize for it. She didn't want to seem ungrate-

164

ful for the work Whitney said she could have. And her mother had thought it was a good career move to be tutored on the set, but she didn't really have a choice if she wanted a major role on the show. And she didn't want to betray her mother now. But she missed school and the company of other children. For three years, almost all her friends had been adults.

"Do you want to do any acting when the doctors say you can go back to work?" Whitney needed to know what to tell Robert, Emma's agent. Emma shook her head and didn't answer.

"I just want to go to school like a normal kid. Do you think Mommy would be mad at that?" She looked worried.

"No, I don't think she'd be mad," Whitney said gently. "I think she'd be proud of you. You have a right to do what you want, Em."

Emma looked relieved when she said it. "I want to be a doctor like you," she said shyly.

"You do? Why?" Whitney looked startled. Her going into medicine had been considered an aberration by her parents, and Paige had always said she thought it was weird that Whitney was a shrink. None of them had ever been impressed by her career in medicine. In their family, only show business counted.

"Because you help people," Emma added.

"There are lots of ways to help people. I just do it this way because I like it." She smiled at her niece.

"I think I'd like it too." Whitney wanted to leave the door open for Emma to choose the right path for herself. She'd been through so much, and when she was ready for school, Whitney thought it was important that Emma pursue a path that excited her.

"Bailey and Amy think you'll be ready to start in September." That would be almost fourteen months after the accident, which was roughly what they had predicted initially, that her recovery would take at least one to two years, maybe longer, but she had made good progress. Belinda was still coming to work with her on her reading twice a week, and it had been slow going. Emma was having a much harder time learning to read again than she'd had at five when Paige taught her. It seemed harder to get going again, and sometimes her brain just wouldn't cooperate. It was frustrating for Emma. Sam wasn't coming to teach them sign language anymore now that Emma could speak again, but he and Belinda were seeing each other. Emma liked playing around with sign language now. She treated it like a game when she didn't want to speak, or didn't want people to know what she was saying to Brett or Whitney.

Whitney talked to Belinda about what she thought of the possibility of Emma going to normal school, and if she'd be ready for it in the fall.

"I think she could manage it," Belinda said cautiously. "She still has memory issues, and she's having trouble reading. She gets burned out very quickly, which never used to happen. She could study a script for hours and never lose her concentration. It's a lot harder for her now. But maybe by September she'll be ready." It was still five months away, lots of time for Emma to work on her reading and brush up on math, which she seemed to have forgotten completely.

"What grade do you think we should apply for?" Whitney asked, concerned.

"She'll be ten by the time she starts school in the fall," Belinda said thoughtfully, "normally that would be fifth grade. A year ago, I'd have said it was no problem. Now, I think you'd be looking at third or fourth, since the accident. And you're going to need a school that will give her accommodations and take the brain injury into account. You can't have normal expectations for her, not even in five months." Whitney nodded. It made sense to her too.

She started looking up schools on the Internet a few days later. Her inquiries were delicate. She explained the circumstances of the accident to the admissions directors, and most of the schools she called said they weren't equipped to teach a child who had suffered a frontal lobe brain injury or had special needs to such an extreme degree. Eventually, she found three schools that were willing to meet her, and if the conversations went well, she would take Emma to see them, and for some testing, but they made no promises as to whether they would take her or not. Some seemed gun-shy about providing tutoring and accommodations, and Whitney didn't want to put her in a special school for brain injured kids. She thought Emma could manage a mainstream school, with Belinda to help prepare her, and maybe tutoring later if necessary. She had always been so bright and done so well in school that it was hard to believe she wouldn't now, and Bailey gently reminded her that a brain injury changed things, and she might have learning difficulties forever. Her personality could even remain altered and subtly different. That was common too.

"Will she ever be normal again?" she asked him with a look of frustration.

"Maybe. But a lot of things change, Whitney. She could have learning disabilities, or react differently than she did before." Whitney had already noticed that Emma was more serious now, but she'd been in an accident, a coma, the ICU for two months, and lost her mother. It was obvious that she'd be serious after all that. Bailey had explained that a frontal lobe injury could alter personality, memory, ability to learn, change her IQ, and cause psychiatric problems. It seemed so unfair to Whitney. Why did Emma have to pay the price of all that because her mother had been texting and driving? Whitney had to force herself not to be angry at Paige all over again. What was she thinking? Or why wasn't she thinking? She should have been if it was going to impact the rest of Emma's life. But at least she was alive, hearing, and speaking again, and some of her memory had come back, even if it was far from perfect. And there was no point being angry at Paige, it wouldn't change a thing. They had to look at the future and leave the past behind.

Whitney made appointments at the three schools, and didn't say anything to Emma. She didn't want her to be disappointed if they didn't think she'd be a match with the school after meeting with Whitney, or if Whitney didn't want her to apply. Two of the schools were well-known private schools and the person she spoke with on the phone had sounded somewhat pretentious but had agreed to meet her. The third school was also private but more alternative, sounded more creative, and was much smaller. Whitney felt as though she were applying herself when she went to see them. And for Emma's sake, she had to get the decision right. Her future academic life was at stake here.

The first two made it clear to her that by the time Emma would start classes in the fall, they expected her to be up to speed and caught up on English and math work, even if she needed some remedial work later, which sounded challenging and like a lot of pressure to Whitney. The third school was willing to design a curriculum for Emma, at the level she would be in the fall, with different levels for different subjects, and they were prepared to help her catch up, as needed. They thought it interesting that she had gone to school on the set for two years before the accident. And they were optimistic that they'd be able to bring her up to speed in all subjects in the course of the school year. They had another student similar to Emma who had nearly died of meningitis and missed a year of school, after suffering a stroke and being in a coma for three months at fourteen. She didn't have a brain injury, but she had memory lapses too. The school seemed ideal to Whitney, and she told Emma about it that night. There were only a hundred and ten students in the school, and the classes were very small. They were willing to offer Emma a place, and wanted to evaluate her in May or June. They suggested she work on her reading until then.

"Do you think I can do it, Whit?" Emma asked her, panicked, when Whitney told her about the school.

"I think you can. You'll have to do your speech therapy, and work with Belinda on reading and math, but she said she'd help you."

"What if they think I'm stupid?" She had tears in her eyes when she said it. She knew she was different now.

"They won't. You're not stupid. You've been sick for almost a year. You have a brain injury. But they're going to accommodate you, and I think you'll be able to catch up."

"Maybe I should stick with tutors," Emma said, looking nervous.

"I think it would be more fun for you to be in school with other kids, don't you? You'll be lonely if you're just tutored at home." Emma nodded. It was why she wanted to go to school, but she was scared too. "Why don't you try it?" Emma wanted to, she just didn't see how she could do it. And when she got nervous, sometimes she still had trouble speaking, or would forget her words entirely for a while.

"Why don't we do something fun to take the pressure off? You can work with Belinda. But why don't you and I take some kind of classes? Dance lessons, or singing, something we can do together." It seemed like a good distraction, and she could see that Emma liked the idea as soon as she suggested it.

"Like what?"

"I don't know. Swimming? Cooking? A dance class?" Emma had forgotten how to swim too, and Whitney wanted her to learn before the summer, so she'd be safe around their pool. She didn't want her to drown if she fell in. She had heard too many horror stories about kids who couldn't swim, like Bailey's brother.

"What about tap?" Emma suggested. "I've always wanted to take it." Whitney knew she'd taken it for several years, but it was obvious Emma didn't remember. It didn't matter if she took it again, as long as she enjoyed it. Swimming would be more useful, but she could do that too.

"I'll check it out," Whitney promised, and called a dance studio on the way to Malibu that offered tap lessons. The traffic would be awful, but they were nice on the phone, and Whitney signed them both up for a beginner's class, which she needed and Emma didn't. It sounded like fun, and Whitney thought it would be good exercise for both of them and a good mother-daughter-type activity. Their first class was the following week.

*   *   *

It took Whitney half an hour to get Emma settled in the car before the dance class. She was always tense and looked panicked whenever they had to drive anywhere. Whitney had medication to give her to calm her down, but taking a sedative before the dance class was liable to knock her out, which seemed pointless, and she was sure that Emma would relax once they got there. She was silent on the ride, and her whole body looked tense when Whitney glanced at her in the rearview mirror. She didn't want her to have an anxiety attack when they got there.

Whitney signed in at the desk when they arrived, and a small, lively, energetic woman in a leotard and tap shoes wrote their names down on a list and confirmed that neither of them had taken tap before. Whitney didn't correct the impression that Emma had never taken tap. It didn't seem important. They changed into leotards in the dressing room, and the teacher had shoes for them to borrow until they got their own.

There were four women and two teenage girls in the class, and the teacher gave a brief demonstration when they started, then showed them each a simple step, and put on some music. Emma was already giggling, and Whitney was trying to remember the step. They were each supposed to take turns showing the teacher what they could do. Whitney felt ridiculous as she tried to get it right, but she managed to get through it, and then it was Emma's turn, and she gracefully spun herself around, and then stopped herself and instantly launched into a professional dance routine that looked like Fred Astaire as the teacher stared at her. Emma flew through the air, tapped her heart out, did a little pirouette, and landed on both feet with perfect precision at the end of the routine. The look on the teacher's face was almost comical, and it was obvious that Emma had taken lessons before, Whitney knew she just hadn't remembered them.

"You've never taken tap before?" the teacher asked her in disbelief, and Emma looked puzzled for a minute.

"I don't remember it, but now that I'm here, I think maybe I might have." She grinned sheepishly at her aunt, who was trying not to laugh. Emma's mind did not remember, but her body and her feet very certainly did. The teacher let her stay in the class, but she suggested an advanced class for Emma the next time.

"I think she thought I was lying to her," Emma said, looking more relaxed as they walked back to Whitney's car in the parking lot after the class. "I guess Mom made me take tap," she added with a grin, still trying to remember.

"And hip-hop and modern dance and ballet," Whitney added for her.

"She made me take all that?"

Whitney nodded.

"Was I any good at it?" She smiled at her aunt.

"Probably about the way you were today. You're a pro, Em." She laughed when Whitney said it.

"How come I don't remember?"

"You will one day," Whitney reassured her. "It will all come back eventually."

"Maybe I'll take ballet too," she said pensively as Whitney watched her put her seatbelt on. She didn't start the car until she had, and then they drove back to Beverly Hills, as they chatted and laughed about the look on the teacher's face, when Emma did a tap dance that put the teacher to shame. "I wish everything else were as easy,"

Emma said with a sigh. "I'm terrible at math, and reading is hard for me. Belinda says I used to remember my lines with one reading."

"You'll probably be able to do it again one day." Emma nodded in answer, and sat staring out the window at the Pacific Ocean. Her mind was a million miles away as Whitney drove them home. Whitney wondered if she was thinking about her mother, but she didn't want to ask. By the time they got back to Beverly Hills, Emma was sound asleep. She'd had a good time tap dancing, but she still tired easily. She went to bed right after dinner that night, and barely ate. The dance routine, the drive, and the class had worn her out.

She was already in bed when Bailey dropped by to see Whitney. Whitney made him something to eat, and they sat at the kitchen table and talked for a long time.

"What did you do today?" he asked after he kissed her. He loved spending time with her and dropping by in the evening. She told him about the tap-dancing lesson and he laughed.

"It bothers her when she can't remember things," Whitney said, and he nodded. And she still didn't remember the accident, if she'd even seen more of it, like the truck bearing down on them, but Whitney never pushed her about it. When the memory finally surfaced, it would be traumatic. All she remembered now was her mother texting, and nothing after that.

"She's come a long way," Bailey said, "and some of it may never come back."

"She says she doesn't want to go back to acting. She wants to be a doctor like us." He smiled when she said it.

"Some days I'd rather be an actor," he teased her, and Whitney laughed.

"Me too." She was seeing her full load of patients again but only working four days a week, so she had more time to spend with Emma.

"Have you thought about the summer at all?" he asked her. He was planning to take time off and wanted to spend it with her. But she was still living day to day with Emma's recovery.

"I'm thinking a house in Tahoe might be fun," she said, and he nodded. They had made no official plans, but were spending more and more time together, on weekends and in the evenings, and he was wonderful with Emma.

"Can I come up and visit you?" he asked shyly, and Whitney smiled at him.

"I think that could be arranged," she teased him.

"So, no trip to Italy this year?" He hoped there wouldn't be, but didn't want to say so. She shook her head, looking serious.

"I don't want to go that far away with Emma, in case she has any problems. Tahoe is far enough." And there was no question of her going on the boat with Chad again.

"She should be fine to go to Tahoe by then," he said, and then pulled Whitney gently into his arms and kissed her. He wanted to spend more time with her, but it was awkward with Emma around all the time, and Whitney didn't want to leave her. She hadn't left her for a single night since July, but she was hungry to spend more time with Bailey too.

"Now I understand why my sister had no love life most of the time. How do people manage it with kids?" she said, and he laughed.

"That's why I never had any."

"Yeah, me too." They were kissing like two teenagers, and she would have liked to sneak him upstairs to her bedroom, but she didn't dare. What if Emma woke up or had a bad dream? She didn't want Emma to find Bailey in her bedroom. At least the night terrors had ended when she started speaking, and she hadn't been aggressive since then either. Being able to talk again had made everything easier.

He finally left around eleven o'clock, and they lingered at the front door, kissing for a long time.

"Maybe I should come to your office between patients," he teased her, and she laughed.

"We'll figure it out one of these days," she whispered, but it made the anticipation sweeter. It was a problem she'd never had before, since she'd lived alone. She waved as he drove away, locked the front door, turned off the lights, and went upstairs. She stood in the doorway of Emma's bedroom. She looked so sweet and peaceful. No one would have guessed that she'd had a brain injury and had nearly died nine months before. Then Whitney went back to her bedroom, thinking of Bailey. She was so attracted to him, but she was afraid too. He was the kind of person who was going to want more than just a casual relationship, and her old demons still haunted her at times. She didn't want anyone controlling her life, or taking over. She loved the idea of spending time with him, and even sleeping with him, but she didn't want anyone to run her life, or tell her what to do. She had promised herself never to let that happen, and if she opened her heart to Bailey, who knew what he would want? Letting someone else run her life was the one thing she knew she could never do. She was never going to let any man control her, the way her father had her mother. For now she was still safe. But for how long, if she got involved with Bailey? Maybe letting herself fall in love with him would spoil everything, especially now with Emma. No matter how much she liked him, and was attracted to him, she was afraid to take the risk. It was easier to be brave for Emma than for Bailey. And in some ways, having Emma around all the time kept Whitney safe.

Chapter 12

Little by little, Whitney was trying to ease Emma into the kind of things that ordinary people did. They went to the grocery store, the dry cleaner, the hardware store, and drugstore. She had Emma help put the dishes in the dishwasher, and learn to make her bed. They did laundry together. Her life with her mother had been fraught with lessons and activities which all centered around Emma's work on the show. They were always rushing somewhere to meet another drama coach, or take another singing lesson, or go to an audition for a commercial, or for the musical in New York. But if Emma wanted a more ordinary life, away from show business, Whitney wanted to get her used to it now, before she started school in the fall. She had never really had a normal life with her mother.

They went to the supermarket together on a Saturday afternoon, when Brett was off. She didn't like taking Emma to places like that in case she got lost. But Whitney kept a close eye on her, and they were in the cereal aisle looking at breakfast cereal together, while Whitney tried to convince her to pick one of the healthier brands. Emma was telling her aunt that her mother had let her eat whatever kind of cereal she wanted, even one of the chocolate ones.

"I strongly doubt that," Whitney said, as Emma gave her a guilty look and giggled. Emma had been pushing the cart they'd already filled with dairy products and fresh vegetables, when a woman behind them jostled Emma and then let out a gasp when she saw her.

"Oh my God, it's *you*! I can't believe it," she said, staring at Emma, who looked confused. The woman was only inches from her face. "I watched the show every week until you left it, and I cried for a week when you died." She was talking a mile a minute, and Emma looked frightened. Whitney wanted to get her away from the woman as fast as she could, but she was blocking them in the aisle with her cart.

"I didn't die, I was in a coma," Emma said, confusing the show with real life.

"No, you were dead, they said so," the woman insisted. "It nearly broke my heart when they wrote you out of the show," she said intensely, and then waved to three friends who were pushing carts nearby, full of laundry detergent and toilet paper. Whitney could see that Emma was starting to look panicked. But by then, the fan's friends had moved their carts toward them, and there was no way for Emma and Whitney to escape, unless they abandoned their cart. The woman who had discovered them was shrieking. "Do you believe it! It's *Emma Watts*!" she said to her friends, as though Emma were an object of some kind, and not a human being. Two of her friends moved in closer then, and one of them took a picture of Emma with her cellphone, literally inches from her face.

"Thanks so much," Whitney said, pushing one of their carts aside, and trying to maneuver Emma forward so they could get away from them, but Emma was rooted to the spot and was terrified. And with that, all three of the women were taking her picture and trying to pose with her.

"We left balloons for you at the hospital after the accident," one of them was saying. "And we were sorry about your mom, that was just so terrible. When are you going to be on a show again?" They were talking at her all at once, as one of them drifted away, talking on her cellphone, and all Whitney wanted to do was get Emma out of the store before the women devoured her. It was the first time anything like it had happened, and reminded Whitney of similar incidents when she was a child, and fans rushed toward her mother and crowded around her, usually followed by paparazzi with cameras flashing in their faces. It had always terrified her, although Paige didn't mind at all. She thought it was funny, and even exciting. Whitney had been phobic about it, and still had a horror of crowds as a result, and she was determined to protect Emma from them. She finally pulled her by the arm, and led her away as quickly as possible to get the rest of their groceries and then stand in line at the checkout.

"I'm sorry," Whitney apologized to her, she could see that Emma was pale and shaking.

"It's okay," she said softly, "it used to happen all the time. Mom always thought it was a good thing, she said it meant the fans loved me on the show." Then she looked at Whitney with a sad expression. "Did they say I died on the show when they wrote me out?" She looked upset about it, and Whitney didn't want to admit she knew.

"I don't know. I never watched it again once you weren't in it. They probably had to do something dramatic," Whitney said calmly, wishing the checker would hurry up. She didn't want to run into the same women again when they were checking out.

The line took forever, and it was a relief when they paid and finally pushed their cart out to the parking lot, but as soon as they came through the doors, a photographer leapt at Emma, and Whitney realized that the women must have called the newspaper, and they had rushed over one of the paparazzi that hung around L.A., stalking actors and actresses and anyone publicity hungry enough to pose for them. The photographer spotted Emma immediately, and he was taking head shots at close range, as Emma turned away to try and avoid him.

"Come on, let's have a big smile for your fans. This is a real 'Where is she now?' moment, your fans are going to love it. . . . Where ya been, honey?" Emma didn't answer, and Whitney wanted to slug him. But the flurry of activity had caught people's attention, and a crowd was forming around them, as Whitney unlocked the car door and pushed Emma in, while she tried to block the photographer with their cart full of groceries.

"Leave her alone, for chrissake," Whitney shouted at him, while he continued to shoot Emma's picture through the back windows, and one of Whitney shouting at him.

"Who are you?" he said in Whitney's face as she shoved past him, threw the grocery bags into the car, closed the doors, and got into the driver's seat, but a dozen fans were crowded around them by then, and Whitney was afraid to run them down. She kept her hand on the wheel, and eased slowly into gear and moved forward, and they parted to let her pass, and then she drove as fast as she dared out of the parking lot, and turned to look at Emma, who was crying.

"They were scary," she said in a raw voice. "Why do they do that?"

"Because you're a star, sweetheart, and they have nothing better to do," Whitney answered as they drove home. She opened the garage door with the remote, and took the groceries to the kitchen through an inside door in case they'd been followed, but everything was peaceful at home. She double locked the front door, then she put her arms around Emma and held her until she stopped shaking. "It's okay, baby, it's all over."

The next day, Brett called them when she saw the story in the tabloids at the grocery store. She brought it over so they could see it. There was a photo of Emma on the front page with the headline, "Heartbroken Child Star Still in Hiding Mourning Mom." It went on to talk about the accident, Paige's death, and the fact that Emma had left the show to recover from her own injuries. They said she'd been in a wheelchair for the last nine months and was learning to walk again, which wasn't true, but that never bothered them if it made for a good story.

"Why didn't they just say I have a brain injury and I'm stupid now?" Emma said, upset by the story when she saw it.

"You're *not* stupid!" Whitney corrected her. "You're one of the smartest people I know, and you're recovering."

"Yes, I am stupid," she said bursting into tears, "I can't remember anything, I can't even play chess anymore, and I read like a five-year-old and I'm never going to get into a normal school. And they probably won't let me in if the paparazzi are chasing me." It was a possibility but Whitney hoped that wouldn't be the case. It reminded her of what Emma's life had been like when Paige was alive. She had cultivated that kind of tabloid interest, which was exactly what Whitney had hated about it for Emma, particularly now, when she was trying to get away from all that.

Emma went up to her room to watch a movie on her iPad, and Whitney was having a cup of coffee in the kitchen with Brett when Belinda called her. She had seen the story too.

"Is she okay?" she asked Whitney, who told her what had happened at the supermarket.

"It was very unpleasant. I always forget how much I hate that."

"They haven't seen her face in a long time, so it's not surprising they're gunning for her," Belinda said sensibly. She was used to tabloids and paparazzi from her work on the show.

"I'll have to be more careful when we go out," Whitney said with a sigh, and after Belinda hung up, Whitney threw the paper in the trash where it belonged. At least they didn't know where Whitney lived, and they hadn't followed them home.

Emma came downstairs a little while later, and looked at Whitney sadly. "Can I ask you a question, Aunt Whit?"

"Of course. What is it?"

"Can I live with you forever?" Whitney's eyes filled with tears as she put her arms around her.

"For sure. Forever. Where did you think you were going to live?"

"I don't know. Mom always said you didn't want kids, and I just thought you might get tired of me someday." Her voice trailed off as Whitney reassured her.

"You can live with me for as long as you want. I'd be heartbroken if you didn't." She meant every word she said and it showed.

"Even if the paparazzi follow me around and you hate that?"

"Even then. It used to happen to my mom when I was a little kid, and I didn't like it then either. It's so intrusive." Emma nodded, although she was used to it from when she was on the show.

Brett went out that night and Emma and Whitney cooked dinner together, and afterward Bailey called her, and she told him about the tabloid fiasco.

"They're such bottom-feeders," he said, sounding disgusted. "Is she okay now?" Whitney said she was, but Emma had nightmares that night and screamed for her mother, and then lay in Whitney's arms and cried until she went back to sleep. The paparazzi attack had unsettled her, but the next day Brett surprised her with some new movies and projects, and Emma was calm and happy when Whitney left for work. Amy called her as soon as she got there. She had a patient she wanted Whitney to see, another young girl with encephalitis, a brain infection, who was exhibiting psychotic behaviors. Amy wanted Whitney's opinion about whether it was entirely due to her illness, or if she really was psychotic or had borderline personality disorder, unrelated to the disease.

"The whole family seems nuts to me," Amy commented, "and I think the encephalitis may be coincidental."

"Where is she?" Whitney asked. She was always intrigued by the cases Amy referred to her, and loved working with her.

"At Cedars."

"I'll go over and take a look at lunchtime, and call you back after I see her."

"I hear the paparazzi were after you and Emma this weekend. How is she?"

"She's okay. It rattled us both. I'm not used to that stuff anymore. She's more of a trouper than I am. I'm out of practice."

"I hate those guys," Amy said. Whitney met with her first patient of the day after she hung up, and at lunchtime she went to Cedars-Sinai to evaluate Amy's patient. The day flew by after that, and Emma was in good spirits and happy with Brett when Whitney got home. It had been a long day, but not a bad one. Amy's case had been interesting. Whitney agreed with her that the whole family sounded dysfunctional, and had a lot more going on than their daughter's encephalitis.

"What am I looking at there?" Amy asked when Whitney called her. Amy knew something was wrong but hadn't been able to figure out what when she saw them. She had a strong feeling that the right diagnosis was psychiatric more than neurological.

"I think the child's mother has Munchausen's by proxy," Whitney said seriously.

"Remind me again what that is."

"The mom finds ways to make her kids sick, or seem sick, so that she gets all the attention and everyone feels sorry for her. I had a case like that last year and it took me about a month to figure it out. She looked like she was the mother of the year, and then I realized she was making her kids sick so she would look like a hero taking care of them. I think that's what you're dealing with here. I'm going to write you a report tonight."

"What do I do to stop it?"

"It's not easy to stop or cure. You really need to get the child away from her. What kind of father do you have on the case at Cedars?"

"Mr. Milquetoast. He doesn't challenge anything his wife says. I think he's afraid of her. Are you telling me the kid's not sick? She's faking it?"

"No, she is genuinely sick, but probably not as sick as she seems, and the mother will interfere with everything you're doing so the kid stays sick, and Mom can pull off her Super Mom act. That's why your specialty is a lot cleaner than mine. You're dealing with genuinely sick people, and all you have to do is cure them. I'm dealing with crazies all day long, and I hate crazies who hurt their own children. They should be watching her closely. I'll keep an eye on her if you like. How's the child doing medically?"

"Not well, it's why I wanted you to consult."

"Your mom over there has the nurses snowed, but I don't buy it."

"Neither did I. I sensed something was wrong, but I couldn't figure out what it was. Maybe I'll put the girl in some kind of quarantine, so I can keep the mother away for a few days and see if she improves."

"That's a great idea," Whitney encouraged her. And then they chatted for a few minutes about how Emma was doing. "She's discouraged about the areas of her memory that haven't come back yet. She keeps saying she's stupid."

"She's the brightest child I've ever seen," Amy said confidently.

"She wants to go to a normal school in September," Whitney told Amy, "and she's afraid they won't let her in."

"I'm sure they will. And her memory should be better by then," Amy said warmly. "Is she remembering anything else about the accident?"

"Not yet, but I hope she will. I think the rest will open up after that."

"I'm sure it doesn't feel that way to you, but she's progressing very quickly. Nine months is nothing in my world, with a brain injury," Amy said seriously.

"My cases usually take longer than that too. The human mind is unpredictable, and so is the brain. Give me a broken leg any day." Amy laughed at what Whitney said.

"We'd both be bored to death with that, wouldn't we? I know I would. I like what I do, even if the healing process takes a long time. At least it's challenging work." She had loved working with Emma, and so had Bailey, and the relationship they'd developed with Whitney. Amy could sense that something more was going on between Whitney and Bailey, but she didn't want to pry. And Bailey was always very private about his personal life, even with her. But she could sense that something was up. He had been happy and upbeat for months.

Whitney was busy for the rest of the day, and spent a quiet evening with Emma after that. Emma had had a nice day with Brett. They'd gone for a long walk in the neighborhood, and Emma's reading was coming along, but slowly. It was still painful for her to read, it was part of the brain function that she hadn't recaptured yet. Whitney still believed that anything was possible. She wasn't ready to give up on Emma reviving her old skills. She was thinking about it that night, lying on her bed, when the phone rang, and Whitney was startled to hear Chad's voice. She hadn't heard from him in seven or eight months, and couldn't imagine why he'd be calling her now. They had left nothing unsaid when they'd last spoken. She wondered if he was in L.A. and wanted to see her, but she didn't want to see him, and didn't want to get tangled up with talking to him either. There was nothing left to say.

"I just thought I'd call and check on you," he said, sounding casual at first, which seemed absurd to her since he hadn't called to check on her during nine months of Emma's illness, so why now? "How's your niece doing?"

"She's recovering slowly. It's been a long haul, but she's speaking again and coming along nicely."

"I'm glad to hear it. I've been worried about you."

"Really?" Whitney sounded chilly with him. He deserved it.

"You took on an awful lot. It can't have been easy for you."

"It hasn't been," she said honestly. She had no intention of letting him off the hook, or easing his conscience. After five and a half years with him, she deserved better than she'd got from him in the end. He had basically made it clear to her that if she wasn't going to institutionalize Emma, it was over between them. He had stuck by that, and never called her again when she refused to abandon Emma.

"I've thought about what you said to me when I saw you in L.A., that love is messy. I guess you were right about that. My son's wife has M.S., and one of my daughters has been in rehab for the last six months. I wasn't expecting that from either of them. And my ex-wife has breast cancer, and has been on chemo for the last four months. I guess families get complicated sometimes. My kids are upset about their mom." Whitney knew he couldn't stand her, so he must not have enjoyed having to help her out either, if he had, or having to be sympathetic to her.

"I'm sorry to hear all that. It sounds like it's been a tough year for you," Whitney said politely, still not sure why he had called her.

"It has been. At my kids' ages you don't expect all these issues to crop up. What's the outlook for your niece?"

"Better than it was when I last saw you. I'm hoping for a full recovery, but it may take a while. She's getting there, though. She'll be starting school in September. She's given up her acting career for now, which is a good thing. She needs some normal kid time, which she never had when her mother was alive."

"And she's living with you?"

"Yes, she is," Whitney said peacefully, with no regrets or apology to him. "It was hard at first, but she's almost back to normal now."

"It sounds like you've had a better year than I have." No thanks to him. "You must be ready for a break."

"Not really. I've been taking on some neurology cases, and I'm going back to work full-time when Emma starts school in September, so I'll be busy. I'm working a four-day week now."

"Any plans for the summer?" he asked, sounding hopeful, and she almost laughed into the phone. He'd had a rough winter and so had she, and now he wanted her to come play with him, so he wouldn't be bored or alone on his boat. She could see him coming a mile away.

"I'm thinking of renting a house in Lake Tahoe. It'll do Emma good," she said casually. Their lives were entirely separate now, which was what he had decided in the fall.

"Can I interest you in some boat time in Italy? That might be a lot more fun for you than Lake Tahoe. You missed the whole trip last year."

"Yes, I did. And I guess I'll be missing it again this year," she said, sounding unaffected by it.

"You don't have to, Whitney. I'd love to have you, if you want to come. We can hang around the South of France, stay at the Hotel du Cap for a few days, and motor down to Italy."

"It sounds great, but I don't think so, Chad. I haven't heard from you in eight months, and I don't work that way. Just hop on a boat with a guy who doesn't call me, cruise around, and then say so long for another year. Funnily enough, that doesn't work for me anymore, the way it used to. It turns out that I like the idea of having someone around for the messy parts too."

"I get your point, Whit. I discovered that myself this year too. I think I was probably a little harsh about your niece. I just couldn't see you taking on a brain damaged kid at this point in your life. That's the last thing you need. But if she's getting better then I'm happy for you. I just thought it might be nice if we spent some time on the boat, for old times' sake. We've always had such a good time together."

"Yes, we did. I've had some great times with you on your boat, Chad, and in other places. I'm grateful to you for that. But I'm not big on the 'for old times' sake' school of romance. My life is more real than that. Or I want it to be. I'd rather be in Tahoe with my brain injured niece than floating around the Mediterranean on a fancy yacht with a guy who can't be bothered to be there for me when things get rough. I just can't do that, Chad. I hope you have a great time. I'm sure you'll find someone only too happy to be there with you. You've got a gorgeous boat, and you're fun to be with. There will be plenty of takers who'll jump at the chance. My life is very different now."

"Don't be that way, Whitney." He sounded annoyed by what she'd said, and shocked. She'd never acted this way before. She was always independent, but he could hear that he'd hurt her with his earlier decision and regretted it now. "I just couldn't see myself hanging around while you dealt with a brain injured kid who's not even your child. I couldn't see the point."

"I got the message loud and clear. She's my niece, and I'm all she's got. That's good enough for me. That *is* the point. Have a great trip. And thanks for thinking of me. Good luck with your daughter-in-law and daughter in rehab and your ex-wife. That's the kind of messy stuff I meant. It catches up with you sometimes. Take care, Chad," she said, and he sounded shocked when she hung up. He was a selfish guy, and always had been. He wanted to be around for the good times and nothing else, and keep just enough distance not to get too involved, which had suited her too. But it no longer did. Suddenly he realized that he'd made a mistake and been cruel in September. And she clearly had no interest in giving him another chance. He wondered if there was someone else. But he realized now he'd probably never see her again. She knew him too well and wanted more than he had to give. He didn't want a serious relationship with anyone.

Whitney felt lighthearted when she hung up. All Chad wanted was a traveling companion. The last nine months had been the hardest in her life, but she and Emma had come through it, and they would make it the rest of the way, without Chad's help, or his boat, or a trip to Italy. She didn't know what would happen with Bailey, maybe nothing ever would. But she'd rather be alone with Emma than sell her soul for a three-week vacation on a yacht with a guy who didn't really care about her, and wouldn't be there for her when she needed him.

She felt like she could conquer the world after Chad's call. She'd been afraid to love anyone before, and have kids of her own. Now she had Emma and wasn't afraid anymore. Whatever happened, she knew she could handle it. Anything was possible, with Bailey, with Emma, or on her own, but not with Chad. She didn't need another glamorous boat trip. All she needed was a real human being with a kind heart. The rest she could deal with herself. Chad had never been that man, and wouldn't be now. And she was fine.

Chapter 13

I n May, the Anderson School contacted Whitney to see how Emma
was doing, and asked her to come in and take some placement
exams, so they could get an idea of where to place her after her unusual schooling until now, and her absence from school entirely for
the past year. Emma was terrified that they wouldn't accept her, and
she froze every time Belinda tried to prepare her. Suddenly her mind
would go blank, her hearing would go dim again, her vision would
blur, and her speech would slur almost as if she was drunk. Sometimes all she could remember how to do was sign, as Sam had taught
her. It was as if her brain couldn't hold up to pressure, and anxiety
would cripple her. Whitney talked to Amy and Bailey about it, and
they said it was normal. Recovery from brain injury was an up and
down, erratic process, and a bumpy one. Emma couldn't handle
much stress anymore. On a good day, she was connected and made
perfect sense. On a bad one, everything she had relearned would
evaporate into the mists again, and she'd have to start from scratch.

She couldn't seem to keep a firm grip on her progress, except when it didn't matter. She had remembered all the tricks of her chess game, and she could beat Belinda at Scrabble, as a spelling exercise, but she lost her ability to speak and her range of vocabulary and couldn't add two and two when she was scared.

"How am I going to get her into a school if she forgets all language the minute she's under pressure?" Whitney said, worried about Emma's future.

"Maybe you don't for now, and wait another year, or they could give her an oral exam in sign language," Amy said practically. "Nothing says she has to be back in school in the fall. You have to keep an open mind about it, Whitney. It's remarkable enough that she learned to speak again, that she regained her hearing, and her vision cleared. You may have to let go of the notion of traditional education for her. In the end, does it really matter? She's functioning and alive, and she may have gaps in her memory forever, too many to be able to go to school at all." Amy was much more willing than Whitney was to let Emma's schooling slide, and be satisfied with the progress she had made, without putting pressure on her. Whitney wanted more for her than that. She wasn't pushing her into an acting career as her mother had. She didn't care if Emma never won an Oscar or an Emmy. But Whitney did want her to have the same opportunities other children had, for knowledge and an education, a job one day, and to become a functioning member of society. She had to go to school to achieve that. It was an advantage Whitney wanted to give her, as a gift after her accident. She could tell that, from a medical point of view, Amy thought she'd never get there and didn't think it was important. Money wasn't an issue, and Emma could be taken care of forever, if that was all she was capable of. Amy was more inclined to celebrate the small victories and not push toward the big ones. Whitney kept telling Emma that anything was possible, and she believed it.

She went back to the school to talk to them herself, and suggested that someone from the school come to the house to meet Emma first, if they were willing. It was an unusual concept, but when Whitney described the nature of her injury, and the progress she had made so far, in less than a year, they agreed to do it. It was compatible with the philosophy of the school, which was that children with all kinds of brains and limitations had the right to an education. They had a child with cerebral palsy, one with severe epilepsy, and two on chemo among their students, along with several with severe learning disabilities. One of their star students had been admitted as autistic, and there was no sign of it in tenth grade after nine years at Anderson, and she had passed her SATs with flying colors. Whitney wanted Emma to be one of their success stories, and her passion about it and certainty that Emma could do it convinced them. The head of their admissions office agreed to spend a morning with Emma at Whitney's home, to get a sense of how she functioned on her home turf. After Whitney's frank description of Emma's loss of speech and hearing and her impaired vision after the coma, the director expected to still see traces of severe limitation.

Instead, Emma was having one of her better days. She was serious and quiet when she met the admissions director, and spoke intelligently and with mature insight about what it had been like to be on a hit television show for two years, and the pressure it put on all the actors, both children and adults. She talked about how it felt not to go to a normal school and how it set her apart from other kids, and was lonely at times, but how it had also provided her with an opportunity to interact with adults. And she spoke honestly about her mother's aspirations for her, and how she had attempted to live up to them with her grandmother as a role model for success.

She spoke poignantly about what she remembered of the accident, and the shock of losing her mother, and she showed the admissions woman a poem she had written about it. Emma sat down to a game of chess with her and beat her soundly, and then she asked her if she'd like to watch cartoons with her. She alternated between acting her real age, with the depth of someone who had suffered, and like a five-year-old. And she shared that she wanted to be a doctor one day, to help others like her who had had brain injuries, and she talked about how lucky she felt every day, even though she had lost her mother. She could speak again and walk, and take lessons, and many others in her situation couldn't. Whitney came and went from the room, so that Emma knew she was nearby, and the rest of the time, she sat in the kitchen, nervously drinking coffee with Belinda and Brett, wondering how Emma was doing. But by the time they were playing chess, and Emma was beating the admissions director, Whitney could see that the woman was bowled over by Emma's abilities, even though Emma admitted to her that some of the time now, she still couldn't remember her last name and had trouble spelling it when she did. She said that having two Ts in it seemed silly and unnecessary, although it seemed fine to her that there were two Ms in Emma, and she said that math was giving her a lot of trouble with her tutor, but she hadn't been good at it before the accident either.

"Congratulations, Dr. Watts," Nora Stratton, the admissions director, said to Whitney after Emma left the room at the end of the lengthy interview, "you've done something very remarkable here. You've given Emma confidence and faith in herself, despite everything that's happened, and some lapses of memory that would have destabilized even the most confident adult."

"I haven't done anything except be here and love her," Whitney said humbly. "It's really all her, and what she has achieved. She's still making progress, and I'd like her to go as far as she can with it. I think she needs a school setting to do that. She deserves more than we can teach her here at home."

"Yes, she does. I agree with you. I'll tell you what, I'll make a date with you for when she graduates from medical school. I've known stories like hers, and there's no limit to what she can achieve with the right support and accommodations. We had an autistic student several years ago who just passed the California bar and became an attorney. He got a job in the DA's office, which was his dream. We believe in making dreams come true at Anderson. She can go as far as she wants to." Whitney had to fight back tears as she listened. She knew they had students without disabilities too, but they weren't afraid to admit unusual students with special needs, and Emma was going to be one of them now. Whitney was convinced that at the right school, Emma could excel. And if she didn't and just turned out to be an ordinary student, with mundane aspirations, that was all right too. But she wanted Emma to have the option, not to push her as Paige had done, but to open doors for her, and let Emma choose for herself which ones she wanted to explore and walk through. It didn't matter if she never became a doctor, or wanted to be a waitress one day, or a salesgirl in a shop. Whitney wanted her to have choices and dreams and options, and how she lived them was up to her.

"I'd like her to fill out a few questionnaires for us, just as guidance about her academic level and general knowledge so we have a better sense of what class to start her in," Mrs. Stratton explained to Whitney after her time with Emma. "And I think she should visit the school, so she's not worried about it all summer. But as far as we're concerned, she's in," she said, extending a hand to shake Whitney's, who was too moved to speak for a minute. One of her patients had told her about the school, because her severely dyslexic nephew had gone there, and Whitney thanked her lucky stars that she had heard about it. It was going to be the perfect place for Emma, and would have been even before the accident. And she had the feeling that even her sister would have approved. She wasn't going to prevent Emma from going back to acting, if that was what she decided she wanted eventually, but they were going to open all the doors of education to her, and let her get a glimpse of a broader world. Their belief was that no one needed to be limited and that anything was possible, which Whitney believed too.

"I think you should start a chess club at school, Emma," Nora Stratton said to her before she left. "You won't have much competition at first, but you can teach some of the other students."

"I play poker too," Emma volunteered. "I used to make a lot of money at it on the set, and blackjack." She looked pleased about it, and the head of admissions laughed.

"We don't gamble at school, but there's always Las Vegas when you're old enough. I used to play poker with my brothers. We'll have to play sometime. Your aunt is going to bring you over for a visit, so you can get the lay of the land, and see the school. You can bring a swimsuit, we have a nice pool." Emma looked forlorn as she said it.

"I can't remember how to swim," she said sadly.

"You can relearn. Babies learn how to swim, so can you. You've relearned much harder things than that." Emma looked cheered by what she said. The school was heavily endowed by grateful parents, and their facilities were impressive. It was about a twenty-minute drive from Whitney's house to where the school was in Hancock Park. "See you soon. And thank you for the cookies." Emma watched her drive away with a serious expression, and then turned to Whitney.

"She's nice. I think I want to see the school."

"That sounds like a good idea," Whitney said and followed her into the house. Emma was exhausted after the long visit, and sat down with her iPad for a little while. It had been a big morning for her. And Belinda and Whitney hugged in victory when Belinda left later that afternoon.

Emma told Bailey about the school when he came to visit them that night after work. He was becoming a more frequent visitor to the house, and Emma considered him a friend. She told him what she knew about the school now, and that she was going to learn how to swim there.

"I wish I'd gone to a school like that," Bailey commented. "I hated my school growing up. There weren't any cool schools in the small town where I lived." It sounded to him as though Whitney had found the perfect school for Emma.

"So how did you get to be a doctor?"

"I went away to a school I liked a lot better. The same school your aunt went to."

"Why didn't you meet her there?" Emma looked puzzled, and Bailey smiled.

"Because I studied all the time, and she probably went out with all the hot guys. And I'm three years older, so we must have kind of missed each other."

"She's forty now," Emma informed him. "She just had a birthday. She kept it a secret because that's old. My mom was thirty-seven." She could remember their ages, but she still couldn't remember how to add, which was the nature of her memory now, with holes in some key places and others that didn't matter.

"Actually, that's not old," Bailey corrected her with a glance at Whitney, who groaned and didn't look happy about it.

"Let's not tell the whole world how old I am," Whitney reminded her, and Emma laughed. Emma was turning ten in a few weeks, and Whitney was going to give her a small party at home, with Amy, Bailey, Belinda, Sam, and Brett. "And by the way, I didn't have a date for four years in medical school, just to set the record straight," Whitney informed them. "I spent all four years in the library and there was nothing cool about me. Your mom was the cool one. She always had a million dates," with all the wrong men, but Whitney didn't add that. Paige had been in her bad-boy phase then, which took her years to grow out of. "She looked like our mother, and she was a lot of fun. I was the dull, shy one." And sometimes she still felt that way, since all she did was work and take care of Emma now. She and Bailey had only been out to dinner a few times in recent months, since they'd admitted their attraction to each other. There was no time or place to do anything about it, and she didn't see how there could be. Her days of glamour on Chad's yacht were over, and she didn't feel comfortable pursuing a romance with Emma having a front row seat to it. It was something they wanted to figure out, but hadn't yet, and Whitney wondered if they ever would. Maybe romance was history for her now, at least until Emma was older.

Bailey was good company, a kind, intelligent man, a good doctor, and very good looking with his dark hair and dark eyes, but he was still kind of a romantic fantasy for her. He was handsome and appealing and there was so much she liked about him, but her life was complicated now, with Emma living with her, and her sole responsibility. And she realized at times that she used Emma's presence as an excuse to avoid getting involved any deeper with Bailey. She wasn't sure she was ready or if she ever would be. Chad had been easy for her, because he didn't want to get too close, see too much of her, or make any deep commitments. But Bailey was different, he was a real person, with real needs, and he wanted to see more of her. For now, Emma was the perfect excuse not to. But Whitney knew that one of these days, they'd have to face their feelings, and that still felt dangerous to her. What if they hurt or disappointed each other, or he tried to control her life? She didn't want any of that to happen, and she didn't want to lose him either. For now, she was free to do whatever she wanted, and that was important to her. Even more so, with Emma. She wanted to make all the decisions about her, with no interference from anyone else. At the same time, she loved being with Bailey and had come to trust him. She wanted to find a way to be close to him, but not give up any power to him, and she wasn't sure how one did that, or if it was even possible. He had never made any permanent commitments either at forty-three. She wondered if they were too old to make the adjustment. Relationships always seemed complicated to her, and very high risk. What if he broke her heart, or their relationship became a power struggle? She didn't want to move into any man's house, especially now with Emma, and she wasn't sure she'd want him living with them either.

"I was born to be a spinster," she said to Belinda with a sigh one day, after worrying about it and mentioning it to her, and she laughed at what Whitney said.

"I'm not sure they call it that anymore. That has a pretty negative connotation. Being single isn't a sign of failure these days, it's a choice. I'm having the same issues with Sam at the moment." They'd been dating for six months, since they'd met during Emma's sign language lessons, and Belinda admitted that they were crazy about each other, and were spending a lot of time together. "He wants us to move in together, and I think it's too soon. I don't want to even think about it for a year. I still want to travel, and I want a career in show business, not just to be a teacher. He wants to settle down and have kids. I'm not ready for that by a long shot. But I don't want to lose him either. I'm thirty-four, which seems so young to me, but I guess if I want babies, I should start thinking about it. But I don't want kids yet. He does. He's only a year older than I am, but all his brothers and sisters are married and have children. Everyone in my family is divorced. That's not exactly an incentive."

"Yeah, I know. My sister and I never got married either, and when she wanted to have a baby, she did it as a single mom and used her best friend as a sperm donor. I've never wanted kids, or marriage. My work has always been a substitute for that, and I've always gone out with men who weren't looking for marriage either. I've always been very honest about it with the men I dated. Bailey and I are a lot alike, he's never been married either. But I think he's a lot less scared than I am. I think he's fantastic but I think this is a serious problem for women of our generation. A lot of us don't want to get married, or give up our freedom. That never looked appealing to me. My mother was an old-fashioned woman. She thought the man should decide everything, and the woman should just follow along blindly, which is what she did. That scares me to death," Whitney freely admitted. "I could never do that and don't want to. Not even for a great guy like Bailey. Marriage scares me to death."

"Maybe you can just figure out some way to live side by side as equals, and find common ground with mutual respect," Belinda said hopefully. It was what she wanted too.

"What novels have you been reading?" Whitney asked her. "That sounds like a perfect world. I don't know a single guy who would agree to that. They're biologically built to call the shots. I hear it in my office every day, from both sides. Guys who want to control, and women who don't want to be controlled. It's the battle of the ages, and sounds like a recipe for disaster to me. Everything goes along great until you fall in love and move in together, or get married, and the next thing you know it's a tug of war day and night, over every-thing from money to kids. It's a nightmare. Bailey is one of the nicest men I've ever met, but we haven't even slept together yet. And if we ever move in with each other, *then* what? Who would have the power then? It's pathological with them, they can't help it. They all want to be the boss." Whitney looked worried as she said it.

"You're scaring me. It sounds like me and Sam. I've even thought of breaking up with him over his wanting to live together, but I don't want to give him up. I just got a new apartment, and I love it. It's not big enough for the two of us, and I hate his apartment, and where he lives. I'd have to commute an hour to work."

"What about getting a new place for the two of you?" Whitney suggested, and Belinda looked depressed about it.

"It's all about sacrifice, isn't it? And I'm not good at that. I had too much of that when I was a kid. Now I've got things the way I want them, and along comes the best guy I ever met, and I'm a goner. It sucks." Whitney hadn't figured out how to solve the problem either, so for the moment, she was making no moves at all. She and Bailey were making out like teenagers, but Whitney was too afraid to make any serious moves or commitment, and taking care of Emma was a convenient place to hide. Turning forty had shaken her too. By now she felt like she should know all the relationship answers, especially as a shrink, and she didn't. Lately she'd been telling herself that she was too old to make changes. But sooner or later, she knew Bailey would do what Sam was doing to Belinda, and lay it on the line, and they'd have a showdown over it, about whether to move forward or not.

Amy had asked her about it too. She was puzzled by their relationship. She knew that Bailey was spending a lot of time with them, at night and on the weekends, more than was warranted by Emma being his patient, but she didn't get the feeling that they were fully involved, and she was right. Whitney was too scared, and Bailey didn't want to push her and risk scaring her off. For the moment, the problem seemed insoluble, and they were circling the issues without having the courage to face them. Amy had tried to encourage them both, but Bailey insisted to her it was still too soon, and he didn't want to push Whitney. She had too much on her plate, and he knew she was scared. But one day, as Whitney admitted to both Amy and Belinda, it would have to be faced. Just not yet. And hopefully not for a while, until she could figure out what she wanted. She knew she wanted Bailey and had never met a man she liked as much, and her breath caught every time he walked into a room with his long legs, warm eyes, and broad shoulders. But she wanted to have her cake and eat it too. She wanted Bailey and her freedom. When she figured that out, she'd be willing to make a move.

Chapter 14

It had taken months, but with a great deal of patience, Whitney had gotten Emma to ride in the car with her, to do errands and go short distances. Emma always remained hypervigilant, as though she expected something bad to happen, and she seemed anxious, but she was slowly becoming more relaxed, and even let Brett drive her too. Emma put her seatbelt on the instant she sat down in the backseat, and watched Brett and Whitney put theirs on too. She didn't like to have the radio on, and never chatted when they were in the car, but by June, she was able to go wherever they had to. Whitney never touched her cellphone when Emma was in the car with her, even to put it on speakerphone, so as not to upset her. Emma remembered all too clearly her mother texting right before the accident, although she didn't remember the rest, and Whitney thought she probably hadn't seen what had happened after that.

Emma was in particularly good spirits the day they went to visit her new school. She was too shy to speak to any of the students, but she had sat in on a class, walked around the grounds, and put her bathing suit on in the locker room and gotten into the pool and held on to the ladder when the other students were in class. The admissions director had introduced her to several of the teachers, and Emma was telling Whitney all about it before they got in the car to drive home.

Whitney had suggested they go out to lunch to celebrate, and Emma thought it was a good idea. Their visit was on the last week of school before vacation, and it was a beautiful warm day in June. Emma was very proud that she had been able to fill out the questionnaire to assess her math skills, and they had given her a reading list for the summer. They had decided to start her in the fourth grade in September, which was only a year behind where she would have been before the accident, which seemed fair, and since Emma didn't know any of the other students, she didn't care that she'd be a year old for her grade. Whitney had reminded her that there was no shame in being a grade behind, and she would catch up quickly. Belinda was going to do some tutoring with her over the summer, to maintain her progress, and so her memory didn't lapse again.

They stopped to do an errand on the way home, and Emma was lost in thought, thinking about the school as they drove along the freeway toward Beverly Hills. Whitney was heading toward the exit to Wilshire Boulevard when a car cut in front of her from the left lane with no warning. She hit the brakes hard and skidded toward the car in front of them. The car that had crossed their path hit another car, and Whitney's car spun around in a circle and came to a dead stop, and the car behind them rear-ended them. It all happened so fast that Whitney barely had time to realize what had happened, only to react as cars screeched to a stop all around them. Emma screamed hysterically from the backseat. Whitney had felt a sudden jolt from the car behind them, but she and Emma weren't injured, just shaken. There was damage to the rear of the car, and several people had gotten out of their cars and were running toward them to make sure they were okay. The minute the car stopped, Whitney turned to make sure Emma was unhurt. Nothing was bleeding, her seatbelt was firmly on, the airbags hadn't opened, but Emma's face was sheet white, her eyes were squeezed shut, and she couldn't stop screaming. Whitney took off her seatbelt immediately and climbed into the backseat to calm Emma down, but nothing stopped her screams as a man poked his head into the car and asked if Emma was hurt.

"She's okay," Whitney said over Emma's cries of anguish, "she's just scared." They could already hear sirens approaching by then, and there were police officers standing next to the car within minutes. Two paramedics came running toward them as Whitney held Emma tightly in her arms. She was flailing as she screamed and fighting to push Whitney away.

"You're okay, baby, you're okay," Whitney kept repeating.

"No!" she screamed piteously. "I told her not to! I told her . . . she was texting . . ." she said, gulping on sobs, ". . . and she flew out the window . . . there . . ." She pointed to the windshield of Whitney's car, which wasn't broken. "She went under the other car in front of us, and then I don't know what happened." Emma was hysterical, but she remembered it all now, the moment of impact, her mother flying through the windshield and under the other cars where she died. Emma couldn't stop screaming, and she fought Whitney like a cat and tried to hit her. Whitney held her tight, and one of the paramedics climbed into the car with them, while two others stood by with a stretcher and a backboard outside the car.

"Is she hurt?" he asked Whitney, and she shook her head. It was too much to explain to him as she tried to get Emma to calm down. The whole rear end of her car had been crushed, her tires were flat, and they were going to have to be towed, but she couldn't get Emma out of the car. She reached over and grabbed her cellphone, scrolled to Bailey's number, and called him. He picked up immediately. All he could hear were Emma's screams, and he was terrified of what might have happened.

"We had an accident . . . we're okay . . . I got rear-ended. Can you come and pick us up?" She told him where they were, while still holding on to Emma, and the patrolman tried to calm her down to no avail.

"Is Emma hurt?" Bailey asked her.

"No."

"Are you?"

"No."

"I'll be there as fast as I can."

Whitney sat in the car, holding Emma, with the highway patrolmen standing outside. Whitney understood now what had happened. Emma had been conscious just long enough to see her mother ejected from the car and only lost consciousness after that. It was the key to everything, the trauma and the loss of memory. She had seen Paige fly from the car to her death and after that Emma had been in the coma. And now she remembered what she had seen that night.

Bailey got there fifteen minutes later, and Whitney was sitting on the side of the road by then, with her arms around Emma. They had gotten her out of the car and she had stopped screaming, she looked glazed and as though she was in shock. Whitney had tried to explain the situation as best she could to the police, and the vehicles that could drive away already had. Whitney's car was being loaded on a tow truck, traffic was moving slowly, and the driver who had cut her off had been arrested for drunk driving. But no one had been injured. What the accident had done was open Emma's final door of memory, and she had remembered everything she had seen of the accident that had killed her mother. She wasn't screaming or speaking by the time Bailey arrived, and she didn't fight them about getting into his car, after Whitney's car was towed away. Whitney sat in the backseat of Bailey's car with her arms around Emma. Bailey glanced at them in the rearview mirror, and said nothing. They were at Whitney's home within minutes, and she gently led Emma into the house and took her upstairs to lie down. What had just happened was a huge shock for Emma. She had relived the accident that had killed her mother.

It was half an hour later when Whitney came downstairs, and Brett went upstairs to sit with Emma, so Whitney could tell Bailey what had happened. He looked as pale as she did when she found him in the kitchen, and she sat down at the kitchen table.

"Jesus, you scared me to death when you called. What happened?"

"The idiot kid they arrested cut me off. Apparently, he was drunk or on drugs or something. I nearly hit the car in front of me, I hit the brakes hard, we spun around, and the car behind me hit us. It was over in a minute, but Emma remembered everything. The truck, the impact, her mother texting, she described Paige shooting through the windshield and flying under the car in front of them, where she died.

I don't know what this is going to do." Whitney was worried about it. "I don't want her to stop speaking again, or regress to where we were last August." She looked panicked as Bailey handed her a glass of water. Whitney's hand shook as she took it. The accident had been traumatic for her too.

"She may regress for a while, but she sustained no injury. This is all about remembered trauma, and releasing the memory she's been blocking for nearly a year. It's better that she remembered what she saw. This was bound to come out sooner or later." They had never been sure until then how much she had seen, but now they knew she had seen her mother fly toward her death. "This is going to be hard for her, and it's a terrible memory to have, but she can heal from it now. It may close up some of those memory lapses for her," he said clinically, and then looked more closely at Whitney. "What about you, are you okay?" He turned her face gently toward the light so he could examine her pupils. "Did you hit your head?"

"No, I'm okay. I have a headache, but I'm fine. She just scared the hell out of me when she started screaming. I'm sorry I called you. I didn't know what else to do. The poor thing, she had a great morning at her new school, and now she remembers everything she saw of her mother's death."

"It was in there anyway, right below the surface. It's better to face it, and to deal with it now, than ten years from now, after a decade of headaches and migraines and nightmares and memory lapses. This is the core of the trauma for her. The physical injury is less traumatic than this." Whitney nodded, and knew it was true. "Do you want me to give her a sedative to calm her down?" Whitney shook her head.

"She was quiet when I left her a few minutes ago, just shocked and sad. It's like Paige dying all over again. I just want to be sure she doesn't stop talking now. She's come so far in the last eleven months. I don't want her to lose that." Whitney looked desperately worried.

"She won't. She has you, and she knows she's safe. She knows nothing bad is going to happen to her now. I think her memory lapses are going to become fewer after this. And the truth is, she may always have some. That's hard to predict. Or she could go all the way to full recovery. Let's see how she reacts to this before we panic. Thank God she didn't get another blow to the head. That would have been really bad." Whitney nodded and noticed that he said "we," she wasn't facing it alone this time. She had Bailey with her, and he cared about Emma too.

He went upstairs to examine Emma a few minutes later and confirmed that she had sustained no injury. She didn't have a concussion or even whiplash and hadn't hit her head, although Whitney had a splitting headache by then from the stress.

"Why don't you lie down for a while," he suggested. "I can stick around for a couple of hours. And I want to see how she's doing before I leave." Emma had spoken to him in a normal voice when he went upstairs to see her, and her speech hadn't altered. She told him what she remembered about her mother flying through the windshield, which was the last time she had seen her alive, seconds before her death. It was a lot for a nine-year-old child to live through, and remember now. But she was handling it better than he'd expected her to, after the initial shock and her intense fear when the car had cut them off on the freeway. It was an instant déjà vu for her.

Bailey sat quietly with Whitney after that, and Emma was up and talking normally when he left to go back to his office. He promised to return after work. It made Whitney realize again what a good man he was, and how dedicated to them. He was someone she could count on. It made everything less frightening, and she could tell that Emma felt that way about him too.

He came back with dinner for them that night, and Emma was subdued and said very little, and hardly ate, but she was speaking clearly, and painfully lucid about what she remembered.

Whitney was putting her to bed after Bailey left, and she spoke to Emma very gently.

"Your mom loved you a lot, Emma. She didn't want any of this to happen to you, or to herself." Emma's eyes filled with despair and tears as soon as Whitney said it, and she turned to her with a look of bottomless grief.

"If she loved me, she wouldn't have texted. I told her not to. She didn't even have her seatbelt on. If she loved me, she wouldn't have died." Emma was sobbing piteously as the realities hit her again. She wasn't angry now, just devastated.

"Sometimes people do stupid things. They think they'll get away with it, or it's just for a minute. She wasn't thinking, but the one thing I do know is how much she loved you. She would never have wanted to leave you. She just didn't think that something like this could happen. I was mad at her at first, because it was such a stupid thing to do. But it was just stupid, and careless. I'm sure she wasn't thinking. She was probably in a hurry." Emma nodded. It was true.

"We were late for my drama coach, and she was afraid he'd leave before we got there. There was a lot of traffic, so she texted him. She was texting so she didn't see the truck."

"The police thought it was something like that. But I'm not mad at her anymore, and you shouldn't be either. The one thing I know for sure is that she loved you every second of her life. She never, ever stopped loving you."

Emma nodded, looking heartbroken as tears rolled down her cheeks. "I'm glad she left me with you, Aunt Whit. I love living with you. I still miss my mom, but I love you so much," she said and slipped her arms around her aunt's neck and held her tight.

"I love you too, Em. We're lucky we have each other."

And then Emma pulled away and looked at her intently. "Do you think my mom would be mad that I don't want to be an actress anymore, and I want to go to school like other kids?"

"I think all she'd want is for you to be happy. It doesn't matter how you do that, or what you decide to be when you grow up. She'd be happy whatever you do, and so will I." Emma nodded and looked relieved. Whitney lay down next to her on the bed with an arm around her until Emma fell asleep, and then she tiptoed softly from the room. She thought about Paige herself all that night, and how ambitious she had been about Emma's career, how proud she had been of her, how much she had wanted her to be like their mother and become a big star one day. She thought of the foolish things they had done together when they were young, how silly Paige had been at times, how daring and how funny, how she flirted shamelessly and how men always fell at her feet. She had been a flake, and a stage mother, a lousy student as a kid when Whitney had written her papers for her, but she had told Emma the truth. Her mother had loved her more than life itself, and had only wanted the best for her. It was a comforting thought as Whitney lay thinking about her sister, missing her, and the memories washed over her again, but more gently now. And the greatest gift of all was that her sister had given her Emma to take care of now, and to love. She was the greatest blessing in Whitney's life, and what she knew she had to do now was be there for her, love her like her own, and help her grow up and forgive her mother. And as she thought it, Whitney's own anger at her sister ebbed away, like the tide going out to sea.

Chapter 15

Emma recovered slowly from the minor accident they had had. It had shaken her up badly, and her final memories of her mother flying through the windshield gave her nightmares several times, but she eventually seemed more peaceful, and her tenth birthday a week later cheered her up considerably. Whitney invited Bailey, Amy, Sam, Belinda, and Brett for dinner. They had pizza and an ice cream cake, and Whitney filled the house with pink and purple balloons. They played music and danced after dinner, and Emma looked happier than she had in a long time. The terrible images of her mother had slowly begun to fade. And with ice cream dribbling down her chin, she announced to everyone that her aunt was thirty years older than she was.

"I just did the math!" Emma said proudly. "It's a subtraction!" Whitney groaned as she said it.

"You couldn't figure out something else to subtract?" Whitney complained, and everyone laughed as Emma put her arms around

Whitney and held her close. She said it was the best birthday she'd ever had, even better than the ones on the set. It was after ten o'clock when everyone went home and Emma slept peacefully that night. She was excited to be ten years old.

Right after her birthday, Emma started on her summer reading list for her new school with Belinda's help. The reading wasn't easy for her, but she improved with each book, and she enjoyed what she was reading, *Little Women, Charlotte's Web,* and *Stuart Little* and some other chapter books. They were going to take a stack of them to Lake Tahoe. Belinda and Sam were planning to come up for a weekend. She had finally come to terms with her difficult decision, and told Whitney she and Sam were each going to leave their apartments and rent a place together in September. She was terrified, but she didn't want to give up and run away from him. It sounded like the right decision to give the relationship a chance, and Whitney had the feeling that it was going to work.

"If it doesn't, I can always find another apartment," she said philosophically, "but not necessarily another guy like him." Whitney was happy for her, and Belinda gave her full credit for introducing them.

"Tell me that if it works," Whitney said, laughing at her. "If it doesn't, it was an accident of fate."

Whitney had called Emma's agent, Robert Jones, by then and told him that Emma wanted to give up acting for a while and was going to start school in the fall. He was disappointed to hear it, and had liked working with Paige a lot better, whose priority had been Emma's career on her path to stardom, not sending her to school like an ordinary kid.

"She can always come back to it," Whitney said quietly.

"That's not always true. People forget. She was a big talent, and she could be a major star, a legend like her grandmother."

"That will still be the case in a few years. She needs a chance to recover from her injury and her mother's death. She has to have time to be just a kid for a while." Whitney was firm about it, and had Emma's best interests at heart. She still had memory lapses, although fewer now, and going to school full-time would be a big change for her after having been tutored on the set for so long. Whitney wanted her to make some friends her own age, not just play poker and chess with the actors she worked with. She could make up her mind later about her career. She didn't need to do it now, at ten.

"I'll call you if any great opportunities come up," he said, clinging to the hope that he could talk her aunt into it, although Whitney sounded like a stubborn woman to him. She had her own ideas about what would be best for the child, and they weren't the same as his and didn't benefit him.

Whitney had rented a house in Lake Tahoe for them for the month of July, and Emma was excited about it. It would be the first summer she'd had when she didn't have voice and drama lessons, no dancing classes, and no lines to learn for the fall. Other than her reading for school, she was going to have the summer off. Whitney had gone up to check out the house. It was a large rambling home with lots of bedrooms, and came with a boat and its own dock. She had invited Amy and her fiancé up later in the month. They had just gotten engaged. And Bailey was coming up for the Fourth of July, during their first weekend in the house.

"And what are you going to let Emma do while she's up there?" Amy questioned her when they saw each other. "Ride a bike? Water ski? Play with other kids?"

"We're starting with swimming lessons at a club nearby," Whitney said vaguely. "She needs to relearn how."

"What about the rest? You can't overprotect her forever," Amy said, concerned that Whitney would try to keep her from normal activities.

"She had a serious brain injury less than a year ago, and a trauma over her mother's death. I'm not going to let her do anything danger-ous on my watch," Whitney said nervously.

"She's almost recovered from her injury, and she may never get back some of the skills she lost. But you have to let her be a regular kid now, fall down, hurt herself a little, get banged up. You can't keep her from that," Amy reminded her, as Whitney looked worried.

"Why not? I don't want anything bad to happen to her."

"Neither do I, but that's part of life. You can't stop her from leading a real life. She's not going to slip into a coma or forget how to speak again, unless she has another major traumatic injury, and chances are, she won't."

"I have a responsibility to her mother," Whitney insisted. "I don't want her to get hurt."

"The only thing she shouldn't do is get a blow to her head. Other than that, she needs to experience being a normal kid. She's never really had the chance."

"I know," Whitney said pensively. All she wanted to do now was keep Emma safe. She couldn't bear the thought of anything bad ever happening to her again, which she knew wasn't entirely realistic, but her sister's death had affected her too. Paige had left her a sacred responsibility, and Whitney wanted to live up to it. She had left her the child that Whitney would never have had the courage to have herself.

"What about you and Bailey? What's happening there? He clams up whenever I ask him." Amy smiled, curious about them. She had grown very fond of Whitney in the past year.

"I'm playing that safe too," Whitney said with a shy smile. "I don't want us to get hurt either. He's coming to Tahoe for the Fourth of July weekend."

"You two should go away somewhere together, and have some fun. God knows you've earned it after the past year."

"Tahoe will be fun. And I'm taking some neurology classes in September. I enjoyed the work we've done together a few times. I want to start seeing some brain injury patients, for the behavioral aspects. It's more interesting than dealing with teenagers smoking too much dope, Beverly Hills housewives with shopping addictions, and corporate husbands who cheat on their wives."

"I want you to come and work with us eventually," Amy said seriously. She had brought it up to Bailey several times, but he wasn't sure where their relationship was going and didn't want to create an awkward situation by working with her, at least not yet. "You two were made for each other," she said. "I wish you'd figure that out."

"Maybe we're too old to take a leap of faith like that," Whitney said thoughtfully.

"I don't buy that. I'm forty-one, planning to get married, and trying to have a baby as soon as we are. People do things later these days, particularly with jobs like ours. It's never too late to take a chance on someone you love. Look at you with Emma. Suddenly, you have a kid. You could even have kids of your own if you wanted to. It's not too late for that either."

"If I had the guts," Whitney said and laughed. "My sister was a lot braver than I am. I have Emma now, that's enough."

"I'm going to try IVF, if we can't do it on our own," Amy confided. "We're going to try this summer, even before we get married. My family will have a fit, if I get pregnant before the wedding, but I'm old enough to do what I want." She envied Amy's ability to please herself and not worry about what everyone else thought. But what was holding Whitney back from throwing her heart over the wall was the same thing that had held her back all her life—the fear of making a mistake, or being controlled by someone else. After generations of divorced parents, it seemed to be what a lot of people worried about these days, and Whitney was no more confident than some of her patients. Her practice was full of women who were afraid to get married, didn't really want to, and decided to have babies on their own, but she didn't want that either. Often their male counterparts saw no reason to marry either. It was the old story of why buy the cow when you could get the milk for free, and there was a lot of free milk around these days. And she hadn't even gotten that far with Bailey. She hadn't gone to bed with him yet. They'd been flirting and kissing and skirting the issue for six months. But what if she did, and lost her head over him? The thought of it scared her to death. Hiding behind her responsibilities to Emma was always safe. There was a guest cottage at the house she was renting in Tahoe, and she was planning to have Bailey sleep there. She didn't want to embarrass Emma, or create an uncomfortable situation by having him in her bed. She had made that clear to him too, and he agreed.

"Well, I hope you two figure it out one of these days," Amy said to Whitney, and she promised to come to Tahoe for a weekend sometime in July. Whitney had met her fiancé, Ted, and liked him too.

Before they left for Tahoe, Whitney took care of something she'd meant to all year. She hadn't had the time or the courage, but the anniversary of Paige's death was in a few weeks, at the end of July. She had never picked her ashes up from the funeral parlor, and she called them, and the cemetery where her parents were buried. She hadn't had a funeral for her, and it seemed late to do a memorial service a year later. Paige had had very few friends, her whole life had centered around Emma.

Whitney was going to bury her alone, without a service, and then decided to tell Emma. Paige hadn't been religious, so she decided to simply make arrangements to bury her ashes next to their parents, with no ceremony. But she didn't want to cheat Emma of the experience if it was important to her.

"You mean bury Mom?" She looked shocked when Whitney mentioned it to her cautiously over breakfast one day. "Where's she been till now?" Emma hadn't let herself think about it, and didn't really want to now.

"Her ashes are at the funeral home, in a box, like about the size of a jewel box. I've been meaning to bury her with our parents at Forest Lawn. They're going to make a little plaque with her name. And I guess I'll be buried there one day too, since neither of us were ever married."

"Is that what people do?" Emma had never thought about it before, and Whitney nodded.

"They get buried with their families, their husbands and wives, and their kids, or their parents."

"That seems really sad. Can I be buried there one day too, with you and Mommy?"

"I hope not." Whitney smiled at her. "I hope you'll have a husband and about ten kids."

"That's too many," Emma said practically, thinking about it. "Why didn't you ever get married, Aunt Whit?" It was a big question which would have required a long answer if she told her the truth.

"I don't know. Scared, I guess. I never really wanted to get married. I was too busy studying to be a doctor, and enjoying my work. And now I think I'm too old to have kids, except for you."

"Mom said she never met the right guy, or she would have gotten married. So she had me anyway. My father was her best friend, but he wasn't really my father, he just wanted to be friends." She said it very matter-of-factly. Her mother had shown her a photograph of him, but she didn't know much more than that.

"I'm glad she had you," Whitney said, although she had been vehement with Paige at the time about what a mistake it was. But now she was glad Paige had done it. It was the right thing after all. So as it turned out, Paige wasn't wrong, even if it had seemed that way to Whitney at the time. Things looked different with the perspective of time.

"I'll come with you." Emma answered her initial question. "Should we bring flowers?" Emma looked serious as she asked, and Whitney nodded. She hadn't thought of it. "My mom liked pink roses and daisies."

"I'll order some," Whitney said softly.

"What about balloons? She liked those too." It sounded a little too festive to Whitney, but why not? Paige belonged to Emma too, and she wanted it to be the way Emma wanted. And Paige had had a childish side to her, even at thirty-seven. In some ways she never grew up, which was part of her charm. Whitney could see that now, although it had annoyed her at times.

"I'll get balloons," she promised.

The day before they left for Tahoe, Whitney and Emma went to the cemetery. The funeral parlor had dropped off the ashes at the cemetery office, in a discreet bronze-lined wooden box with a bronze heart on it. They walked to the grave site where two of the cemetery workers were waiting for them with the box. The small hole had already been dug. The monuments to Whitney's parents were a pair of white marble angels that stood about five feet tall, side by side, holding hands. It seemed the perfect memorial to them. The small spot next to them for Paige seemed dwarfed by the angels, and looked insignificant when one of the workers put the box into it. Whitney had ordered a heart-shaped white marble marker with Paige's name on it, which wouldn't be ready for several months, which she explained to Emma. Whitney was carrying the bouquet of pink roses, and Emma held the daisies, and the bunch of pink and white heart-shaped balloons were fluttering in the breeze, as though struggling to be free as Whitney held the ribbons that hung from them.

Emma and Whitney stood holding hands as the box with Paige's ashes was lowered into the grave, and then they each laid the flowers down on the place where she should have been for the past year, next to her parents. It was a beautiful cemetery with rolling hills and a view of the L.A. skyline, and many famous actors buried there.

"Is there anything you want to say?" Whitney whispered to her and Emma thought about it for a minute.

"I love you, Mommy. Sweet dreams," she said in a soft voice, as Whitney thought about it too.

"Thank you for Emma, Paigey. I love you too." There was no anger left, no resentment for what had happened. That was all there was left to say. Then Emma reached up and took the balloons from Whitney and gently let them go, and they watched them drift away. They watched them for as long as they could see them in the sky. Then Whitney kissed Emma's cheek, took her hand, and they walked back to the car and drove home. They both felt an overwhelming sense of peace.

Chapter 16

The house that Whitney had rented at Lake Tahoe was even better than she remembered from when she drove up to see it, along with several others. It was a big beautiful old home that belonged to a family whose children had grown up and now had children of their own, according to the realtor. They still used it in August, but had decided to rent it in July for the first time. There were six bedrooms, a bunk room on the top floor, enough bathrooms for everyone, a huge living room and dining room downstairs on the main floor with fireplaces tall enough to stand in, wooden beams and paneling throughout the house, and a big slightly old-fashioned kitchen where you could prepare meals for an army. There was an outdoor barbecue. And down the slope at the edge of the lake, there was a boathouse with two speedboats in it, a sleek modern one and an old wooden Riva that had been impeccably cared for. There was a jet ski, and a long dock that jutted out into the water.

The whole property was ringed with beautiful old trees, and there was a tennis court behind the house that had been built fairly recently for teenaged grandchildren. A small guest cottage with two bedrooms was next to it, away from the hubbub of the main house. It had everything they could have wanted, more bedrooms than they needed, and it was all impeccably maintained. Emma was thrilled when she saw it, and ran from room to room trying to decide which one to sleep in. The master bedroom had a big carved antique wooden bed, and an enormous bathroom. Emma chose the bedroom next to it, with twin beds covered in pink floral chintzes, a dressing table with a matching skirt, and more pink floral fabric at the windows. It looked very English.

They'd stopped to buy groceries on the way, and after they put them away, Whitney made sandwiches for them, and after she put the dishes in the dishwasher, they walked down to the lake to explore the boathouse, and Emma jumped up and down when she saw the jet ski.

"Can I use it?" she asked Whitney, who looked at it nervously, remembering Amy's warning not to overprotect her.

"Have you ever used one?"

"I don't know," she said honestly. "I can't remember." Whitney smiled at her answer.

"Maybe we should use it together. They can be powerful, and dangerous." She knew there were frequent accidents on the lake in the summer, and she didn't want to be careless. "And I want you to wear a life preserver whenever you're down at the lake," she added, "until you learn to swim again." She noticed that there were half a dozen bicycles leaning against the wall, with helmets on pegs above them. They'd been told that there were tennis rackets in the garage, and the realtor had said that there were public stables nearby, if they liked to ride. Whitney hadn't ridden since she and Paige were children, and she didn't want to start again now at her age. It had been too long, and she'd never been a terrific rider.

They sat on the dock after they'd looked around, and dangled their feet in the water. It was freezing cold. The water at Lake Tahoe was always freezing, and swimming was always invigorating. They went back up to the house after that, and put their bathing suits on, and then came back, and Whitney got a life jacket from the boathouse and made Emma put it on.

"It's too small, Aunt Whit," Emma complained. "It's squeezing me."

"Then go grab a bigger one. You're not going in without one."

"I'm not two years old, you know," she grumbled over her shoulder and came back a minute later with a slightly larger one over her bathing suit. They got into the water together, and they both screamed at first at how cold the water was, and Emma said her feet had tingles. They floated around together close to the dock, and were shivering when they got out. Whitney toweled her off as they both giggled about how cold it was. They lay in the sun for a while on dry towels, and at the end of the afternoon, they went back up to the house. Bailey called to see how they were and asked if they needed him to bring anything they'd forgotten. He was going to leave at five in the morning and hoped to be there by three in the afternoon. It was a long drive from L.A. Whitney had left even earlier. Emma had slept most of the way.

They were cooking an early dinner of hamburgers when he called them, and Whitney sounded relaxed and happy.

"The house is perfect," she told him. "Bring your bathing suit, you don't need your tennis racket, they have some here. We found bicycles in the boathouse. Wait till you see it!" She sounded as happy as Emma. They were planning to stay there for a month, and Bailey was coming up for four days over the long weekend. They had checked out the guest house on their way back from the lake. It looked like a little English cottage in a fairy tale.

"Maybe I'll try to leave a little earlier," he said, "so we can swim when I get there."

"They have a jet ski too," Whitney added. "Do you know how to drive one?"

"Of course. I'm a pro. I can't wait to see you both." Whitney was excited to see him too. For all her nervousness about embarking on a relationship with him, they had gotten used to seeing each other almost every day, and she was excited about spending the four-day weekend with him. "I'll get there as soon as I can," he promised. "If they have a barbecue, I'll make dinner tomorrow, and maybe we can go night fishing sometime. We might even be able to catch crayfish right from the dock." Everything he suggested sounded like fun to Whitney. They talked about it over dinner after he hung up.

"Can I go night fishing with him?" Emma asked.

"Sure," Whitney said, without giving it further thought. She knew Bailey wouldn't do anything dangerous with her. She'd be in good hands with him, even on the jet ski. It was going to be nice having a man there to help them. Brett had come up with them too and had friends staying nearby.

Whitney thought of Chad as she did the dishes after dinner. This was an entirely different experience from his luxurious yacht with the huge crew but it felt more like a real vacation, with lots of space

230

to move around in. She was glad she had rented it. It reminded her too of vacations she had taken with their parents, with big comfortable houses they had rented in various locations when she and Paige were little and their mother was between films. They had even gone to Africa on safari once, under very luxurious circumstances, when they were in their teens. Their mother had hated it and been frightened of animals and snakes the whole time, but the girls and their father had loved it.

Emma slept peacefully after their swim in the lake, and Whitney woke early the next morning, and put two vases of flowers from the garden in the cottage for Bailey, and then came back and made breakfast for Emma when she woke up. She made pancakes and bacon, and then they walked back to the lake, and lay in the sun on the dock again, with Emma in her life jacket.

Bailey left L.A. two hours earlier than he said he would, and reached the house at one, just as Emma and Whitney were finishing lunch. Emma let out a squeal of delight when she saw him, and gave him a tour of the whole place, including the boathouse, the jet ski, and the dock. Then she showed him his cottage, which Whitney had left open for him. He admired the well-kept tennis court on their way to the house, where Whitney had been organizing what they were going to have for dinner.

"The old Riva they have in the boathouse is a beauty," he said admiringly, as he kissed her when Emma went upstairs to get something in her bedroom. "Thank you for having me up here. My grandparents had a house like this on a lake in Wisconsin. We used to go up there every summer, until my brother's accident. I loved it." The house Whitney had rented had a wonderful old-fashioned feeling to it, and everything was in mint condition. The family who owned it obviously loved it.

"How about a swim in the lake?" he suggested when Emma reappeared.

She looked glum for a moment. "Aunt Whit says I have to wear a life jacket till I learn how to swim again."

"That sounds sensible. Then let's get started right away so I can get you up on water skis before the end of the month," he said, and Emma clapped her hands with glee. He was hoping to be invited back for at least one more weekend, or several.

"Will you take me on the jet ski?" He looked to Whitney for his cue, and she nodded.

The three of them went down to the dock. Emma put the life vest on, and Bailey dove smoothly into the water, swam underwater for a few minutes, and came up spluttering with the cold.

"It's even colder than I remembered from the last time I was here," he said and climbed out to lie in the sunshine with them, and a few minutes later, he took Emma in swimming and kept a firm grip on her life jacket, and Whitney joined them, but they didn't stay in long.

"Can we do the jet ski now?" Emma wanted to do everything with him.

"How about doing that tomorrow? Why don't we drive the boat around before dinner?" He took the Riva out with great care a little while later, made sure that there was gas in it, and then drove along the shore to take a look. They all enjoyed it. And he wiped it down and covered it carefully when they brought it back. "That is an absolute gem," he said to Whitney.

As the sun was setting, they went up to the house and started dinner. Brett was at her friends' that night. Bailey lit the barbecue, and Whitney had chicken and steaks ready for him to cook. Then he went to his cottage to change and put on jeans and a sweater as it started to get chilly. Whitney sent Emma to her room to get a sweater too.

It felt like a family being together. Whitney was enjoying it thoroughly and so was Emma. She liked having a man around to do things with, and had had too little of it in her lifetime, since Paige's romances were always brief, and never with men who were interested in children. Bailey was having fun with them, and was suggesting they go fishing the next day and check out the dock for crayfish that night, with a net, some bait, and a flashlight to attract them.

"How do you know all these things?" Whitney asked him as he prepared a tray of the meat for dinner.

"I'm a guy. Guys know about things like barbecues and fishing," he teased her, leaned over to kiss her, and Emma saw it and giggled, but she didn't disapprove. "And tomorrow the jet ski, I promise." He wanted to get in everything that Emma wanted to do, and still manage to spend time with Whitney. But there would be plenty of time at night when Emma was asleep.

The steaks and chicken he grilled for them that night were delicious, and Whitney made baked potatoes and corn on the cob to go with them. Then Bailey put together s'mores for dessert from some groceries he had brought himself, and they ate them outdoors near the open fireplace. Emma got the gooey marshmallows and melted chocolate all over her face. She looked like she was in heaven, and Whitney had one too.

"Oohhh, these are so good," Emma said, helping herself to a third one, and Bailey laughed watching her.

"Did you ever go to camp, Em?" he asked her casually, and she laughed at him.

"Are you kidding? I was on a TV show for two years. I had to learn lines every day, and during the hiatus, I had drama coach and voice lessons, and tap, hip-hop, and ballet." She remembered it all now. "There was no way I could have gone to camp. My mom wouldn't have let me."

"Maybe next year," Bailey commented with a glance at Whitney, who didn't respond. Amy had made him the same speech about not overprotecting Emma.

"Could I go to camp, Aunt Whit?" Emma asked hopefully, and Whitney looked vague about it.

"We'll see, a year is a long time away," was all she said, and Bailey questioned her when Emma went inside for a minute.

"You don't want her to go to camp?"

"I don't want her to get hurt again. She could have an accident at camp. We just got her back in one piece. I don't want anything happening to her." He nodded, and understood.

"She's having a ball here," he said as he put an arm around Whitney's shoulders and she thanked him for the delicious dinner. She was enjoying having him there too. "I'm the master of the barbecue. And the jet ski." Whitney looked nervous when he said it, but didn't respond.

They told ghost stories at the outdoor fireplace until Whitney sent Emma to bed, and went to tuck her in, and then she came back and sat outside with Bailey for a long time enjoying the sounds of the night and the glorious sight of the moon over the lake. It was an incredibly romantic spot, and he kissed her longingly. He didn't comment on the fact that she had assigned him to the cottage and not her room. He understood why, because of Emma. It would have been too awkward to do otherwise.

He kissed her again before he went to bed, and when he walked into the main house in the morning, Whitney had made waffles, and there was a plate of crisp bacon on the table. She had learned to cook simple meals in the past year.

"What's our plan this morning?" he asked as he finished breakfast and thanked her. "Fishing or jet ski?"

"Jet ski!" Emma said immediately, and he looked at Whitney, who nodded with a sigh.

"Just be careful, and hang on to Bailey extra tight," she told her niece. She watched from the dock when he took the jet ski out of the boathouse a little while later, and Whitney could see that he was being extra cautious and didn't go at full speed with Emma sitting behind him. He only went faster after she had gotten off, and then he took it out for a spin on his own and had some fun with it. Whitney was grateful that he was careful with her. That afternoon he took Emma fishing for a while, before they all went swimming together, and the water was colder than ever.

They made hamburgers and hot dogs on the barbecue that night, and Emma watched a movie and fell asleep with a bowl of popcorn sitting next to her that Bailey made her, after he made some s'mores again.

"You're going to spoil her forever," Whitney said, cuddled up next to him under the stars, sharing a blanket. "You're a tough act to follow," she added contentedly.

"That's the whole point. This way, she'll beg you to have me up every weekend. Next time I think I might fly to Reno. It would be quicker." It had been a long drive.

"I love having you here," Whitney admitted. There was something so easy and comfortable about being with him. He was such a warm, kind person, and incredibly patient with Emma.

"She didn't have much of a childhood before the accident," he commented, "the life of a child star."

"My sister was the original stage mother. But we didn't have much of a childhood either. We were always meeting our mother somewhere that she was making a movie and couldn't be with us, or being chased around by paparazzi. I hated it. Paige loved it, she loved basking in our mother's glory . . . and then Emma's."

"Do you think Emma will miss it?"

"I hope not," she said with considerable feeling. "I want her to have a better life than that. Paige and I used to argue about it. I just don't think it's a good life for a kid, either as an actor, or the child of one. It's not a healthy life. People dream about it, but they don't know what it's really like."

"It's so different from the way I grew up in the Midwest. Everything you did sounds so glamorous. I feel like a bumpkin compared to you. You must think I'm a real rube."

"Of course not, you're a doctor. And that life isn't glamorous. It may sound that way from the outside, but it's not. It's too much pressure as a kid, and even more as an adult. Everything's for show, while the press chases you around. Nothing about it is real. It's why I never wanted to have kids, or even get married. I'm not sure what I think about my mother anymore. I don't know if she loved her life with my father, letting him make all her decisions for her. Or if she hated it

236

and dementia was her only way out. It's hard to understand other people's relationships. I can't even figure out my own." He smiled when she said it. But she seemed more at peace than she had before. "I hated the fact that Paige dragged Emma into show business. She had her modeling at six months, and auditioning for parts at six."

"Emma has a better life now, thanks to you," he said quietly. "Is that really why you never married?"

She paused before she answered. "It just seemed too complicated to me. My father ran my mother's life as though she were a child. He made every decision for her, what movies she was in, what parts she played, what she wore, how she did her hair, who her friends were, what the press saw, what they didn't. He controlled every moment of her day and world. That's what marriage meant to me when I was growing up. I never wanted someone to do that to me." She had said it before and he could see that it had marked her deeply.

"I've been afraid of that all my life, that a man would try to control me the way my father controlled her."

"Are you afraid of that with me?" he asked her for the first time, and she nodded. She wanted to be honest with him about her fears, so he would understand her hesitations. "I'd never do that to you, Whitney. That's not what I want to share with someone. Marriage is a partnership, not a dictatorship."

"People say that, and then things get out of control. I never wanted to take that chance." Which explained why she'd chosen men like Chad who kept their distance and never got involved too deeply. Bailey was different. He was right up close, which felt frightening at times, and so appealing at others.

"So you stay alone forever? Or you keep people at arm's length?

That doesn't sound like a happy life either. In fact, it sounds like a sad existence to me," he said gently.

"The other way is worse," she said quietly, and he knew what he was up against. He had sensed it since he'd met her, from things she said.

"Would you ever want to live with me?" She was startled by his question, but it was the crux of it for her.

She didn't answer for a long time. "The thought of it terrifies me. Not just with you. With anyone. It's tempting but so damn scary and potentially dangerous."

"The alternative is very lonely," he said, sorry for her. He could sense how frightened she was, and how isolated she'd been until Emma. Emma had begun to open doors for her that had always been closed before.

"It would kill me if someone tried to control me the way my father did to her. He wanted us to go into the business too. Paige tried, but she didn't have the talent. And I ran. I hid in medicine, and he couldn't do anything about it. And then Paige dragged Emma into it. It's an insidious business that eats people up and spits them out. I'm happy I escaped it." But she hadn't escaped her demons yet. The specter of her father loomed large. And she was describing a life and a world that Bailey knew nothing about and he wouldn't have wanted either. It was a sophisticated world that came at a high price. His parents hadn't been happy either, after his brother's accident destroyed them, but he still believed that two people could be happy together, and he wanted to try it with her, if she'd let him, which was not a sure thing by any means. She had built powerful walls around herself and hidden behind them, and in the past year with Emma, her walls had begun crumbling. He understood who she was now, and the battles she had fought, and her honesty only made him love her more. He just had to figure out how to help her get over her walls. He had been fighting his own demons for most of his life, and the memory of his parents' unhappy marriage, but he knew that with Whitney, it could all be different. He had never felt that way before. Watching Whitney with Emma had taught him something about courage, and being with her made him feel brave. Maybe brave enough for both of them.

As he lay in the cottage that night he was overwhelmed with tender feelings for her, this woman who had fought so hard to save her niece and honor her sister, to forgive her parents and be free.

And in her bedroom in the main house, Whitney was thinking the same things about him, and what a good man he was. In the last eleven months, she had come to trust him. It was a first for her. She wasn't sure yet if she wanted to live with him. But the one thing she did know was that she loved him, more than any man she'd known before.

Chapter 17

The rest of Bailey's stay with them in Tahoe was perfect and sped by too quickly. They caught crayfish at the dock at night, and ate them for lunch the next day. He took them fishing, and Emma caught a tiny little fish and he cooked it, which delighted her.

He gave her swimming lessons in the shallow water at the edge of the lake, and she started to remember how to float and dog paddle. He gave her rides on the jet ski, and they took the Riva out again. He wanted to go horseback riding but they didn't have time. Emma and Whitney were both sorry to see him leave on Sunday afternoon. There had been fireworks the night before for the Fourth of July, and a parade in the town nearest the house. He enjoyed every moment with them, and Whitney invited him back the following weekend. He agreed to come, and said he'd fly so he'd have more time with them, instead of wasting it driving up from L.A.

Whitney and Emma enjoyed their time together alone during the week too. Brett went back to L.A., and they went for long walks, and

Whitney worked on Emma's swimming with her. They looked through the shops in town, bought groceries, and did some baking. And they sat on the dock and talked about Emma's mother.

"I miss her a lot sometimes, now that I remember more about her. She was fun to be with. We did silly things sometimes. Once, we squirted whipped cream all over the neighbor's car because he was mean to us and said we made too much noise."

"That sounds like your mom. She used to do things like that when we were kids too. She taught me how to egg cars. My dad had a fit when he found out, when someone called the police. And then she blamed me and said she didn't do it. I was mad at her for months afterward, because I got grounded and she didn't. She was kind of a pain in the ass when we were kids." Whitney smiled at her niece and Emma laughed.

"She was kind of a pain in the ass with me sometimes too. But I loved her anyway. I really didn't want to be in that musical in New York, and I thought she was going to make me do it. Maybe she would have. She thought it was a big opportunity. I wanted to stay on the show in L.A. She never listened to what I wanted. She always said she knew what was best for me."

"My dad was like that too. I guess she was more like him than I realized," Whitney said thoughtfully.

"You listen to me, and you care about what I want to do," Emma said.

"Maybe it's easier because I'm not your mom. She had put a lot of time and energy into your career. I think you can always do that later, not at your age."

"She never asked me if I wanted to be an actress. She just expected it of me, so I did it. Sometimes it was fun, but a lot of the time it wasn't. It's hard work."

"I think my mom felt that way too. I'm not sure she ever really enjoyed being the big star she was. Sometimes maybe, but not always. Once she told me it scared her. It would have scared me too."

"It didn't scare me, it just wasn't fun a lot of the time," Emma said quietly.

"Being a doctor isn't fun every day either. It's the nature of work. Sometimes it's hard too."

"But you help people. You make them better. Like Bailey and Amy."

"I try. I don't always get it right."

"I think you do," Emma said in an admiring tone. "I think you're a good mom too. You should have had kids of your own."

"I don't need to. Now I have you." She smiled at her, and after that they went up to the house and made dinner together. They made s'mores, although Emma said they weren't as good as Bailey's.

They had fun with him when he got back from the city. He came up on Thursday, and was planning to stay until Monday morning. And they caught crayfish again the first night he was there and cooked them for dinner.

He looked happy to see Whitney, and relaxed, and told her about the cases he had worked on that week. He was writing another paper on brain injury, and he showed her the rough draft, and then he asked her a question she wasn't expecting. He'd said it casually before, but this time he asked her very directly.

"Would you ever consider coming into our practice with us? Amy and I have been talking about it for months. I want to have a psychiatrist in our group to deal with that whole end of things. It would make our group a lot stronger. Would you consider it?" Whitney paused as she thought about it and nodded.

"Yes, I would consider it. We've talked about it before, and I agree with you. I think psychiatry and neurology are more related than people think, in the case of brain injury, and working with both would make my practice much more interesting than it has been for the last few years. I think I'm ready for a change. When were you thinking?"

"As soon as you're ready. I think Amy's about to have some big news. She wants to get married and have babies, and she's been thinking about going back to Colorado where she came from and setting up a smaller practice there, but I don't think she's going to do it immediately. She's tired of L.A. and wants to move back to Denver sometime in the next year. You could join us in September. You can still see some of your regular patients if you want, but you could see ours too." It sounded exciting to Whitney, and they talked about it until late that night. "We have an empty office you can use," he added, as he smiled at her, and then he kissed her. "I know it seems complicated if you work with us, and you and I get involved too. But I love the idea of both. Do you think you can handle a double header like that?" That sounded challenging and appealing to her too.

"We could try it. If it doesn't work, or we fight all the time, I can go back to my old practice. We could do it as an experiment for a while." But he seemed easy to get along with, and they hadn't had any major disagreements so far, about Emma or anything else. "What does Amy say about it? Is she okay with the idea? She's mentioned it, but I wasn't sure if she was serious."

"She told me not to screw it up and scare you off, or she'd kill me."

They both laughed. "So I think she means it," he said, "and I do too." It was all Whitney needed to hear.

They talked about it again the next morning over breakfast, and then they went down to the lake and Bailey gave Emma another swimming lesson. She was feather kicking through the water with her life jacket on, and she took it off for a few minutes, and she still managed to slice through the water. Her body was remembering what her mind had forgotten, which happened to her about many things. A lot of her memory had come back, more than Bailey had expected. It was what Whitney had hoped.

"You don't give up easily," he said quietly, when they were watching Emma in the water one afternoon.

"I like to think that anything is possible," she said, and he looked into her eyes.

"So do I. I don't give up easily either. I love you, Whitney. I want this to work between us, however you want to design it, whatever the terms. A relationship, a marriage, a joint practice. I think we both bring a lot to the table. I don't need to get married, or have kids if that's not what you want. I'm not going to try to control you. I'm not your father. And you're not your mother. You're not helpless and powerless. We're two people who love and respect each other. I don't need to put a ring or a leash on you to do that." What he said moved her deeply and she didn't know what to say at first.

"Thank you" was all she could muster. He had understood how terrified she was of falling into her father's trap.

"I'm scared too, you know, I've never put my heart out there for anyone the way I have for you. If you walk away, it will break my heart."

"I'm not walking away," she said softly. "I think I'm walking toward you, I'm just slower than most people."

"You're like a wild horse," he said gently, "but they're the best ones. I'm here, Whitney, whenever you want me to be." She nodded, and they lay down next to each other on the dock. It felt good just being near him, and knowing he wasn't going to try and force her into anything she didn't want. She loved the idea of joining their practice. He had given her a lot to think about.

The three of them played Scrabble and chess and poker at night. Emma beat them soundly a number of times, and she laughed whenever she did. She beat Bailey out of five dollars at poker and he told her she was a little bandit. Then she beat him at chess too.

"I think I liked you better before your memory came back," he growled at her, and she laughed. She still had frustrating moments every now and then when she came up against a hole in her memory. It was always unexpected and inexplicable. Some small thing she couldn't remember, a word, or an answer to a question. It annoyed her whenever it happened, and she said it made her feel stupid.

"You're not stupid," Bailey explained to her again. "It's part of your injury, like a weak ankle or a weak wrist. Some things take longer to get strong again than others. Or sometimes you have a little weakness forever. You're almost as strong as you were, just not quite."

"Do you think I'll have trouble in school?" she asked him seriously. She was worried about it, and had said it to Whitney too.

"No, I don't," he answered. "You can't be good at everything, so you'll be better at some subjects, but you're not going to forget your

name, or how to read or how to add. All of that is behind you, Emma."
It took a year, but as brain injuries went, that was fast. And youth
was on her side, as they had said.

"Do you think I'm too stupid to ever be a doctor?" she asked him.

"What kind of doctor?"

"A neurologist, like you and Amy. I want to take care of kids like
me, with brain injuries." She seemed serious about it, although she
had years ahead of her to change her mind and do something else, or
even be an actress again.

"I'll tell you what," he said with a solemn expression. "If you go to
medical school and become a neurologist, if I'm still practicing when
you finish, I guarantee you a place in our practice, and I'll put your
name on the door right next to mine. Is that a deal?" He held out a
hand to shake hers, as she studied his expression to see if he meant
it, and he looked like he did.

"How long would it take me?"

"About thirteen years, including college, medical school, and residency. So that's about twenty-one years from now. You'll just catch
me before I retire so you better hurry up."

"It's a deal," she said soberly and shook his hand. "I'll be there."

"I'm trying to get your aunt to come in with us too," he said, looking pleased. "And remember your aunt's motto, 'Anything is possible,'
so don't go giving up and telling me how stupid you are halfway
through medical school. I'm expecting you to go all the way."

Emma nodded as she looked at him, and a long, slow smile lit up
her face. Whitney saw it as she walked over to them.

"What's going on here? More poker games?"

"I'm recruiting child labor," he said, looking pleased with himself.

"Emma and I just made a deal. So you'd better get your ass in gear, before she gets her name on the door first." Whitney laughed out loud at what he said.

On Saturday, Bailey got his wish, or one of them. He called the stables nearby to see about renting horses and a guide for a leisurely ride in the hills. He was an experienced rider, and Whitney said she hadn't ridden since she was a kid but didn't want to be a poor sport and stay home, so she agreed to go. Bailey said he'd ask for an easy horse for her, and for Emma. She had ridden a few times on the show. And riding with Bailey sounded like fun to her.

Whitney got nervous about it as they got in the car to drive to the stables, and she spoke to Bailey in an undertone. "Do you think this is a good idea? For Emma, I mean."

"It's fine," he said reassuringly, "those rented horses for hire are always hacks at stables like this. We'll have to beat on them to keep them going. I wouldn't suggest it if I thought it was dangerous for her. And they'll make us wear helmets anyway, or I will if they don't." Whitney felt better when he said it, and got in the car, and Emma hopped onto the backseat in jeans, and boots with heels as Bailey had told her to. She was wearing a pair of red Doc Martens and looked very cute, with her long hair in pigtails. Whitney had done her braids, and was wearing short boots too.

They were surprised by how crowded the stables were when they got there. A dozen horses were tied up in a corral, six others were being saddled, and there were people milling around, asking questions, getting on horses, and putting helmets on. By the time they got to Bailey, they said they had run out of their newer helmets, and handed him two old, beaten-up ones for him and Whitney, and a small newer one for Emma. Bailey told her to put it on and checked the strap himself. The horses they'd been given looked ancient, and their guide even more so. He was Native American with deeply leathered skin, long braids, and a turquoise belt buckle. He said they were going to follow an easy path along the lake, and the ride would take an hour. They had too many reservations to keep them out any longer today, but if they came some other time, he'd take a different path for two or three hours. Bailey figured an hour would be long enough for Emma, who had little experience, but she was excited to go. And Whitney didn't want to ride for longer than an hour either and knew she'd be sore the next day after not having ridden for so long.

They finally left the area outside the barn half an hour later, and Harry Running Bear, their guide, led the way, across the highway, to a series of trails, and picked one. It all seemed a little too tame to Bailey, who was already bored on a half dead horse who could barely pick up his feet and stopped to graze every few minutes, along with Whitney's horse, who seemed even older.

The whole thing was beginning to seem like a bad idea, when Emma's slightly younger horse pricked up his ears, started moving sideways, and then bolted when he saw a rabbit run across the path. The horse shied away, wild eyed, before Bailey could grab his bridle, and took off with Emma looking panicked. Bailey chased after Emma as fast as his horse was willing to go, which wasn't fast enough. He couldn't close the distance between them, as Harry Running Bear stared at them in astonishment and did nothing, and Whitney screamed at Bailey to catch them. Just as he got to Emma, holding on to the saddle for dear life, her horse bucked neatly and Emma flew through the air like a bird and landed on the grass, winded, as her horse ran back toward the stable. Bailey dismounted and ran toward her. She was staring up at the sky expressionlessly with her eyes open when he got there and didn't make a sound. She looked dead for a minute and then she turned her head slowly toward him and moaned. She was alive, and she was wearing a helmet, but she could have been concussed or have injured her neck. He felt it gingerly with his fingers, as Emma looked at him and whispered.

"My head hurts."

"Don't move, Em," he said gently as Harry Running Bear finally got to them and Bailey told the guide to call an ambulance on his cellphone.

"I don't have one," he said awkwardly and Bailey handed him his own, as Whitney rode up, jumped off her horse, and ran over to Emma and Bailey. He was telling her not to move or sit up and Whitney knew he feared her neck was broken. Whitney looked panicked and was fighting back tears.

"Is she okay?"

"I think so," he said calmly. "She's winded, and her head hurts." Whitney could imagine another year of brain injury and was furious with Bailey for suggesting the idea, and herself for agreeing to it.

"The ambulance will be here in ten minutes," Harry announced. "Should we ride her back to the stable?"

"I think we'd better wait here," Bailey said, sounding tense.

Emma was lying on the grass with her eyes closed, and they fluttered open from time to time. When the ambulance arrived ten minutes later, it was a Jeep with two paramedics in it, who hopped out with a stretcher to put Emma on, and she started to cry when she saw it. It had bad memories for her too.

They lay her on the backseat of the Jeep, and Whitney rode with her, sitting on the floor of the car while Bailey rode ahead back to the stables, and Harry led Whitney's horse home.

Emma sat up and threw up as soon as they got to the stables, which Bailey and Whitney both knew meant she had a concussion, and the Jeep drove Emma and Whitney to the hospital while Bailey followed in their car, feeling like a monster for suggesting they go riding in the first place. He had apologized to Whitney about a dozen times before they took off for the hospital.

He met them in the emergency room and demanded to see the neurologist on call for a head injury.

"We don't know if it's a head injury yet, sir," the nurse snapped at him, and he replied just as quickly.

"I'm a neurologist, and I know. She's got a concussion, and a previous head injury. We need a CT scan, an MRI, and EEG stat," he leveled at her, and she looked startled and picked up the phone, and then turned to Bailey again.

"The doctor will be here in an hour. He's in Truckee." Bailey resisted the urge to scream at her, and went to find Whitney and Emma in the exam room where they'd put them. Emma had just thrown up again, and Whitney looked as pale as she did, and barely spoke to him, as she nodded and sat down after they cleaned Emma up. She was looking very pale, and lying with her eyes closed, and Bailey stood next to her talking to her. He was telling Emma that he didn't want her to go to sleep, and kept a running banter going with her, to keep her focused and engaged. And finally, over an hour later, the doctor walked in, looking faintly annoyed.

"What's the big excitement here? I hear this young lady fell off a horse." She nodded and then winced at the pain in her head, and Bailey asked to speak to him outside for a moment. They walked out together, and Bailey gave him the rapid version of the past year, her car accident a year before, and weeks in a coma, due to brain trauma as a result, and recent recovery.

"I understand your concern," he said seriously, "let's have a look at her together." Bailey stood aside as the neurologist examined her. He had already noticed that there were more than twenty orthopedic surgeons listed on the board in the emergency room, and only three neurologists. It was a ski community in winter, and they saw more broken bones than head injuries, but the doctor seemed competent enough as Bailey watched him, and Whitney stared at them both.

"All right," the middle-aged neurologist agreed with Bailey, "let's get a CT and an MRI on her, and an EEG to be on the safe side, but I think we're looking at a mild concussion. It isn't what I'd want to see happen after a brain injury, but I think we may have gotten lucky on this one. She was wearing a helmet?"

"Yes, she was." Bailey nodded, feeling sick himself at what had happened. He hadn't dared look at Whitney since they'd walked in, and she wasn't speaking to him.

They completed the scans within the next hour, and the neurologist came back to confer with Bailey. "The scans all look good. She's awake, she's alert, she's talking to us. I think with a few days in bed she'll be fine. But I think maybe we want to skip riding lessons after this, if you agree." He was smiling and Bailey looked immensely relieved.

"God, yes. It was entirely my fault. It was my idea. The horse saw a rabbit, bucked, and took off."

"They're a bunch of old broken-down nags in that place anyway. But I think Emma should skip riding after this, for the sake of your nerves and mine, and her mother's," he said, glancing at Whitney, and they didn't bother to explain. He had obviously assumed that Bailey was her father. "You should check her every two hours tonight when she's asleep. I'll leave that up to you."

"Thank you, Doctor."

"Anytime. I'm glad it was nothing worse," he said and hurried out with a wave, as Bailey turned to look at Whitney. She looked like she was going to faint. Emma already seemed better when she sat up, and had color in her face.

"Are you ready to kill me? You should be," he said to Whitney with deep remorse. "I'm so sorry," he said to both of them.

"It was fun, until I fell off," Emma said as she got off the exam table, and Bailey groaned.

"It was not fun before or after you fell off, and it was a terrible idea. I'm really sorry," he said, as Whitney nodded and followed them out of the room, and then out to the parking lot. They were all grateful that Emma had been wearing the helmet. Without it, she might be in a coma again, which Whitney and Bailey were both well aware of.

"It wasn't your fault," she finally managed to say to Bailey. "It was mine too. I let her do it, even if I was nervous about it. Amy told me I shouldn't overprotect her, so I was trying to be grown up about it."

"So much for that. Your instincts are better than Amy's. Emma's not her child, she's yours." Whitney smiled weakly at what he said. She called Brett a few minutes later and asked her to fly up to Reno. She'd been due back in a few days anyway, after her time off. She was shocked when Whitney told her Emma had a concussion and had fallen off a horse. And she agreed to be there in a few hours. They were going to take turns watching her during the night. Bailey would be watching her too, and said he'd stay a few extra days if Whitney would let him, which she said he could. She was grateful to have him near at hand.

"It could have happened some other way," she said graciously, once Emma was settled in bed with her iPad, watching a movie. "She could have tripped and fallen, she could have fallen down the stairs. She could bump her head. Amy's right. I can't protect her from everything. She can get hurt in school in September, although I hope not."

"Putting her on a horse was stupid," he continued to berate himself, and he sat in the kitchen with her while they waited for Brett to arrive. She pulled up in a cab at four o'clock, and Whitney looked relieved when she walked in, and she went straight upstairs to Emma, who was delighted to see her and told her all about her big adventure.

Bailey and Whitney walked down to the lake then, and sat on the dock, trying to calm down themselves. It had been a stressful morning.

"Can you forgive me?" he asked her mournfully after they'd been there for a while and Whitney admitted how terrified she'd been when she saw Emma fly off the horse and couldn't stop her, and neither could Bailey.

"There's nothing to forgive. It'll give us something to talk about years from now."

"I'd rather be talking about something more pleasant than when she got a concussion because I was an idiot and suggested we go horseback riding."

"We scared the hell out of Harry Running Horse or whatever his name was. I think we were a lot more than he bargained for," Whitney said, grinning, now that the worst was over, and they were reassured.

"No wonder you don't want anyone controlling your life. You do it better than anyone else. You don't need me screwing things up and getting Emma concussed."

"She'll be fine in a few days. You heard the doctor. Don't beat yourself up."

They sat on the dock for a long time, until the sun started to go down, while Brett stayed with Emma and played games with her. She said her head felt better, which Brett reported to Whitney when they walked back in, looking slightly more relaxed.

"I don't suppose this is going to help convince you to join our practice, or to trust me as the man in your life," he said unhappily.

"It doesn't change anything," she said gently. "And we were lucky, since Emma is okay."

He went to bed early after all the excitement of the day, and Whitney lay in bed thinking about him that night. She had checked on Emma, who was sound asleep, and Brett was in the other twin bed in the room with her, and Whitney had instructed her to check Emma every two hours. It allowed Whitney to relax and think about Bailey. She felt sorry for him. He had been so distraught when Emma got hurt, and so remorseful afterward. It wasn't his fault, and she knew he meant well, and how much he cared about Emma.

She still wanted to join him and Amy in their practice. Nothing that had happened changed any of that. She wanted to work with brain injured children, and on traumatic head injuries, in addition to her psychiatric practice. The look on his face all afternoon had gone straight to her heart. It made her think of what she had said to Chad almost a year before, when he had come to Los Angeles to have lunch with her and convince her to institutionalize Emma so she didn't have to deal with her. She shuddered at the thought, and her response had been the right one.

She got out of bed as she thought about it, and put a robe on. She knew what she wanted to say to him, although she didn't know how Bailey would respond. But he had been so kind to them for so long, she could at least put him out of his misery and reassure him that she wasn't angry at him. She had agreed to take Emma riding. The fault was hers too.

She walked silently down the stairs, and out the kitchen door. There was a bright moon overhead, and she saw two falling stars when she looked up. She smiled thinking how absurd it would be if she got attacked by a bear on the way to the cottage. The realtor had warned them that there were bears in the area, and they had to be careful at night.

She walked along the path to the cottage, and knocked on the door when she got there. The lights were off inside, and she hated to wake him, but she knew how upset he'd been about Emma, and it was only ten o'clock. Bailey came to the door very quickly and pulled it open, and looked startled when he saw her standing there in her bathrobe and pink ballerina slippers.

"Is she all right?" He looked panicked and ready to run to the main house.

"She's fine. She's asleep and Brett is with her. I just wanted to come over and tell you I'm sorry about today. It was an accident. It could have happened doing anything. I know how bad you felt."

"I could have set her back a year, right into a coma," he said, looking tortured.

"But you didn't. That's all that matters. I'll be more cautious next time, and so will you. Shit happens." He smiled when she said it, and stepped backward into the room. "And she's okay, that's all that matters."

"Do you want to come in?" he asked, she nodded and walked in, and she could see a reading light on next to his bed. He hadn't been asleep.

"I thought about something just now, when I was thinking about you. That's why I came over, in case you were awake."

"What were you thinking? That I'm an idiot, and you don't trust me? I don't blame you." He still looked deeply unhappy.

"No, that love is messy. It just is. We all do dumb stuff and make mistakes. Don't ask me why, but my sister was texting, with the most precious passenger of all in the car, the person she loved most in the world and gave up her life for. She was usually a maniac about seatbelts and they didn't have them on that one time. It was so unlike my sister. And look what happened. I nearly got us killed in an accident on the freeway that wasn't even my fault. We got rear-ended and I scared Emma to death. Things happen in life. As soon as we love someone, it has the potential to be a mess. I could hurt you, you could hurt me, we could disappoint each other, or do something stupid that changes everything or kills one of us. Once you love somebody, there's no protection and nothing is safe, and the stakes are high. There are no guarantees in life, ever. My mother adored my father, and I thought he screwed up her life, but she loved him anyway. And she died, and it ruined what was left of his. And I think he did his best for her, no matter how I see it."

"What are you saying to me?" he asked her as she stood just inside the doorway of the little cottage. "That love is too dangerous to take a chance on, and you don't want to risk getting hurt for me?" It was the perfect end to an already horrible day, and he looked heartbroken as he asked her the question. He wished she hadn't come to the cottage to tell him that.

"No, I'm telling you just what I said, that love is messy. We get hurt, we get broken, we make mistakes but we have to take the risk. Life without taking those risks is meaningless. I've been too terrified to move forward since the day I met you, but I'm going to get hurt again one day anyway. I can't hide under my bed or in a closet forever. And if it's a mess, and I get hurt, I'll recover from it. It won't kill me, and it's better to take the chance and live, than never dare to love anyone and not take a chance on them.

"I love you, Bailey. That's all I know. I think you're worth it. Let's be brave and give it a whirl. If you scare me to death, I'll tell you. And if you turn out to be like my father, then that's bad luck for me and I'll leave. If you want me, I want to give it a chance, whatever happens. I can handle it. So can you. We're grown-ups, and I think we love each other, no matter how messy it gets. Life just isn't perfectly clean." As she said it, she held her arms out to him, and he pulled her close to him so tightly that it knocked the air out of her, and she gave herself to him heart and soul as he held her. She followed him into the bedroom where he'd been reading, and he gently took off her robe and her nightgown and they dropped to her feet, and she pulled away the T-shirt and underwear he'd gone to bed in, and she gasped as she felt his hands caress her. She had never wanted any man more, and the terrors of the day were forgotten, along with all her fears since they'd met. She knew that whatever happened, he wouldn't be her father, trying to control her, and she wasn't her mother, helpless and vulnerable and afraid to think for herself. Or even Paige, who had been a flake right to her final hour, texting while she drove so Emma's drama coach wouldn't leave before they got home.

That wasn't how life worked. Neither of them were the ghosts of the past coming back to haunt them. They were who they were, as they were meant to be, and they'd have to find their way on their own, and do their best not to hurt each other.

After they made love, she lay in his arms and looked up at him, as he smiled at her. "Am I dreaming this? Will I know I imagined it when I wake up tomorrow morning?"

"You're not dreaming," she said sleepily and kissed him. "Maybe I am. I don't know why you'd want me anyway. I'm a terrible cook, I'm neurotic about marriage . . . I don't want kids, except for Emma . . . you could do a whole lot better."

"Just shut up," he said and kissed her. "Don't talk like that. I love you . . . and I guess you're right. Love is messy. I've been waiting to find it neatly tied up all my life, and it doesn't work that way. Will you come work with me too? I want the whole package, and Emma, if you still trust me with her."

"You've got it," she said happily, and fell asleep as he lay next to her, smiling. It had turned out to be a very good day after all. And love wasn't nearly as messy as she'd thought, and had been well worth the wait.

Chapter 18

Bailey took the last two weeks of July off and stayed with Emma and Whitney in Tahoe. He took Emma swimming every day, and took her out very gingerly at low speeds on the jet ski, even though Emma accused him of being a coward, but he wasn't going to take another risk. And Whitney slept with him in the cottage every night, and let Brett know where she was, in case they needed her during the night. But Emma hadn't had a night terror in months, or even a nightmare recently, after she'd remembered the accident. There were no ghosts left in her past, only tender memories of the mother she had loved. She laughed at the stories Whitney told her about when they were young, and Paige got her in trouble. And Emma embarrassed Bailey and her aunt when she asked them casually one morning over breakfast why they didn't sleep in Whitney's room, instead of the cottage every night.

"What makes you think we're sleeping in the cottage?" Bailey put his best poker face on, and Emma laughed.

"I always peek in to check on her in the morning. She hasn't slept in her room since you got here. She told me she makes her bed before I get up, but her corners are always messy. Besides, I looked out my window the other day and I saw you kissing." He glanced across the table at Whitney, who was smiling too.

"You're not old enough to know stuff like that," Whitney said, as she sat down next to her.

"Yes, I am. I'm ten. I was on an adult drama. Everyone was sleeping with someone on the show. Are you and Bailey getting married?" she asked in a matter-of-fact way, and Bailey was blushing.

"Not that I know of," Whitney answered for him.

"Mom said you're phobic about marriage," Emma said and helped herself to a cinnamon bun.

"She was probably right," Whitney admitted.

"Can I be in it if you get married?"

"Of course," Whitney said nonchalantly, and Bailey looked like he'd been in the spin cycle of the washing machine by the time Emma left the table with Brett and went back to her room to dress.

"How does she know all that? Your sister must have been very open with her."

"Probably too much so. Ten is the new twenty."

"Are we getting married?" he asked her, trying to look casual about it.

"I hope not. At least not yet. Why don't we try working together and living with each other for a while and see what happens?"

"What if I get pregnant?" he asked, and Whitney laughed.

"I'll have Emma explain to you how that can be avoided. Belinda taught her sex ed. I think she was eight at the time."

"This is all much too grown-up and sophisticated for me. You Hollywood folk lead X-rated lives. I'm a country boy."

"You're doing just fine."

He moved into Whitney's bedroom when Amy and her fiancé came for the weekend, and they let them stay in the cottage. The following weekend Belinda came up with Sam. They had found an apartment and were moving in together, and Amy was delighted to hear that Whitney was joining their practice, particularly since she had just found out she was pregnant, and they had managed it without IVF. Bailey was right. Amy said they were going to move to Colorado in a year. And she was pleased to see that Bailey and Whitney had come to some kind of arrangement and they seemed happy. She didn't ask for the details and figured they were old enough to work it out.

They told Amy about the horseback riding incident, and she groaned. "Are you both crazy?" she asked Bailey. "I said not to overprotect her, not to try and kill her on a horse. Thank God nothing worse happened."

They spent the last few days at the lake without guests, and then they drove back to Los Angeles. They were all busy. Whitney was closing her Beverly Hills office to move in with Bailey and Amy, and would see all her patients there. Emma was getting ready for school with Belinda's help. In the midst of it, Bailey moved in to Whitney's house. They had decided that they liked her house better than his, and Whitney didn't want to move for him.

It had been a turbulent but productive year for all of them, particularly Emma, who had her first nightmare in months the night before she started school.

263

She was too terrified to speak at the breakfast table, and Bailey wished her luck when he left for work.

"See you later," he said to Whitney and she nodded. She was worried about Emma, who hadn't touched her breakfast and said she wanted to stay home.

"You can't miss the first day," Whitney said as she walked her to the car, and watched Emma put her seatbelt on. Her new backpack was on the backseat next to her. It was pink with a big green neon heart on it. They had bought it at Target when they'd gotten her school supplies. The school had sent out a list. Emma had picked her outfit carefully two days before. She was wearing pink jeans with a white sweatshirt and pink Doc Martens, and Whitney had given her her own iPhone so she could call anytime if she had a problem. She knew she had to turn it off in class.

They were halfway to school when Emma finally spoke, in barely more than a whisper from the backseat. But Whitney heard her.

"What if they all hate me?" she said. She was the new girl in class for the first time in three years.

"They won't. They're going to love you. By tonight you're going to tell me how many new best friends you have," Whitney said as she drove and kept her eyes on the road. They didn't need an incident that morning.

"What if my memory goes again, and I can't remember anything?" She was terrified.

"That's not going to happen. Your brain is fine now. And you remember what they told you. They're going to go at your speed for a while. You set the pace."

"What if I forget how to talk or read? No one will understand if I sign."

"You won't need to sign," she reassured her. "What if a bomb hits the school, or a comet?" Whitney teased her and Emma laughed.

"That might mess up my new shoes, or my phone," Emma said. She was very proud of her pink Doc Martens, and they had gotten new red ones too. She had outgrown the old ones. Whitney was just sorry Paige couldn't see her. But if she'd been alive, Emma would have been heading to the set to be on the show, or maybe in New York performing in the musical she'd auditioned for. Her life would have been very different if her mother was alive. But Whitney would give her a good life too, none of it was wasted. Her years as an actress had taught her many things, and her new school would be entirely different and good for her too. It was all part of life.

"I forgot how to spell the word 'calibrate' last week," Emma said, sounding worried. "Maybe that means my brain is acting up again."

"I forget how to spell it too, and my brain is fine. You have my cellphone number in your phone, and you know how to reach me if you have a problem."

"I'll call you at lunch," Emma said, and her eyes looked huge as Whitney pulled into the drop-off line, and they approached the entrance of the school. "I feel sick. I think I'm going to throw up. Take me home," she said in a desperate whisper.

"You're going to be fine. You'll never get into medical school if you can't make it through fourth grade." Emma grinned at that, and a teacher opened the door and helped her out, and recognized her immediately.

"Good morning, Emma. Welcome to Anderson. We're all excited to meet you." She wanted to crawl back into the car and into the womb, but she walked bravely to the front door and turned to wave at her aunt.

"Have a great day!" Whitney called after her and pulled away as Emma disappeared into the school. She suddenly looked tiny and vulnerable, and Whitney's heart ached for a minute and then she told herself Emma would be okay. She'd been through so much worse, and she had so much to look forward to, so many people to meet and things to do, and adventures to have. And even if this was different from Paige's plans for her daughter, Whitney knew that Paige would be proud of her too. It was all up to Emma and what she wanted in life now. She had to discover who she was and who she wanted to be when she grew up, and this was just the beginning. She had the world in her hand, and anything was possible.

Whitney drove the twenty minutes to Bailey's office. It was her first day there too. She knew that he was waiting for her. They had cleared an office for her, and she was seeing her first patient there that afternoon.

He was waiting on the street for her when she arrived. The sun was shining brightly, and he walked her inside. She felt like the new girl in school too, just like Emma. After the year they'd had, she knew she could do it. She set her briefcase down and looked around, as Bailey brought her a cup of coffee and set it down on the desk. He kissed her and smiled at her. It was the right time to start a new life, for her, and for Emma, for Bailey, for all of them. It was a perfect day for new beginnings, and whatever came next.

Epilogue

Emma Watts parked her car in the lot outside the building. They had told her which space to use. There was one for each of the doctors, and the rest were for patients. Her heart was pounding and it reminded her of her first day at Anderson, in fourth grade, when everything was new. And instead of pink Doc Martens, she was wearing black high heels and a gray suit. She was thirty-one, and she felt like the new girl at school again. She had finished her residency in pediatrics and a second one in neurology, which had taken thirteen years from when she started college. She stopped and smiled when she saw the brand-new brass plaque on the door next to Bailey's, with her name on it. It was shinier than the others, they had just put it up the day before. Bailey had put it there himself. He had kept his word. The other brass plaques were weathered and had been there for a long time, and a few had changed.

Amy Clarke had moved back to Colorado twenty years before. She was practicing medicine with her husband in Boulder, and had three children. Two of them were premed now too. Whitney and Bailey were still going strong and practicing together. It had worked out well. They had invited Emma to join them just as they said they would. It had been twenty-two years since the accident. She had never wavered since her recovery about wanting to be a doctor, and going to Anderson had helped her get there. She had specialized in neurology in med school and her residencies were in pediatric brain injuries. And now here she was, ready for her first day working with Whitney and Bailey.

Some things hadn't changed. Whitney and Bailey had been living together for the last twenty-one years. They had never married and said they didn't need to. They were as married as two people could be, and Whitney thought making it official would ruin everything. Bailey had kept his word and didn't mind.

Emma could hardly wait to get started. This was the fulfilling of the dream she'd had since she was ten years old. It was a dream that had followed a nightmare. She was ready to join them now.

Whitney was waiting for her when she walked in, hugged her, and showed her to her office. Bailey had painted it for her himself, and Emma had brought her framed diplomas from UCLA and Yale to hang on the wall. Emma had reached all her goals, one by one. It had taken a long time to get here, but it was all worth it in the end. Bailey was smiling at her from the doorway of his office, as Emma beamed at him. Whitney watched her proudly. She had taught Emma everything she knew and believed in, that anything was possible and to never give up her dreams. It was all she had ever needed to know. Now Emma was here at last, and all her dreams had come true. Whitney had never expected anything less of her, and had never let her down. Motherhood was the gift Emma had given her.

About the Author

DANIELLE STEEL has been hailed as one of the world's most popular authors, with almost a billion copies of her novels sold. Her many international bestsellers include *Turning Point, Beauchamp Hall, The Good Fight, The Cast, Accidental Heroes, Fall from Grace, Past Perfect, Fairytale,* and other highly acclaimed novels. She is also the author of *His Bright Light,* the story of her son Nick Traina's life and death; *A Gift of Hope,* a memoir of her work with the homeless; *Pure Joy,* about the dogs she and her family have loved; and the children's books *Pretty Minnie in Paris* and *Pretty Minnie in Hollywood.*

Daniellesteel.com
Facebook.com/DanielleSteelOfficial
Twitter: @daniellesteel

About the Type

This book was set in Charter, a typeface designed in 1987 by Matthew Carter (b. 1937) for Bitstream, Inc., a digital type-foundry that he cofounded in 1981. One of the most influential typographers of our time, Carter designed this versatile font to feature a compact width, squared serifs, and open letterforms. These features give the typeface a fresh, highly legible, and unencumbered appearance.